Love Finds You™

IN

Sunflower

KA

Love Finds You™

IN Sunflower KANSAS

PAMELA TRACY

summerside
PRESS™

Summerside Press™
Minneapolis 55438
www.summersidepress.com

Love Finds You in Sunflower, Kansas
© 2012 by Pamela Tracy Osback

ISBN 978-1-60936-594-3

Scripture references are from The Holy Bible, New International
Version®, NIV®. Copyright © 1973, 1978, 1984 by Biblica, Inc.™ Used by
permission of Zondervan. All rights reserved worldwide.

The town depicted in this book is a real place, but all characters are
fictional. Any resemblances to actual people or events are purely
coincidental.

Cover design by Garborg Design Works | www.garborgdesign.com
Interior design by Müllerhaus Publishing Group | www.mullerhaus.net

Cover photo of sunflowers by Bigstock.
Back cover photo of sunflower field by Gina Collecchia.
Photo of Sunflower Army Ammunition Plant by Ben Anhalt.
Photo of downtown Bonner Springs courtesy of Bonner Springs Tourism,
bonnersprings.org.

*Summerside Press™ is an inspirational publisher offering fresh, irresistible
books to uplift the heart and engage the mind.*

Printed in USA.

Acknowledgments

A few months ago I made a phone call to a minister in Bonner Springs, Kansas. I asked him, "Who in your congregation likes to read?" He gave me the name of Kay Tinsley. I promptly called, and a friendship was born. Throughout the writing of this novel, Kay has been the expert on the look and feel of small-town Kansas. Thank you so much, Kay.

Thank-yous wouldn't be complete if I didn't thank my son and husband, who often find their way to my office to say, "Come play," when I should be writing.

Also, to my critique group—Libby Banks, Connie Flynn, and Cathy McDavid. You keep me from using the word *look* a million times. You keep me from letting the heroine and hero stay apart too long. And you remind me that writing is a whole lotta fun. We've been together ten years; I say let's do ten more.

Thanks to my wonderful agent, Steve Laube, who keeps me grounded.

And, of course, to the team at Summerside, especially Rachel Meisel and Ellen Tarver, who made it all happen.

Sunflower, Kansas

Bonner Springs, Kansas

IT'S NOT SURPRISING THAT KANSAS SHOULD HAVE A TOWN NAMED for its state flower. And true to its name, the area around Sunflower, Kansas, boasts at least eleven varieties of sunflowers.

Sunflower, at first glance, is not a place to put down roots. Yet it manages to have its roots grow in two directions—Johnson and Wyandotte Counties. This historic area has always been a hub, thanks to the Kaw River. Some claim it as the oldest area in Kansas. But, to believe that, you have to believe that Coronado, the Spanish explorer, made his way here in the mid-1500s. He was searching for love but instead found a place to stay near one of Kansas's many springs.

The Wyandotte Indians and Delaware Indians migrated here. Soon, fur traders and trappers called it home. Then came trading posts. The most famous one in the Sunflower area was called Four

Houses. Eventually, there was a ferry across the river that helped expand the area into a settlement. Then steamboats came along and did their share. They were followed by the railroad, which helped make this region just outside of Kansas City one of the most populous in the state.

Searching a map will indicate that a place called Sunflower, Kansas, exists right by the town of Bonner Springs. Farmers once populated this area, but nothing resides in Sunflower anymore except a now-defunct ammunition plant. Today, Midwestern values and the quest for good times and fellowship (think outdoor concerts, Tiblow Days, and a Renaissance festival) make for a great place to live.

Pamela Tracy

Chapter One

....

"Just about anybody, except a convicted felon, can become a private investigator."

Burt Renfro's words did not make Annie Jamison feel any better.

Anybody, in this case, happened to be her mother.

Leaning against the kitchen counter, Annie closed her eyes, hard, opened them again, and slowly peered around the corner into the living room. No matter how many times she did this—by her count, she'd just reached fifteen—the fact remained that her mother was *not* entertaining the Thursday morning ladies' Bible study group.

"Yup," Burt continued, "your mother told me all about it. Pass an evaluation, pass a background check, pass a test, and get a firearms permit. That's pretty much all there is to it."

"My mother has a firearms permit?"

Burt held up his hand. "I don't believe she has a firearms permit. Nor am I certain she really plans on becoming a private investigator. All I said was, it looks like she's on her way."

"Mom never does anything halfway," Annie muttered, peering into the living room again to get a good look at her mother.

Gone were the simple pullover shirts and blue jeans that had been Willa Jamison's mainstay. Instead, Mom wore a gauzy, flowing skirt of orange and red swirls topped by an oversized bright yellow blouse. Annie figured the outfit would look more at home on her sister Cathy. It certainly didn't look at home on her mother, at least not the Sunday school–teaching, cookie-baking, carpooling mother of her memory. After scrutinizing her mother's outfit again, Annie breathed a little easier.

Nowhere did she see the telltale bulge of a gun.

Interestingly enough, of the four people sitting in the living room, all from her mother's forensics class at the local college, her mother looked the sanest. A young man enamored with his laptop computer sat cross-legged on the floor. His name was Leonard. What he lacked in social skills, he more than made up for in keyboarding skills. His fingers flew across the keys. He'd only managed a shy, mumbled hello to Annie and then had gone back to his computer. He was definitely the behind-the-scenes guy, the computer geek. The two women on the couch watching the *Jack and Janice Morning Show* wore flowing black wigs—so obviously wigs that even Annie noticed—and had storybook names. The taller one was Alice, the shorter one was Wendy. Wendy was flamboyant with shocking red lipstick and a cobalt-blue pantsuit complete with rhinestones. Alice was a little more subtle. She chose pale pink lipstick and a sky-blue pantsuit with rhinestones. They had to be pushing eighty, yet their animated hand signals and spirited conversation mimicked pure youthful energy. Annie was exhausted just from watching them. They were the salespeople, talking up the ArmChair Detectives' potential and spitting out advertising ideas as if it were an up-and-coming contender in the world of private detectives. Unfortunately, not everything Wendy said made sense.

"You need me to stick around?" Burt asked gently. As their across-the-street neighbor since before Annie was born, he'd seen everything the family had to offer. He, like Annie, probably never expected this.

"No," said Annie, "and let me apologize again for thinking you were pulling a belated April Fools' joke. I'm really thankful you called me. I have no idea what my mother's thinking."

Burt smiled a bit, enough so Annie *almost* felt better. "You were the only one I felt I could call. Good thing you have a presence on the Internet. How are your businesses doing?"

"Even with the downturn in the economy, people still want their homes cleaned," Annie replied. "As for Jamison Jewelry, it's slow but sure. I make most of my money at the weekend bazaars, not off the website. I'm not a name."

"Yet," Burt said encouragingly.

"Speaking of keeping me busy…" Annie peered into the living room for the sixteenth time.

"Don't be too hard on your mother. She's gone from wife and mother to widow and empty nester in just a short time. She's trying to fill space. My wife turned our house into a gym after our youngest got married, exercise machines in every room. Great dust collectors. I hang my shirts on the stair-stepper."

"That was five years ago," Annie remembered.

"I've lost fifteen pounds," Burt joked. He moved toward the kitchen door and continued. "Thanks to a bike that never leaves the family room."

He shrugged into a light jacket as Annie opened the door for him. "I was on that bike," he said, "when your mother and her friends carried that sign across the yard and into the house."

Annie's mom lived in a fairly upscale neighborhood in Tucson,

Arizona. Annie didn't even want to know what the rest of their quiet, conservative, upper-class neighborhood thought when they saw her mother and her friends toting a large hot pink ARMCHAIR DETECTIVES FOR HIRE: WE FIND LOST THINGS sign.

No doubt it was a Wendy and Alice design.

"There really is no such thing as an armchair detective," Annie muttered. "They only exist in fiction."

Before Burt closed the door behind him, he chuckled. "I know that, and the really good news is, most of them don't have, need, or even want firearms."

The kitchen door didn't stay shut for long. Annie hadn't even made it back to the living room when she heard tires screeching and Burt's cry of welcome. Finally, her sisters were here. They'd had a longer drive than she. Phoenix, where they both lived, was two hours away; Casa Grande, Annie's home, only an hour. Annie headed outside and watched as Beth pulled her silver Taurus into the driveway.

Beth bolted out of the car and met Annie in the driveway. Cathy followed, more leisurely. Beth got right to the point. "Where's Mom?"

"In the living room," Annie said. "Mr. Renfro was right. She's involved with kooks. I'd call them harmless except they're actually starting a business. They've got a website, business cards, and everything. Whenever I try to get Mom to talk to me, she tells me a statistic. Did you know that every twenty-four seconds a car is stolen in the United States?"

Beth, law degree duly framed, bar passed just last year, gave Annie a look of disbelief and headed for the front door. She disappeared inside. Annie and Cathy looked at each other for all of two seconds before hurrying after her.

Leonard, the laptop computer guy, caught sight of Beth, turned bright red, and said hopefully, "Have you lost anything lately?"

Annie had to give Beth credit. She didn't lose her temper. Ignoring Leonard, she went straight to the source of the problem. "Mother, this is ridiculous. Have you been to the doctor?"

Their mother simply smiled and said, "Let me see my friends to the door, and then we'll talk." She turned to her classmates. "What a surprise. All my children are here for a visit at one time."

Alice and Wendy insisted on shaking Beth's and Cathy's hands. They'd already cooed over Annie. Now, Wendy mentioned her own children and expressed envy at their mom having all her brood home at once. Alice apparently considered Wendy's children her own and talked about grandchildren. Mr. Laptop, who probably didn't have children, seemed disinclined to leave. Clearly smitten with Beth, which was strange because Cathy usually garnered the most attention, he lingered in the living room until Beth's glare and Annie's nudge urged him out the front door.

Cathy headed for the green armchair in the corner—their father's favorite—and pulled a Spanish book out of her bag. Of all the sisters, she was the one who typically went with the flow. "I have a test on Monday," she said in response to Beth's glare. "And finals are next month!"

Beth was more than annoyed. "Is that all you're worried about?"

"Those ladies were nice. The guy was a bit weird, but he looked harmless." Cathy glanced down at her book and grimaced. "I can tell you exactly what this class cost and how much time I've put into it."

Annie knew something Beth didn't. Cathy was in danger of flunking out of her Spanish class and had a right to be concerned.

"Plus," Cathy continued, "you guys might be worrying for nothing. Mom's gone through these phases before. Remember cake decorating? Tole painting? Scrapbooking? Pilates?"

"She's as bad as Mom," Beth mouthed to Annie.

No, not really, Annie knew. Beth just saw the glass as half-empty while Cathy saw it as half-full. Annie, always busy, wouldn't even take the time to consider the question. She'd just be busy trying to fill it the rest of the way.

Their mother swirled into the room. Like a child home from school with lots of news to share, she plopped down on the couch and faced her daughters.

Beth wasted no time. "Mother, are you going through the change?"

Mom laughed gaily. "At just over fifty, I hardly think so. But, yes, I suppose I am going through *a* change. A most spectacular one, and it's way overdue."

"Mother, this nonsense has to stop!" Beth frowned at a giant blue book that lay centered on the coffee table. Annie watched as Beth picked it up. Raised gold lettering proclaimed *What Every Detective Needs to Know*. Judging by the wear and tear, the book was circa 1940.

Beth looked like she'd just eaten a pickle.

Cathy shut her book, keeping her page marked with a finger. "Mom, I'm sure you know what you're doing. I think starting a business is incredibly brave." She stood and gave her sisters accusing looks. "I'm going to my room. I have to study."

The slamming of Cathy's bedroom door spurred Annie's mom onto her feet. She started picking up the drinks, napkins, and such, left by her earlier guests. "I have a lot to do, and you girls worry too much," she said. "This is just something new in my life. I don't have a college degree, I don't want to be just a volunteer, and I don't want to stay home watching television all day." She frowned at the television where Janice, from the *Jack and Janice Morning Show*, was highlighting wedding dresses.

She sighed before turning it off. "I want to do something different." She looked down at the dishes in her hands. "Something fun."

Annie waited until Mom left the room and then looked at Beth. "Fun? I don't think detectives, even armchair detectives, have fun."

"If that's all she were doing, I wouldn't worry. That might even be fun, except armchair detectives don't leave the house, and she definitely needs to get out more. Mom's taking on the role of amateur sleuth. Very Jessica Fletcher. Mom, do you hear me?"

"I do," Mom called back, "but 'Amateur Sleuths for Hire: We Find Things' didn't sound as marketable."

Beth opened her mouth and closed it again. Annie rarely saw her older sister speechless. If it weren't such a serious time, she'd enjoy it.

"I blame Edgar Allan Poe for all of this. He introduced the world to detective fiction, and Mom reads it all the time."

"*Murder, She Wrote* was my favorite show," Mom added. And then said loudly, "This is a perfect job for me."

"Mom, I'm not sure Jessica Fletcher really had fun," Annie responded, just as loudly. "Every vacation was ruined by a dead body."

"Yes," Beth agreed, the pickle look back on her face. "If Jessica Fletcher were real, which she's not, she most assuredly didn't have fun. Most of the time, in today's world, sleuths—which I guess would be a private detective, really—are either trying to catch a spouse cheating or they're looking for missing people who want to stay missing."

"A child goes missing every forty seconds," Mom called.

Beth lowered her voice. "And since fifty percent of the US population cheat on their spouses, private detectives have job security." She raised her voice. "Mom, you don't need a job."

"Yes, I do."

"Mom," Cathy called, coming out of her bedroom. "We're your job."

"Not enough anymore," Mom insisted. The sounds of the sink being turned on and glasses and plates being washed came from the kitchen. They were the sound of home, of normalcy. Annie fingered one of the cards left on the coffee table. "According to the business cards and the sign in the laundry room, she and her friends are going to focus on finding lost things."

"There's a sign in the laundry room?"

"Hot pink," Annie answered. "I think the big-haired sisters designed it."

"Mom!" Cathy yelled, as if cued. "I can't find my Jars of Clay CD!"

"It's in the drawer by your bed! Under the book I gave you to read that you didn't read."

"It's midlife crisis. Has to be," Annie joked.

Beth completely missed the joke. "Midlife crisis? At fifty-three? That means she'll live to be a hundred and six! I don't think we're up to that. Try again."

"She's bored." Cathy exited her bedroom and disappeared into the kitchen. Annie noted that she wasn't carrying her Spanish book. When Cathy returned to the living room, she had a soda in hand.

"Burt said the same thing," Annie said. "After we left the nest, she had Dad to take care of. He's gone, and we're scattered. It makes sense that she's looking for something to do. We need to devote more time to Mom."

"How?" Cathy sat down on the couch and propped her head on her hand.

"One of us needs to move back home, at least for a little while," Beth said matter-of-factly.

Cathy's hands went in the air, waving a negative. "I can't possibly, at least not right away. This semester is crazy and—"

"I wasn't thinking about you," Beth said coolly. She looked down at her left hand where a split shank diamond engagement ring glittered.

Annie wanted to laugh. *Who* Beth was thinking about was obvious. Cathy was two years away from her teaching certification and usually attended summer school. Beth was a brand-new associate at a law firm. She was also getting married in a year, to a stuffy man with a stuffy, upper-crust family and political aspirations. Beth intended to have the wedding of the century.

The only Jamison daughter not caught in a crucial time of life where weeks and months made a difference was *Annie*. She'd bypassed college, to her parents' chagrin, and gone right into the business world. She and her best friend, Rachel, had started their own business, OhSoClean, cleaning houses.

Cathy wanted to hire her; Beth wanted to hide her.

Annie shook her head. "I can't. Our business is still new. We're making a profit, but if we have to hire a temporary replacement for me, then we'll go in the hole. Plus, Jamison Jewelry has shows coming up soon. It's too late to get a refund and I need the exposure. Besides, I think you're overreacting just a little. Maybe we could each take a weekend—"

The phone rang.

"She needs more," Beth insisted.

"I can help with the shows," Cathy offered. "You can pay me a percentage like you did last time. I'll just bring my books so I can study during the downtime."

Annie shook her head. She knew Cathy tried, but it wasn't a very good option.

The answering machine clicked on. "Yes," came a raspy, hesitant voice, "I saw your advertisement in the newspaper. I'd like to meet. You see, I'm convinced my husband didn't die of natural causes, and I can't find the will. You can call me back at 555-3745."

Chapter Two

A week later, Annie pulled into her mother's driveway with two suit-cases, her jewelry supplies, and a backpack full of paperwork she'd been meaning to do for OhSoClean. She was temporarily returning to the nest. Mom kept insisting it wasn't necessary and even spouted the statistic. Nineteen percent of today's youth return home to live. Well, this bird wasn't returning home for free rent or free food. This bird was returning home to make sure Mom wasn't going cuckoo.

Beth had wanted Annie to move back home the same day they'd all visited. Cathy, of course, didn't see a need at all. And Annie, as usual, decided on the sensible route. She'd cut her hours, drive back and forth from home to work, and in a few weeks everything would be back to normal. Her business partner, Rachel, claimed she didn't mind shouldering more during the two weeks Annie was part-time. As a matter of fact, she wanted more responsibility.

"You do way too much," Rachel had said.

Annie had her doubts. Rachel was a good worker and dependable, but she wasn't organized. She couldn't do things the way Annie did. Rachel hadn't grown up with Beth as a big sister. Of course, Rachel had grown up seeing what all three sisters were like. She'd lived five houses away and had been Annie's best friend since third grade.

Rachel wasn't tough at all. She felt helpless when employees called in sick, didn't know how to field complaints, and was too understanding when customer payments came in late or short.

With any luck, two weeks would be enough time. After all, surely Mom just needed company, just needed to know her daughters loved her and wanted to spend time with her. When all was said and done, Annie knew she was the logical choice. Beth would tie Mom up in knots and make things worse. Cathy would probably start dating the laptop guy and want her name added to the business cards.

"Mom!" Annie unlocked the door and entered an eerily quiet kitchen. The air conditioner was off, that was the first clue. The coffeemaker was unplugged, that was the next. And in her mom's bedroom, a huge empty space in the closet was the biggest clue. Either Mom had had a garage sale, or...

Annie heard the doorbell. "Tell me you're moving your mother in with you," Burt said when Annie flung open the door.

"No."

"She's not with you?"

Annie felt the first nudge of concern. "Burt, what are you trying to say?"

"That I made a mistake. She left two days ago. One of her friends arrived, they loaded two suitcases into the trunk, and off she went big as you please. I didn't call because I thought maybe you girls had insisted she come stay with one of you."

Annie shook her head, a helpless feeling settling in the pit of her stomach. "I'm sure we'll figure this out. I'll call you as soon as I know something."

After Burt left, Annie checked her phone. Sure enough, it was on vibrate—she'd forgotten to return it to sound. The message from her mother, left hours ago, said for Annie not to come because Mom was away on business. Annie listened to it twice, hoping for more, but all her mother said was: *We actually have a client from out of town. I've gone to help him locate some missing items. I should be back, hopefully, within the week.* Her mother's *"Don't worry; I'll be fine"* didn't help matters at all.

Annie felt her mouth go dry. She couldn't imagine her mother acting like a detective. What would she be looking for? Where did she go?

Immediately, Annie hit speed-dial and called her mother. The pre-recorded message "I am currently unavailable.... Thank you for calling..." was the only response. Next, Annie sent a text but didn't get back a response even though she sat on the hard kitchen chair and stared at her phone for five minutes.

Great, just great.

A few hours later, Beth and Cathy arrived. Beth was looking for any hint that Mother might have left behind.

At a glance, there was none.

Then Cathy and Annie got to work calling Mom's friends— the ones they knew, at least. All were somewhat concerned, but most were not surprised. "She's been thinking about getting a part-time job," more than one said. "Good," another said. "I told her she needed to get away."

Ten unanswered phone calls to Mom later, the girls started systematically going through the house looking for anything that might tell them where their mother had gone.

"I can't believe they put their number on a business card and then all we get is an answering machine," Beth complained. "We're going to have to search harder. Somewhere, Mom's left a clue."

"They'll call us back," Cathy soothed.

Cathy wasn't fooling anybody. Annie had caught Cathy standing in the doorway of their mother's room with her head bowed, praying. Annie thought about joining in, but her sister had looked so, well, so enveloped that Annie didn't want to intrude.

And somehow Annie had lost the ability to pray spontaneously. When she tried, she usually only got as far as "help" and "please."

So far the only hint of their mother's whereabouts was the word "Max" written on the tablet by the phone. Of course, Max could be the new lawn care man.

"Remember, you're not cleaning," Beth reminded Annie more than once. "You're searching for clues. This isn't the time to make beds and straighten shoes. And make sure your phone is set to ring."

"Sometimes it's when you clean, really clean, that you find the unexpected."

Beth snorted but didn't argue. Cathy looked sympathetic. That is, until Beth focused on her. "And there's no time for getting all melancholy over old pictures of Daddy or the feel of his favorite chair. You're searching."

"Mom will call eventually," Cathy said. "She's avoiding us right now because she doesn't want to hear what we have to say."

Annie shook her head. "That's not like Mom. She'd never make us worry."

Cathy disagreed. "She feels strongly about this. We didn't respond like she hoped. We weren't encouraging at all."

"When someone goes missing, the first twenty-four hours are crucial." Beth probably didn't realize how much like Mom she sounded.

Beth divided up the house. Annie wound up with the master bedroom. No way would Cathy have made it in this room with its memories and smells.

Dad's dresser was right inside the door. A family photo sat on top. Next to it was a bowl containing a set of car keys, a few pens, and a pocketknife. All nice and neat, the way Daddy liked.

Dad's stuff still waiting.

A clothes hamper and a blue chair, both piled with Mom's clothes, came next. For the first time, Annie thought about the changes in her mother's life. Mom usually straightened things up immediately. She might have changed the way she dressed, for now, but she hadn't gotten rid of her old clothes. Besides the clothes stacked on the chair and hamper, there were two green garbage bags in the back of the closet, stuffed with old T-shirts, jeans, and even some of Mom's nice church outfits. Funny, Annie hadn't realized how many clothes her mother had.

Also in the back of the closet were the paintings, almost a dozen, covered with a blanket. Annie didn't take the time to go through them. They were her mom's past.

"I thought I wanted to paint," she said, "but then I discovered I wanted to be a wife and mother."

Beth had asked, "Why can't you be both?"

Annie had been little that long ago day and didn't remember her mother's answer, just that it apparently hadn't satisfied Beth.

Mom's towering stack of books—and, yes, Edgar Allan Poe was

in the mix—leaned against a dresser with not one but two working clocks. The biggest had been a gift from Cathy one Christmas. The other had been a wedding gift more than thirty years ago. Jewelry, most of it made by Annie, was scattered across the dresser top as well as receipts and a collection of pens that read ARMCHAIR DETECTIVES: WE FIND LOST THINGS.

Clothes were folded neatly in the drawers.

Last time Annie sat on her mother's bed rummaging through old papers was when Dad died.

Okay, that was something to discuss with her sisters. It was better to have an armchair detective for a mother than no mother or a really unhappy mother. Annie hesitated. She and her sisters had marched in here like prison guards, intent on making their mother see the error of her ways.

What if they were the ones who were wrong?

Before Annie could take that thought too far, she pulled what looked like a magazine from the drawer of the nightstand by her mother's bed. It was a newspaper, tabloid layout, very small.

The little newspaper, called the *Chieftain*, was maybe eighteen pages in all, and the banner on the front proclaimed BONNER SPRINGS, KANSAS. It was full of brief summaries from the town's politicians, human interest stories, and community announcements: a wedding, some birthdays. The last page contained advertisements. Somebody named Molly was willing to babysit. Another person offered piano lessons. The biggest advertisement, right smack in the middle of the page, highlighted the armchair detectives with a contact number in bold, capital letters.

"Beth! Cathy!"

PAMELA TRACY

Before they could answer, the phone rang. "I'll get it!" Beth yelled. Annie and Cathy made it to the kitchen just as Beth said, "Look, Wendy, we need to know where Mother is. We're hoping you can help us."

Beth's frown let Annie know that whatever Wendy replied wasn't much help.

"This makes no sense," Beth finally said. "Why would she go to Sunflower, Kansas?"

Annie held up the newspaper and pointed to the word *Kansas*. Beth sat down at the kitchen table, clutching the phone tightly, quickly perusing the paper and saying crisply, "We have a newspaper from Bonner Springs. Is that near Sunflower? Did someone there hire her? What was their name? Was it Max? She wrote the name *Max* on a tablet. How do I find them?"

Judging by the pursed lips and shake of Beth's head, someone had hired their mother.

"What do you mean you can't give out the client's name? She's our mother. No, no, please don't hang up." Beth knew how to work a jury, but she obviously didn't know how to work an armchair detective.

Annie took the phone and identified herself. Keeping her voice calm, she asked, "Are you sure she went to Sunflower, Kansas, and not Bonner Springs?"

"I really don't remember," Wendy said, "but we sent her off two days ago. I can't believe we have our first case. This is so exciting. Don't you think?"

"Thanks for giving us the information. It certainly is exciting," Annie agreed. She doubted Wendy realized that in this case, the Jamison girls didn't think "exciting" was good. After a few more

25

minutes on the phone, she hung up. Wendy honestly didn't remember much of anything except the name Sunflower, Kansas.

"No, no way," Beth said, after reading the ad. "This must be one of those fake newspapers you buy at the mall. My boss has one in his office with his face on the cover of *Newsweek*. Mom—"

"It looks real to me," Cathy observed.

"No way, Mom would not go off to the middle of nowhere, especially without letting us know. And, she'd answer her phone!" Beth pulled out her phone. "I'll find Sunflower, Kansas."

Annie again tried her Mom's cell phone. No answer. No surprise.

Stop worrying, she told herself. Half the time, Mom forgot to keep the thing charged. Plus, Mom believed her cell phone was only for emergencies, and on her end, this wasn't an emergency.

"You'd think since she's heading off on a business venture, and her associates would need to get a hold of her, she'd answer," Beth muttered. Then she said, "Got it!" and held up her phone so her sisters could see.

Bonner Springs was there. A place so small it didn't even rate a decent-sized period on the map, more a micro-dot, a mere nano of a spot. Sunflower didn't rate a mention. While her sisters looked over her shoulder, Beth googled Sunflower. Again, she could find Bonner Springs, plenty of info about Bonner Springs, but every link to Sunflower came with a Bonner Springs address.

"Could there really be a place so small it's not on a map?" Cathy asked.

"Bet you've never heard of Why, Arizona," Beth said. "But it exists, just not on many maps. Bonner Springs has plenty of listings, including the sheriff's number."

Once she got a hold of someone in law enforcement, she hit the speaker button, and they all listened to Sheriff Steven Webber. He was to the point. No, he couldn't give any information about Willa Jamison, although he did admit he had no one by that name in his jail. Yes, if he saw Mrs. Jamison, he'd pass on that her daughters were looking for her and that she needed to call them.

Next, Beth placed a call to a church too small to have a secretary but with a friendly minister who answered and informed them that Willa was working for the former minister of the congregation and yes, that man's name was Max.

"Thank God," Beth breathed.

The minister wasn't willing to give out the man's last name or phone number, nor was he willing to share the reason behind their mom's "business" venture, but he'd pass on that her daughters were looking for her. The look on Beth's face said it all. She wanted to throw the phone, yell at the preacher, or at least threaten him with contempt if he didn't cough up the information. Instead, she asked in a no-nonsense voice, "Where's the nearest airport?"

"Near is relative, ma'am." The minister chuckled. "You'll have to fly into Kansas City International, rent a car, and make the drive. We don't have an airport."

Chapter Three

....

While waiting for the airline to call her plane's departure, Annie called Rachel to let her know that instead of going part-time for two weeks, she was taking two weeks completely off.

Rachel did what she always did. Offered to pray.

Annie laughed. "I think I'm going to need more than prayer."

There had once been a time when Annie prayed, but the habit was gone. For the last year, at OhSoClean, instead of praying, Annie just got busy trying to fix whatever needed fixing, soothe whatever needed soothing, and recover whatever needing recovering. Praying took valuable time.

"I'll pray anyway," Rachel promised. "And I'll call my dad and see if he can come into the office and help a bit."

Rachel's dad had moved to Casa Grande a year before the girls. He'd raised Rachel after her mother walked out on them when Rachel was just six. In Casa Grande, he'd been responsible for securing their first few clients.

"I appreciate that," Annie said. "Be sure to pray not only for my mom, but for OhSoClean."

Then finally, Annie heard her flight called, got on the plane, and spent the flight thinking about what she and her sisters had discovered.

It wasn't much.

Thanks to Burt Renfro, they knew their mother had left on Friday morning. Wendy saying Willa had been in Kansas for two days confirmed that. None of Willa's church friends were aware she was leaving, and as she'd not signed up to help prepare communion, help in the nursery, or be a greeter for the month of May, there was nothing for her to cancel. Beth had called the number on the Armchair Detective business card again, wanting to talk to either Alice or laptop guy—what was his name? Something with an *L*—but it seemed the Armchair Detective Agency appreciated their call, was away on a case, and would return the call as soon as possible.

Beth decided that in order to speak to a "live" armchair detective, she needed to be at the local community college Tuesday evening when their class met.

Annie almost wished she could be there. The instructor wouldn't know what hit him. Beth might just take over the class.

Annie's plane finally taxied onto the Kansas City airport runway. She, the sister who rarely took risks and never acted rashly, had booked a last-minute flight. With no time to think twice, she'd taken her two suitcases, her jewelry supplies, and the backpack and made it to the airport on time.

A few hours later, after waiting for her luggage and grabbing something to eat, Annie drove down a dark and lonely Kansas highway.

Time had really gotten away from her.

Annie figured the biggest headache she faced was the GPS system. It made the roads leading to Bonner Springs look like they should be straight. They weren't. As if realizing the mistake, the GPS began sputtering "recalculating" every few minutes. The roads taunted the GPS. They curved to the right, swayed to the left, and once a lonely cow stood in the road, unperturbed by the honking of Annie's horn.

The GPS recalculated the cow.

The gas gauge trembled lower as the sun dipped. She had a dozen text messages from Beth. Rachel also called. Seemed two of their clients had cancelled because they only wanted Annie to clean their homes. If they couldn't have Annie, they'd wait for her return.

This meant lost revenue for OhSoClean. Plus, the girl they'd hired to fill in for Annie now had a reduced load and would earn less money than she'd been promised. Annie couldn't call her clients right now to assure them personally. Nor could she call the new hire and reassure her.

She would have to wait until morning, and boy, was she looking forward to morning. She needed to get her well-organized life back on track.

She glared at the GPS one more time. She'd followed its every direction, and the only thing she knew for sure was that she was lost. Lost at a road that came to a T. Annie could either go right or left, and the GPS remained silent. She was on her own.

Two roads diverged in a wood, and I—
I took the road less traveled by,
And that has made all the difference.

The difference, Annie thought an hour later as she stared into the night. The reason why any sane person—especially a female traveling alone—would choose the well-traveled road was because Robert Frost's road less traveled by didn't have lights, a Circle K with a phone, or gas.

Of course, back at the T, both directions had looked less traveled by.

The car sputtered to a halt. She'd lost the train track more than an hour ago. Cornstalks shimmered in the night, looking like giant scolding praying mantises. Crickets added to the late-night cacophony. A sudden chill overtook her, but not from the cold night air. It wasn't really that cold. It was fear—fear of being in the middle of a strange nowhere with no immediate possibility of rescue.

* * * * *

The sun peeked over the horizon as Joe Kelly's old Ford truck crested the top of Steventon Drive. Jacko, a purebred golden retriever found abandoned and hurt in the middle of the road, obviously neglected, and now completely devoted, stuck his head out the window.

"I don't smell that bad," Joe insisted, rolling down his own window. The early morning was shedding the night's chill, and the scent of cow was as strong outside the truck as in. Birthing a breech bull calf, a big one at that, at almost four in the morning did little to start a day right, let alone a week. After a birth that took almost two hours and then another two hours spent trying to get the mother to stand, Joe felt like he'd arm wrestled with the two-thousand-pound daddy bull.

And lost.

Still, there were two prizes. One, he'd helped prevent the Hickses from losing money. The calf was worth something—his father was a champion. Two, Mrs. Hicks was the best cook in the county. After Joe stepped out of his overalls, he hit the restroom for a scrub and then sat down to a whopping helping of scrambled eggs and ham, plus fresh milk. She wouldn't let him say no, and she fed Jacko.

So, Joe ate the breakfast, all the time remembering how often he'd eaten there as a young boy and then a teenager, back when their youngest son, Kyle—Joe's best friend—helped with the farm and wanted to someday take it over. Back when Joe didn't think of her as Mrs. Hicks but instead thought of her as a second mother. Back before their families landed in the middle of a misunderstanding, and decades of friendship were followed by a decade of polite business exchange.

He managed to clear his plate, thank her, and head for the door, Jacko at his heels. Mrs. Hicks acted like she wanted to say something, but a look from her husband prompted her to nod her head and hand him a brown lunch sack. "I made blueberry muffins yesterday. I remember they're your favorite."

"Send the bill," Mr. Hicks said.

Joe took the muffins and headed for his truck. All he wanted was to get home, take a shower, turn off the light, and catch two hours of sleep before office hours began.

He had left the Hickses' property, smaller now than it used to be, since neither of their boys was around to take it over, when he got the first inkling that home and a few hours' sleep wasn't going to happen. Up ahead, in the sea of waving green and yellow stalks, a little red car stood out like an oversized fire hydrant. There were no orange cones signaling the need for help. No one was about. Joe, always cautious when things looked out of place, drove past slowly.

Jacko barked.

"What is it, boy?"

Turning frantically in the car and looking out the back window, Jacko whined and scratched at the glass.

The retriever had good instincts. Joe did a U-turn and pulled in front of the car. It looked deserted. Deciding to check it out, he shut off the engine, stepped out, and ambled toward it. The front seat was empty, but curled up in the back, beneath what looked like a blanket made of clothes, lay a woman. She was a sleeping beauty, but as stupid as all get out to pull off the road in the middle of nowhere to catch some shut-eye.

Joe rapped on the window.

She stretched and turned over. Her knees went up, fetal-style, and she tucked a hand under her cheek.

Joe whistled softly. He wanted one of these under his tree for Christmas. It didn't even need to come wrapped. He liked her exactly the way she was—hair sticking out at all angles and a face that seemed meant for a smile. He rapped louder, and her eyes opened. For a moment she stared at him blankly. Then she scooted to an upright position and to the other side of the car. She wasn't smiling.

Joe bent down and peered at her through the car window. "Do you need some help?"

"No."

"Really? Well, okay. I'm Joe Kelly, one of the vets in Bonner Springs. You're just outside the Hickses' land. They have a home down the road a ways." He pointed and waited for the wary look to leave her eyes.

It didn't.

"Do you want to use my cell phone?" he offered.

She scooted toward the door and cracked the window. Just

enough for the cell phone and a question. "What did you say your name was?"

"Joe Kelly." As if he needed to prove his words, he pointed to his Ford. His name and business information were stenciled on the door.

She punched some numbers and spoke in hushed tones. After a moment, she pushed the rest of the clothes off her. Opening the door, she gingerly stepped out of the car and nervously twisted one of the bracelets on her arm. "Sorry, I'm still half asleep and feel a little vulnerable out here in the middle of nowhere. My cell phone's battery gave out hours ago. The dispatcher says you're okay. I described you."

"You called the police?"

"It was all I could think of."

"You know the Bonner Springs police phone number by heart?" He was impressed.

She looked a bit embarrassed. "My big sister is a bit of a worrier. She wrote it down in my planner."

"It's always good to have someone watching out for you," he said. "You trust me enough to let me take you into town?"

Two suitcases, a backpack crammed with folders and paper, and a bag of something very heavy later, Joe turned on the ignition and took another look at the woman.

"So, do you have a name?" he asked.

"Annie."

Joe watched as she stared out the window, still looking tired and wary. While she didn't wince at the sloppy kiss Jacko awarded her, she didn't look thrilled.

"Jacko," Joe said. "Give the lady time to get to know you before you kiss her."

Jacko didn't even bother looking guilty, just wagged his tail.

Joe noticed that Annie looked a bit concerned when he placed her stuff next to his veterinarian equipment, old blankets, and soiled overalls. Then, to his amusement, she reorganized the front seat so it looked, well, a little neater.

Definitely a city girl.

Still, she did halfway smile when Jacko put his nose on top of her pant leg and gazed up at her adoringly. Something must be on this woman's mind. Jacko usually acted as a babe magnet, and half smiles were rare.

As he drove, Joe surmised that Annie couldn't have gotten much sleep. Her hair was flat on the side facing him, but that didn't diminish its shine. She must have noticed his glances, because she seemed nervous and started playing with the bracelets on her arm. She was uncomfortable, even though she'd gotten the dispatcher's reassurance of his identity.

"You're lucky I had an early morning call at the Hickses' place. This road doesn't get much traffic."

"And how far are we from Bonner Springs?"

"About thirty miles."

She looked perturbed. "I knew my GPS wasn't working right. I'm glad you know where everything is. Can you tell me about Sunflower? I asked back at the airport when I rented the car. They couldn't find it on any of their maps."

"There's nothing in Sunflower but a closed plant, lots of open space, and some deserted farms. Why would you want to go there?"

"I don't want to go there, but I might have to. I thought it was a really small town."

"I would call it nonexistent more than small. I should know— long ago some of my ancestors actually farmed there."

Before he could say anything else, her stomach growled. He reached behind the seat and snagged the sack of muffins.

She didn't hesitate, took one, and sank her teeth in appreciatively.

"When did you eat last?"

She laughed. "I ate peanuts on the plane yesterday, and then I grabbed something in Kansas City on my way out. But I always eat when I'm stressed, and believe me, last night driving around lost, I was stressed. You wouldn't by any chance have some coffee to go with these muffins?"

"No, no coffee."

She folded the bag neatly, brushed a few crumbs from her pants, and asked, "Are we almost to Bonner Springs yet?"

"It's five minutes ahead. Do you have a place to stay? Where do you want me to drop you off?"

"For now, just a motel."

"Which one?"

"One that's central."

"Central to what?"

"Downtown."

"We have two motels, both by the highway. There are a couple of bed-and-breakfast establishments, though, more centrally located."

"Just take me to one of the B&Bs. I'd really appreciate it."

He stopped asking questions. She seemed to relax, hesitantly petting Jacko, and stared out the window of his truck.

"So, what do you do for a living, Annie?"

"I make jewelry and I have my own business cleaning houses. But I'm taking two weeks off because of some family business. My first time off in years." She checked her watch and sighed. "Too early to call and check on things back home."

He wanted to ask, "What kind of family business?" but he didn't. Instead he let her enjoy the scenery.

"My mother's acting a little strange," Annie finally offered. "Then again, maybe my mother isn't acting strange, maybe we are. It's just my sisters and I are worried about her. But you don't need to know about all this." She yawned and held her hands out in front of her in an elegant stretch. Silver bracelets with blue stones jangled as she pushed up the sleeves of her shirt and gave a smile that had him contemplating giving up the two hours' sleep in order to help her get situated. Then, he really started thinking about her words. *My mother's acting a little strange. My sisters and I...*

Joe's foot moved to hover over the brake. No, it couldn't be. Bonner Springs was small, and Joe knew everybody. If he hadn't spayed their cats, then he'd mowed their lawns or sat next to them at church or in school. Indeed, there was a strange woman in town, a woman who'd proudly shown a picture of her three daughters after church yesterday. He'd chosen to do no more than glance at it but now regretted that decision. "What did you say your last name was?"

"I didn't, but it's Jamison. I'm Annie Jamison."

Tires squealed as the old truck came to an abrupt halt. He felt the hardness of the steering wheel under his grip and fought to gain control of both the car and his emotions.

A fool gives full vent to his anger, but a wise man keeps himself under control. The sermon yesterday, from Proverbs 29, had quite a bit to say about making choices. Joe had listened, just as he had listened to sermons all his life. So, instead of depositing her on the side of the road to look for another way into town, he just stared at her.

Jacko gave a low growl, clearly picking up on his owner's animosity. Annie gave him a wild look and fumbled for the car's door handle. "What's wrong with you?" She turned to look him straight in the face, surprise and anger evident in her expression. There was something else there, too, something that almost made him feel ashamed.

She looked ready to bolt.

"Your mother's the armchair detective?" he finally managed to say. His knuckles were white on the steering wheel. He brushed a lock of hair away from his eyes, and his hat fell off. He left it. He was tired, too tired to deal with this right now.

"No—yes…kind of. How'd you know?"

Jacko spoke, a singsongy yowl that Joe's friends called dogspeak.

He saw the resemblance now. Their hair color was the same dark blond. Both women favored straight styles that were somewhat short and choppy. The same texture even—thick and healthy. Of course, Joe wasn't exactly sure that Willa's hair glistened in the morning sun like Annie's did, and he didn't care to know. Annie's dark brown eyes, more wary than when he'd rapped on her window this morning, glared at him.

"No, yes, kind of," he ground out. "Is that a no, Willa Jamison is not your mother, or no, yes, kind of, Willa Jamison is not a licensed detective."

"She's not a licensed detective."

He clenched his teeth so hard they hurt, started the truck, and pulled out onto the road, driving faster than the old vehicle should or wanted to go. He still gripped the steering wheel hard enough to make his fingers hurt. "I can't believe you have the gall to sit here and admit your mother's a crook."

"What? I admitted no such thing. My mother is not a crook! How do you know my mother?"

Joe finally made it to Swingster Road and drove straight to a clapboard house with a bed-and-breakfast sign hanging on the front porch. Then he calmly reached across her lap and opened the car door.

Jacko barked.

Annie's mouth opened in protest. Joe felt a moment's hesitation, but her current expression reminded him of her mother—a woman he'd met exactly three times and a woman he wished would disappear.

With a huff, she grabbed her purse. "Are all the residents of Bonner Springs as rude as you, Mr. Kelly?"

"No, only the ones who don't like watching their fathers get ripped off by con artists. You're what I call an accessory. Why don't you save all of us time and heartache? Turn yourself in."

Chapter Four

....

His father? Her mother?

She'd managed to slam the car door with poise and anger both. It was a trait she'd learned from Cathy, who'd had more dates in high school than Annie and Beth combined. She took a step toward the bed-and-breakfast and then faltered. Her belongings were in the backseat of Joe Kelly's truck.

Great, just great.

So far, Bonner Springs, Kansas, was sadly lacking in the "We're Glad You're Here" category. When she caught up to Joe Kelly, she'd give him a piece of her mind and then retrieve her clothes. Only, maybe she ought to do it in reverse order.

The nerve! So the former minister had a good-looking son who was no gentleman. Well, most likely the father wasn't a gentleman either. No, the father was the worst kind of man—one who took confused mothers away from their homes and pretended to believe their shenanigans.

Annie headed toward the B&B's entrance, but according to the note posted on the door, the owners had an emergency and would be back at the end of the week. They listed a phone number for another B&B. Since Annie's cell phone wasn't charged, phone numbers were nothing more than teasing.

On a whim, Annie hit her heels together three times, but for now, Kansas was home until she convinced her mother otherwise.

Five was even too early for the small café on the corner. If Annie wanted a cup of coffee, she'd need to wait until six when the place opened, and judging by the looks of the place, it would indeed be coffee—no cappuccino, no latte. Nope, just plain old coffee—the kind meant to say good-bye to the weekend and hello to a definitely muddling and misguided Monday.

Annie sure wished it were six. Coffee, even some strong enough to put hair on your chest, sounded good.

What she really needed was a good old-fashioned phone booth, one with a phone book chained to it. She wasn't sure such things still existed. She took one step toward the café—surely someone was inside. Maybe they could help her.

The road, deserted just moments earlier, suddenly came to life. A car slowed, sped up, and slowed again, this time to a halt. The woman behind the wheel stared at Annie and frowned before rolling down her window, leaning toward the passenger side, and asking, "Are you lost, honey?"

"I—I sure am. I was hoping to stay at the bed-and-breakfast, but it's closed."

"Did you have a reservation? They called everyone and sent them other places before they left. Where were you supposed to go?"

"I didn't have a reservation. I just…" Annie paused. Telling her life story to complete strangers was not something she was comfortable with. "I just need to find my mother. That's all."

"Who's your mother?"

"Willa Jamison."

The woman's lips pursed as she stared at Annie. Then her eyes lit up and she smiled. "Oh, I know who you're talking about. I met her at church this past Sunday. What a charming woman. Well, hop in. I'm Carolyn Mayhew. I'll take you to your mother."

Great, not even a week into residency and already her mother was an icon, a charming icon at that. Shrugging away a lifetime of "Don't get into the car with strangers," Annie pushed aside the boxes of cosmetic supplies taking up the majority of available space and crawled into the passenger seat. That's when the snout of an overgrown bear, pretending to be a dog, made its way to her shoulder.

"This is my day for dogs," Annie muttered.

"What?"

"Ack, nothing, just talking to myself." Annie started to open the door, intent on exiting, but Carolyn laughed and pushed at the dog.

"Rambo is nothing but a big baby. He thinks you must be here to make friends with him. Right, Rambo?"

Rambo let out a low-pitched woof. Annie assumed it meant agreement.

Gingerly settling into what space remained, Annie had to admit that maybe it was a good thing *that man* had her stuff. There certainly wasn't any room for it in this vehicle. Besides one oversized dog, boxes of samples were crammed in the backseat. Unfortunately, not all the samples were contained. Annie carefully placed tiny nail polish bottles on the dashboard.

"You're certainly out and about early," Carolyn observed. "When did you get into town?"

"Just this morning. I rented a car in Kansas City yesterday, but it broke down in the middle of a cornfield."

"Oh, what happened?" Carolyn managed to look distraught and intrigued at the same time. "How did you get this far?"

"The local veterinarian picked me up. My rental is out of gas back near the Hickses' place."

"Dr. Joe picked you up. Wonder why he didn't take you to his dad?"

Annie decided not to answer that one. Carolyn didn't seem to mind answering it herself. "He must have had another call. You were at the Hickses' place, huh? That's a distance. How'd you wind up clear out there?"

"I blame my GPS."

"I can't even find my GPS," Carolyn confided cheerfully. "It's somewhere in the car. It fell off the windshield and I've just not bothered to find it. I never leave Bonner Springs anyhow. Well, don't worry. If Dr. Joe knows where your car is, he'll make sure it gets to his dad's place. Both those men know how to fix little problems."

Annie didn't mention that those men were part of a *big* problem. One *she* needed to fix.

Carolyn Mayhew's Volkswagen either didn't do over forty or Carolyn Mayhew wasn't willing to go over forty. Annie's hand tapped an impatient beat against the side of the door.

Carolyn took the opportunity to suggest a shade of eye shadow Annie should wear. Then she segued into the importance of the right foundation. She didn't seem to require responses from her captive audience. But after a few beauty tips, she must have noticed her passenger didn't even wear makeup and spent the rest of the short drive talking about the Kelly family.

Max was a retired minister and a widower. He lived in a

Victorian house that his father, also a minister, had inherited from his father. Carolyn wasn't sure about the father before that.

Joe, now, was a surprise. Dr. Joe was an only son who didn't choose the ministry. Nope, he was a vet, and not a girlfriend in sight. That he'd dated Carolyn's daughter for only a short time was a surprise, Carolyn confided, but said daughter was happily married now—a farmer's wife—with grandchild number two on the way.

Carolyn didn't have time to share any more. Annie was delivered right to the door of a big yellow Victorian house, and the Volkswagen puttered away.

The timing couldn't have been more perfect. The front door opened, and her mom stepped out and bent down to retrieve a newspaper.

As if she belonged. As if she lived in the house.

When she looked up and saw Annie, instead of smiling, Annie's mother frowned.

"Mom?"

Her mother straightened, shook her head as if in wonder, and then, finally, the edges of her lips turned up. "Okay, you found me. When the minister relayed your message, I knew it was only a matter of time. Truly, though, I expected a phone call. Why'd you come all this way?"

"We've called a dozen times, Mom. We've been worried sick. You're not answering your phone. You're not responding to text messages."

Willa had the grace to look guilty. "I need to charge it. I keep forgetting. I've been using Max's."

"Then you should have called us on his."

"I planned to but wanted to wait until I had something to share besides a location."

"All we wanted," Annie said, trying not to sound angry, "was the location. Mom, you scared us to death. Why didn't you at least leave a note, send an e-mail, something?"

"I started to, but I couldn't get the words right. I had an opportunity with the new business and I wanted to take it. I knew you girls wouldn't understand."

"You got that right. We were so worried."

"Days go by without phone calls from any of my daughters," her mom said evenly. "Life gets hectic. I know that. And, yes, I know, you text me, but I'm not glued to my phone, and that's not hearing your voice."

Annie took a breath. Her mother told the truth. Annie got busy, sent a quick text because it was less time-consuming than calling. Her sisters were the same.

"I should have called," Mom said gently.

"It would have helped. I found the ad in the Bonner Springs newspaper and then we managed to get a hold of one of the armchair detectives. Wendy. She said you were in Sunflower, though."

Her mother turned and Annie followed her through the front door into a spacious living room. A braided rug lapped against a faded blue couch. The furniture looked well-used, well-loved, and sturdy. A faint odor of lemon reminded Annie of days spent helping her mother clean.

"Wendy's starting to forget things. I'm staying with Margaret— that's Max's sister, right next door. I'm sure she'll make room for you. I'll take you over and introduce you and—"

"Mom, I didn't come to stay. I came to take you home. And, if you're staying with Margaret, why are you over here this early?"

Her mother didn't even blink. "I'm working. Today I'm tearing apart the attic. I intend for my first case to be a success. So, did you bring any suitcases?"

"Oh man." Could this day get any worse? Annie could only shake her head and moan, "I left them in his car."

"Whose car?"

Annie ran her hand along the curve of the knob at the staircase's base, forcing herself not to ask why her mother already acted like this was her home. "The vet's. The son of the man you're—you're working for. We had a slight misunderstanding about…" Annie wasn't sure exactly what to say. The only thing she was sure about was that she was tired, dirty, and seriously out of her element. "I imagine he'll turn up any minute now."

"Okay, honey. Why don't you freshen up? The bathroom's at the top of the stairs. It looks like you slept in your clothes." Mom peered closer. "And they're covered in animal hair. Hurry, Max, Margaret, and I are about to have breakfast. He'll be thrilled to meet you. He's heard all about my girls."

"Who is this guy, Mom? What are you doing here? This is Kansas! Why didn't he hire someone local? I can't believe you left without even telling us. Why?"

"Why? Because of the attitude you're showing now. You girls forget that besides being your mother, I'm also an adult, fully capable of making my own decisions. This is business, like you have your business. I'm just starting my career a little later in life. I don't want you interfering or poking fun at it, and if that means I have to do my first real assignment three states away, then so be it. Now behave, or you can just go home."

Before Annie could utter a surprised "Mom," she disappeared down the hall.

Annie thought about following, but truthfully, since hand-cuffs and kidnapping were out of the question, what was she to do? Besides, right now all she wanted was a restroom, a clean washrag, a lint brush, some soap, and two minutes with a toothbrush.

Traipsing up the stairs, Annie took in her surroundings. No wonder her mother already felt at home here. Max Kelly was as big a packrat as her mother. Pictures were on every wall, and knick-knacks were in abundance.

The first door Annie opened at the top of the stairs was not a bathroom. It had obviously housed a boy at one time. There was still a border around the ceiling featuring different sports figures. The shelves underneath boasted trophies as well as photographs—some professional, some not. The walls were painted hunter green. The oak floor was polished to a shine.

The next door revealed the small bathroom. The carpeting was a bland brown that needed replacing. This room was in dire need of a makeover. A quick look in the mirror showed Annie that she, too, could use one. First, there was the punk hair. Not in color, mind you, thought Annie, but there were rock stars who paid good money to have the left half of their hair erupt at such an impossible angle like hers did now.

"Annie, are you about done? Your clothes are here."

Quickly, she splashed water on her face, brushed her teeth with finger efficiency, and hurried downstairs.

She heard his voice before she saw him.

The front door was open. Her suitcases and backpack were just inside, and Joe Kelly was carrying her jewelry bag up the front walk.

Her mother and Joe eyed each other warily.

For a moment, Annie didn't know who to feel more sorry for. He set the bag in the lap of an easy chair and scowled at her. "What's in there? It weighs a ton."

He made the living room look smaller somehow. He was a bear of a man, with shaggy brown hair, impressive biceps, and deep brown eyes. Annie imagined an unruly boy leaving muddy footprints on the faded carpeting as he ran through the room with a football or baseball bat.

"I make jewelry," she explained, "and I'm pretty good at it. I have some commissioned items that I need to complete, so I brought supplies with me."

He made a noise that reminded her of an annoyed horse, perfect coming from a veterinarian.

The dog didn't share Joe's distaste for the Jamison women. Jacko, tail wagging, leaned contently against Annie's leg.

Joe gave Annie a steely look, snapped his fingers at the dog, and headed for his truck. Obviously, conversation was not on his list of things to do today. The dog gave Annie an apologetic look and followed his master.

"Joe didn't stick around?" The deep voice belonged to a man tall enough to have played basketball against Michael Jordan. Annie saw where Joe got his impressive bicep genes. Thick silver hair fell in waves behind this man's ears. Glasses, similar to Benjamin Franklin's, made this man almost too darling to dislike.

"He had an early morning call," Annie said. "At the Hickses' place."

The man raised an eyebrow, clearly curious how Annie could know so much.

"You must be Annie, Willa's middle girl. She's shown me your picture. I'm Max Kelly. Pleased to meet you."

"Pleased to meet you, too," Annie responded automatically, reminding herself that she did *not* return the pleasure. This must be where Joe got his height. Twinkling eyes ran in the family, too. Although Joe's too easily went from appreciation to ire. Well, maybe Joe had something to be annoyed about. Again, Annie noticed that her mom looked entirely too comfortable in Max Kelly's home.

"Mom, are you okay?" Annie dogged her mother's and Max's steps into the kitchen. She looked okay. She looked better than okay. She didn't wear the gauze and loose-fitting tops from a few weeks ago. She was back to a simple shirt and pair of jeans.

"I'm fine. Sit down, dear." Mom pulled out a chair and said to Max, "Margaret says eat without her. She's tidying up the guest room."

It took all of Annie's willpower to sit across from the congenial man at the breakfast table and not warm up to his personality. He talked about his son and the veterinarian practice he'd started because his mother loved animals and because of a tadpole experiment in third grade. Max downplayed his time as a minister and instead highlighted his current job at a local museum. He was only a volunteer, he stressed, but the history of the town offered enough so that he discovered something new every week. "Our town started out being called Four Houses," he shared. "Then it changed to Tiblow."

He didn't sound like a nut.

Sitting in the middle of Bonner Springs, Kansas, on a Monday morning and trying to figure out the best way to put her mother in a straitjacket was too weird to believe. There was not a thing she could do now. It was time to get to know the enemy. Annie pointed to the Blue Willow plates on a ledge that spanned the perimeter of the kitchen. "You have a great house."

"My late wife was quite a decorator."

"How long has she been gone?"

"Four years. I miss her every day."

Just a few years longer than Annie's dad.

"Why did you bring my mother here?"

"Annie, I told you, it's business and I—"

"No secret," Max interrupted. "We're looking for a few coins I lost."

"And you've lost them recently?" Annie pushed the last of her pancakes away.

"No, the last time I saw them was when Joe was in high school."

Uninvited interest spread through Annie. Just how old was the son? *The great-looking son who dumped me in front of a bed-and-breakfast to be picked up by a chattering granny with too much time on her hands.*

"How long ago was that?"

"Let's see. Joe graduated high school ten years ago."

Okay, that put Joe somewhere in his late twenties. A little older than most of the guys Annie dated. Wait! Where were these thoughts coming from? The Kelly men were part of the problem. The dad's charm had gotten past Willa's defenses. A mother who refused to allow her daughters out after midnight, who sent their father to find them if she thought they'd gotten themselves in trouble, and who believed that any movie her daughters thought worth seeing, she'd be seeing, had traveled three states to help a strange man.

Annie squirmed and wished like anything that her sisters were there. What made them think she could rationalize with her mother and get everything back to normal? Fatigue, as palpable as a blanket, urged Annie back toward the coffee cup in front of her.

After a scalding, numbing, long drink, she glanced around the kitchen and wondered how many nooks and crannies the house had and immediately knew. *Way too many.* Another shot of coffee failed to diminish the overwhelming reality of just how many hiding places were in this house. She swallowed before asking, "So, how did you lose these coins?"

"I didn't. Joe was showing them to a friend, and somehow three of them disappeared." Max gave a sad smile. "We were hosting the church's youth group that night. He and his best friend went into my office. Kyle Hicks collected coins, too. Joe just wanted to show off my Stellas."

At Annie's blank look, Max explained. "Stellas are a coin issued in 1880. They feature a coiled hair type designed by George T. Morgan. They're valued at almost fourteen thousand dollars apiece. Willa's going to help me find them."

"Maybe Kyle would be better at the job."

Max shook his head, a hint of sadness in his eyes. "Kyle doesn't know what happened to them, and he no longer lives in these parts." He started clearing the table, still talking. "So, Annie, how long will you be staying?"

Mom frowned at Annie, clearly communicating how displeased she'd be if Annie mentioned that the Jamison daughters thought their mother was nuts or that they thought they could dictate how long she, the mother, stayed.

"I'll be here until I'm sure Mom is all right."

"I'm fine, dear."

"But, Mom, there are only strangers here. This is crazy."

"Strangers who are quickly becoming friends. And starting a business from scratch, like our Armchair Detectives or your OhSoClean, is not crazy, as you well know."

There was a big difference between cleaning people's houses and traveling three states to look for lost coins. And what was with friends who came out of nowhere? Annie suddenly felt alone and vulnerable. Staring at her mother, who looked perfectly comfortable, perfectly content, and perfectly at home, Annie knew that in order to get her mother back to Arizona before Mr. Museum Man became Mr. Yes Dear, she needed to become a big part of the "we" in *We Find Lost Things*.

Chapter Five

....

Annie followed her mother on a well-worn path from Max's house to the house right next door. It wasn't nearly as big and definitely wasn't Victorian. It was small, painted white, and had a half porch. The yard was a riot of flowers in all colors, sizes, and shapes. Annie knew if not for her mother's situation, she'd like this Margaret person.

Willa knocked on the door and then pushed it open, walking in and hollering, "Margaret. It's Willa. I have my daughter with me."

Annie followed her mother into a living room. The floor looked to be hard pine, aged to a reddish hue, well taken care of, and beautiful. Hand-knotted rugs were placed in areas of high traffic. A comfortable-looking beige couch was against one wall, flanked by armchairs that matched the red of the pine floor. A television dominated the room.

A woman who looked like Max, only more compact, came into the room. "I saw Carolyn dropping someone off and figured it might be one of your daughters."

Unlike Max, Margaret didn't look 100 percent inviting. She looked wary.

"This is my middle daughter, Annie."

"The one who makes jewelry, has her own business, and lives to work." It wasn't a question, it was more a statement.

Annie frowned.

Her mother managed to look a little guilty at the description, but not guilty enough to appease Annie.

"Really," Annie protested, "I can stay at a motel or find a bed-and-breakfast. I don't mean to impose."

"I have the room," Margaret said. "Besides, I'm finding this whole business fascinating."

"Fascinating?" Annie said. "You're kidding."

Margaret reached for one of Annie's bags. It felt surreal to surrender it. Annie felt like taking charge, convincing her mother that it was time to stop playing this game and come home, and yet, instead of fixing the problem, she was being drawn into a game she didn't know the rules to and had no hope of winning.

* * * * *

It was after seven when Joe finally trudged up the stairs to his living quarters. He checked Jacko's food and water, then showered and changed. A predawn adventure, spent with animals and a strange woman who needed rescuing, did not bode well for clothes. Finally, he grabbed a bag of chips from the top of the refrigerator and headed back downstairs with Jacko at his heels.

He had about fifteen minutes before his receptionist arrived and his day began. He was bone-tired and not looking forward to this particular Monday. He had three distant farms to visit. His focus for today: Holstein dairy cows. He'd be checking pregnancies and any other health issues.

And the farmers were smart. At every single farm, he'd hear, "Since you're here, Doc…"

Usually he loved it. Usually he wasn't this tired. Usually he wasn't worried about his father. But now, not one but two females seemed to have practically moved in with him.

His veterinary clinic had at one time been a modest two-story house. Then, about twenty years ago, a small-animal vet had opened practice in it. Two years ago, he'd retired and sold his practice to Joe. Joe expanded to farm animals and sank his money into more tools of the trade. Instead of investing in another house, he took up residence on the second floor.

Granted, the top floor was more a glorified attic and smaller than what Joe wanted, but after he'd looked at his student debt, he'd decided that remodeling the upstairs into an apartment made a lot of sense. It put him where he needed to be if an emergency arrived. That and, after eighteen years of being a preacher's kid and eight years of living in either a noisy dorm or a crowded apartment, he liked being alone.

Unfortunately, when he'd moved back to Bonner Springs for good two years ago, his father had realized that the house the Kellys had owned for more than a century was too big for one man. He'd started grumbling about selling it. He made sure his grumbling took place whenever Joe was nearby. What Dad really wanted was to give the house to Joe, as soon as Joe acquired a wife and the potential for lots of grandchildren.

Joe thought he had time. In all honesty, school had been a 24/7 study experience. Back in Bonner Springs, starting a practice had been not only a 24/7 work experience, but also an I'm-getting-even-further-into-debt experience. Adding more bills, a wife, and kids was just too overwhelming a concept for Joe to consider at the moment.

It looked like Dad was tired of waiting and might seriously be entertaining thoughts of actually selling the house.

But Joe didn't have time to worry about either scenario. He'd spent way too much time in melancholy. Instead of using his fifteen minutes before the day started wisely, he'd wasted thirty minutes. And since his receptionist hadn't called his cell phone to see why he wasn't prepping for the day, it looked like she was running late, too.

It was going to be one of those days.

Well, she'd call when she got in. This wasn't the first time she'd been late.

Joe idly rubbed Jacko between the ears. The dog pranced away and went to sniff at the door leading down to the clinic.

"I'm coming. I know it's time." Even the dog was acting strange. Jacko had been acting fickle ever since this morning, cozying up to that crazy female as if all were well with the world.

* * * * *

"I've already moved my stuff into his sister's house," Annie informed Beth. The small bedroom at Margaret's had flowered wallpaper and a full-sized bed with a pink comforter. At the end of the bed was an eggshell dresser with gold trim. Next to the bed was a small round table with a tatted doily and a lamp.

Annie already knew the small table would become her somewhat cramped work station. She needed to work on turquoise bracelets, just not at this moment. At this moment, she just wanted to enjoy the room's ambiance. It smelled of lavender, and more than anything, Annie wanted to kick her shoes off, sink into the bed, fluff the pillow, and read until she fell asleep and had herself a good nap. She mentioned as much to Beth.

"No," Beth insisted. "Don't let yourself get comfortable. You need to insist that Mom pack up and leave with you."

"It's not going to happen anytime soon," Annie said. "My rental is in the middle of a cornfield. Mom insists that she's quite fine and keeps reminding me that until she got this 'job,' we didn't seem to need her."

"What was that last?" Beth asked.

Annie had already closed the door to her temporary lodging. Margaret was hard of hearing. Whatever judge show she had on the television could probably be heard by the whole neighborhood. Raising her voice, Annie said, "I said, Mom keeps reminding me that we didn't need her. Of course, now she's also reminding me that I need her help. I have to go. We're heading out to retrieve my rental."

"But—"

Annie didn't wait for Beth to go on. Beth had a half-dozen orders to give. It wasn't that Annie minded Beth's input, but Beth wanted everything done *now*.

"I need to go," Annie finally said. "I promised Mom I'd be back at Max's as soon as I got situated here."

Beth was still talking when Annie hit the OFF button. She was tempted to follow her mom's example and turn her cell phone off. Sticking it in the side pocket of her purse, she let herself out of Margaret's front door and met her mom and Max at his car.

Max drove, Mom was in the passenger seat, and Annie felt like a distressed child sitting all alone and miserable in the backseat while

Max talked. He didn't seem to need many responses. Maybe he'd heard enough back when he was a minister.

"You'll have to tour the Moon Marble Company. Joe and his friend Kyle worked there one summer after they turned sixteen. The place has a bunch of antique toys and such. Your mom likes antiques."

Annie wanted to ask, "How do you know all this about my mother? You've only known her a few days." But questioning Max while he helped her felt rude. Annie was also pretty sure her mother wouldn't be pleased by the questions.

By the time they got to her rental, Annie was pretty sure she'd promised Max that she'd not only go with him to see the National Agricultural Center and Hall of Fame, but also some speedway.

"You coming back to Max's?" her mom asked.

Annie looked at her mother. "You mean Margaret's?"

"No, Max and I will probably eat lunch—"

"And then I volunteer at the museum," Max added. "You're welcome to join us and then come look at—"

"I think I'll explore the town. I'll stop by if I can."

Once Max had filled the tank of her rental car, he and her mom left. Annie leaned against the car but she didn't get to relax, because her phone beeped, again. It had been signaling messages since it charged. She'd ignored it in the car, not wanting her Mom and Max to hear the one-sided conversations about them. Annie couldn't ignore this one. It was work related. Rachel had sent a one-word text message: *help.*

"That should be my middle name," Annie muttered. It took only a few minutes to call OhSoClean and hear Rachel's breathless story about an employee who'd gotten a little too vigorous while cleaning an antique mirror. She had somehow loosened the mirror from its wall mount, and then—for an hour—had held the mirror in place so there'd be no chance it would hit the ground and crack before the owners got home.

Owners upset, employee upset, Rachel upset.

Annie called the home owners. Soon she'd arranged for a handyman to be there later in the afternoon to check that the mirror was securely back in place. Then, she offered a free house-cleaning to make up for the inconvenience. The homeowners were appeased. Finally Annie was able to take a look at the rest of her messages. She'd read some of them in the backseat during the drive but decided not to acknowledge Beth's questions until she had some answers.

None were from the employee who'd loosened the mirror. Cathy hadn't texted or called. She had classes this morning and had prioritized well. Beth, not so much. A dozen texts, all left in the last few hours, proved that she was still agitated by their mother's actions and threatening to come to Bonner Springs. If Annie were 100 percent sure that Max Kelly was a con man, she'd have welcomed Beth's presence, but so far all the man had done was be nice, talk about his lost coins, be nice, help carry her belongings to his sister's house, be nice, drive her out to her rental, be nice, insist she make herself at home, and invite her to explore the town.

The most recent text, sent a mere ten minutes before Rachel's, was a bit different. It simply said the word "sad."

Annie hit the number 2 on her phone's speed dial. Beth answered on the first ring. Annie had been expecting an "About time!" but instead got an "I am so, so sad."

"Quit worrying," Annie advised. "I'm taking care of everything. I'll have Mom home in a day or two."

"I believe you, although I really wish I were there." The words were Beth through and through, but the tone wasn't.

"What's wrong? Is there something with this detective thing that I don't know about?"

"No, although I think the computer guy is losing interest in the business venture. Last time I talked to him, he said if he wasn't paid more for designing and keeping up the website, and soon, he had something else he'd rather do."

Annie started to say "good," but Beth wasn't finished. "It's Charles."

Glad that Beth couldn't see her, Annie made a face. Charles Simon Reinfeld was not her favorite person. He was engaged to Beth but had two mistresses. The first was named Career. The second was Social Ambition. Beth thought she and Charles had a lot in common. Annie and Cathy prayed Beth would open her eyes and run.

"Is he out of town again?"

"No, but he's busy, so busy he thinks we might want to slow down the relationship. You know we'd set the date. I was so excited. I've been watching the *Janice and Jack Morning Show*. Janice is about to get married. This morning, she toured all kind of wedding venues. I took notes. Then, Charles calls and says he doesn't want to set a date. He isn't ready. He wants to take things easy. He says maybe it's too early to set a date."

Annie almost snarled, *It's been six years!* but Beth was the sister who snarled. Annie was the sister who fixed.

"He's an idiot."

"No, he's just really busy and when he gets busy, he tends to try to rearrange things."

"You don't rearrange the person you love."

"Ack," Beth said. "I need to meet with a client in five minutes. I gotta go. Keep me informed."

Beth hung up before Annie could call Charles an idiot a second time or find out if he'd asked for his ring back.

Would Beth have given it back?

After one quick text to Cathy—who Annie was now starting to believe was the sanest sister—alerting her as to the latest developments, Annie drove to Bonner Springs to explore. She needed time to think and plan. It would be good if she could find out a little more about the Kellys, too.

An hour later, she knew that within a mile of Max's house were three antique shops. She passed by them and put them on her *If there's time* list. Her explorations took her past Page's World, a used bookstore, housed in a garage of all things. City Hall reigned in the middle of town.

Joe Kelly's veterinarian clinic was at the end of a street that tapered off into miles and miles of trees. It looked like it belonged on an Irish hillside. It had dark brown beams and light brown paint with big inviting windows. It was, quite simply, quaint and inviting. It fit Joe's scraggly personality.

But Annie didn't want to find anything to admire about the man who thought her mother was a crook.

As vague sunshine glanced off the windshields of parked cars at Bonner Spring's biggest store, Annie hugged her sweater to her. Compared to Arizona, Kansas was downright chilly. There was only one thing to do: spend money on items she'd have to pay extra for to mail back home.

It took the purchase of a decent coat, a heavier sweater, two pairs of jeans, and a pair of tennis shoes before Annie felt almost normal again. She headed for the two-story library she'd seen on Netteton and Insley, pushed open the front door, and walked into a wonderland.

The smell of books greeted her, luring her in, and reminded her that there were still checks and balances in the world. The library had always been a safe haven, especially during the days when being the middle daughter seemed more than she could handle.

A librarian looked up and smiled. "I don't think I've seen you before. You new?"

"I'm Annie Jamison and I'm visiting—"

"Oh, you're Willa's girl. I'll bet you're the one who cleans houses for a living. I wish you lived here. I'd hire you in a red-hot minute. Willa said you make jewelry, too."

"That's me. How do you know my mom?"

"I attend the same church as Max." The librarian had a few things to say about the Kelly men, mostly what the Volkswagen makeup saleswoman had said, minus the "Joe didn't seem interesting in dating my daughter" bit.

"Right now," Annie said once the librarian paused, "I'd just like to find out some of your town's history."

A minute later Annie was sitting at a table turning page after page of old newspapers. The same community-based ones she'd found in her mother's drawer.

Going through the dusty stack took hours, and even then she

didn't finish, but some of that was due to Rachel's calls from Casa Grande. The air-conditioning had gone out in the office and three potential clients had called requesting estimates. Rachel hated doing the first home visit and talking fees and contracts.

"You're going to have to deal with it," was the only advice Annie had. After all, Annie was having to deal with a lot worse: a runaway mother who'd chosen a destination three states away and in a town where everyone knew everyone and everything without the assistance of the evening news.

No wonder their newspaper was so small.

Small and full of information. Annie found more than twenty articles featuring the Kelly family. They covered everything from Joe—referred to as Dr. Joe—catching the largest bullhead during last year's annual Fish Fry to Max Kelly donating the statues in front of Bonner Springs's Museum.

"He loves that museum," the librarian said, looking over Annie's shoulder.

The Kelly name was on a few other buildings, too. Not too bad for a family of preachers. Why did such a man need to con her mother? It didn't make sense. What could he be hoping to gain? And, even more worrisome, if it wasn't a con, what was it?

* * * * *

Joe hadn't been raised on a farm. Oh, he'd lived in a farming community, but as the preacher's kid, that meant he was the kid who was always thrilled to be riding somebody else's horse or watching somebody else show their prize pig at the local 4H competitions. His mother was the animal lover in the family. Not only did she think every home needed two cats and a dog, but she also thought every human needed to give a hand to nature. At five years old, Joe knew how to bottle feed baby squirrels who'd lost their mother. He knew to avoid raccoons because of rabies. And he knew that wild animals were only temporary in his home and needed to be released the minute they could survive on their own.

When he went to earn his veterinarian degree, an impassioned professor convinced Joe to specialize in large food animals as well as pets.

The first time Joe had to treat a bull, he'd almost regretted his decision not to stand behind the pulpit. Surely standing behind a pulpit was safer than standing beside a bull, looking it in the eye, and saying, "Yes, I'm here to do something you might not like."

Bulls have one goal in life, and playing nice with the vet is not it.

It was almost eight when Joe parked in front of his clinic home, and actually, he was in a pretty good mood. His assumption that he'd be seeing more than Holsteins was correct. He'd examined a few pigs, one sheep, and a bull. Bruno, because he'd been bottle fed, actually had personality. Joe had rubbed its back while examining a few skin problems. The danger, Joe knew, was thinking that if Bruno the Bull had been a cat, he would have rolled over and purred. Docile bulls like Bruno were the most dangerous. Mean bulls were always mean—they let you know you were enemy number one the minute you drove up. Docile bulls gave no warning. Joe could become enemy number one simply because the wind changed.

The place was quiet, but then, most people knew that Monday

Dr. Joe was on the road. He'd only fielded a few calls. Surprisingly, he hadn't heard from his receptionist.

His note, with his list of things to do today, was still on the desk. Hmm. Taking out his cell, he called his receptionist and left a message.

Joe quickly took care of the two cats that were penned downstairs in the clinic. He hoped they found homes soon. Then he headed upstairs and right to the shower.

After sticking a frozen pizza in the oven, he settled behind his computer. Since it was on the kitchen table, dining, entering notes on the animals he'd cared for that day, and googling went hand in hand.

He was a bit distracted this evening and twice had to go back and make corrections on medication he'd prescribed for two different cats. He blamed Annie Jamison. She'd been on his mind all day. He'd called his father twice. Once Max had been eating lunch with Willa but not with Annie. Later, Max had been at the museum. He had been full of details about Annie and the drive to fetch her rental. Right now, to his dad's way of thinking, two Jamison females were better than one.

It wasn't hard to find mention of the Jamison girls on the computer. Annie was easy, thanks to her businesses: two to be exact. The website for OhSoClean was informative and easy to navigate. It showed Annie—curvy, smiling, and all business—in the process of cleaning a house. There were testimonials and a rate schedule.

Hmmm, maybe she made more than he? He liked the way she'd listed price packages and holiday specials. Not that he could offer holiday specials…could he? Neuter your cat and get a free poinsettia.

No, that wouldn't work. Maybe neuter your cat and get a bag of free pine-scented kitty litter.

Her second website featured jewelry. Well, that made sense. She wore a dozen bracelets if not more, and he'd carried in a heavy bag she claimed had jewelry supplies. He'd not noticed anything else. But here was her site. At the top left was a picture of Annie stringing a necklace. Underneath that was a brief history of how she got her start—she thanked her grandparents and mom—and how long she'd been selling her wares. There were a hundred pieces advertised, most between fifty and a hundred dollars, but a few were as high as five hundred. He could push on the shopping cart icon and purchase icon, and could even save on the item of the day if he wanted.

Interesting, but he wasn't in the market for a bolo tie.

Ten more minutes, he told himself, and then he had to go to bed.

The oldest daughter, Beth, had more initials behind her name than Joe. The youngest daughter, Cathy, was the most photogenic and had the largest presence on the web. She and her friends made good use of both Facebook and Twitter. Joe would need a whole day just to understand her Facebook page. He was a bit surprised to see she was majoring in elementary education—she looked like she should be doing commercials or modeling.

Joe found an obit for Annie's father. He'd been dead over a year, just as Annie and her mother claimed. It didn't say how he died and listed that he was survived by a wife and three daughters. Donations could be made to one of the cancer charities.

Reading the obit brought back memories of his mother. The family, per Elizabeth's wishes, asked that donations be made to the Bonner Springs Animal Care Center.

As for Annie's mother, she really didn't have a web presence. There was a homepage for the Armchair Detectives, but it was vague, and when he clicked on links, most were still under construction. Either the Jamisons were new to the con game or very good at it.

He'd finished the bag of chips, Jacko was asleep at his feet, and, judging by the darkness outside, Joe should go to bed. It had been a long day.

Instead of sleep, he checked on the two cats and one ferret who had been his guests downstairs in overnight care and then returned to his computer. He went back to the OhSoClean website again and studied the photos of Annie. Of the three girls, she appealed to him the most.

This morning, bright and ridiculously early, even with her hair mussed from a backseat snooze, Annie had looked, well, she'd looked better than anything he'd seen in quite a while. Better than Honey Smith, owner of a spoiled rotten Chihuahua, who thought small-town veterinarians made money. Better than Betsy Mayhew, who had managed to sit next to him every Sunday morning at church until finally realizing that Joe only planned to say "I do" if someone happened to say, "Hey, who knows how to treat ringworm?"

Chapter Six

....

"Dr. Joe!"

Joe opened one eye. Someone was standing outside and hollering.

"Dr. Joe!"

It had been years since he'd fallen asleep at the computer.

"We open in about ten minutes, just take a seat," he called down the stairs. Right, like whoever was outside could hear him. He grabbed his jeans from off the floor, hurried down the stairs, opened the front door, and greeted his first appointment of the day. "I'll be right with you."

"Okay!"

His first thought was, *Where is my receptionist?* Unfortunately, his next thought was, *Guess I'll be looking for a new one.* This one had already called in sick more than a dozen times during the three months she'd worked for him. If she'd called in today, he'd not be running late. The phone would have woken him up. He quickly changed out of his jeans and into his work clothes, meaning a fresh pair of jeans and a shirt stenciled with *Kelly's Animal Clinic*, and then put a lab coat over the shirt before taking the stairs two at a time.

"Thank you for waiting," he said to Julie Marsh as he headed for the front desk. She nodded, unperturbed. The oldest of seven children, and pretty much raising the younger six, Julie no doubt considered sitting in an empty office and leisurely reading a magazine a treat.

"Just give me one more minute." Joe frowned as he pulled the file on Oscar Marsh, the cat he'd held overnight for observation. Oscar no longer had fur on the nape of his neck. His family, who dearly loved him, insisted that Joe watch the cat and try to figure out what the problem was.

Joe released Oscar and told Julia that Oscar's fur loss had something to do with the two-year-old twins he shared a last name with.

Two hours and three clients later, Joe finally had time to call his receptionist on her parents' landline instead of her personal cell phone number. Her weeping mother answered. Lucy had taken off yesterday and was probably on her way to New Orleans or maybe even Denver or Omaha.

His last three receptionists had all left for greener pastures. What they didn't seem to realize was that New Orleans, Omaha, and Denver didn't really have greener pastures—just more fast food restaurants, movie theaters, and pavement.

At least the previous three had given notice.

Tuesday was the day he operated a small pet clinic. Without someone manning the front desk, it meant putting out a yellow pad and letting people write down their names when they arrived. Not his favorite way to do business, but he'd done it before. He was still small, that helped.

And hurt.

Cats and dogs made up most of his in-town business. Oh, there were a few ferrets, birds, and one potbellied pig tossed in for good measure. An hour later, Joe smiled at little Ashley Bond, all of five years old, as she held her cat tightly against her. Tiger Bond was scheduled to become a soprano.

"Of course I won't hurt him. I'll do the surgery, and you can pick him up tonight." Joe bent down. "He'll feel a little sore and need lots of petting. Think you can handle that?"

Ashley nodded and loosened her grip. Joe had to admit that Tiger was a good-natured cat. Feline fur clumped in damp patches where a little girl's love had clasped too tightly. Tiger hadn't even meowed.

"I was hoping to ask you about his claws," Dan said.

Joe had his own opinion about the importance of claws to a cat, but he'd learned to pick his battles.

"Have you tried double-sided tape?" he asked.

"What?"

"If you put the sticky tape on the area he's scratching, that might stop him."

"Please, Daddy."

Dan looked like the scratching dilemma might deduct lives from Tiger's original nine.

Joe took advantage of Dan's indecision. "There's also a spray that leaves a scent humans can't smell, but animals despise. Try that."

Tiger nuzzled into Joe's neck, as if thanking him for saving his claws.

After the Bonds left, Joe rubbed Tiger's neck. "I think you lucked out this time, but I'd rethink my choice of a sharpening tool."

"A dog just threw up in your waiting room."

It was her, Annie Jamison, standing in the door of his examining room and looking like she belonged.

For once, the perfect response came. "Well, maybe you can put on your OhSoClean apron and get rid of it."

"I'd rather put on my OhSoClean apron and get rid of you."

Had anyone else been that quick with a comeback, Joe would have laughed. Unfortunately, Annie probably wasn't joking. "What do you want? I'm busy. My receptionist quit on me, no notice or anything."

"I can see that. I put out a new yellow pad. You were on the last page, and it's full."

"Don't do me any favors."

"Don't worry, I don't plan to." She turned, flipping her hair in a sign of anger that only women could manage.

The Jamison women, at least the mom, had tilted his perfectly balanced life. And now there was this one, who, for some reason, he didn't want to let waltz out of his examining room. "Wait! Just why did you come here?"

"Because it seems to me we're on the same side." She was at the door, holding it open, and tapping long fingernails against the frame.

"Same side? Us? I don't think so."

"Mr. Kelly. You obviously don't want my mother here. Well, guess what? I don't want her here, either. And as soon as I figure out if those coins can be found, I'll be working on finding them and getting my mother home to Arizona. It seems to me, if we work together, we can solve both our problems."

Her cheeks flushed pink. He wondered if they were as smooth and warm as they looked. Tiger let out a low growl and squirmed.

Her bracelets jangled back to her wrists as her hands went to her sides. Her eyes flashed. Her green earrings sparkled under the harsh light in the examination room. Green meant "go" and, oh, he wanted to. He wanted to go wherever this lady was leading.

If only her mother wasn't taking advantage of his dad. Joe had tried calling him twice. "Where are our parents today?"

"I'll tell you where they're not. They are not tearing that house apart looking for the coins. Instead, they went to some farmer's market somewhere."

"Harrumph" was the only response Joe could think of.

Annie stood half in the room and half ready to flee. "There's a diner at the corner of town. I passed it on my way into town yesterday morning when a *kind* stranger picked me up and took me to the B&B. If you're interested in talking, meet me at your dad's at seven tonight."

"Well, work is—"

"What time do you finish, Mr. Kelly?"

"I don't know. Today's going to be a long one. Why don't you—"

"Let's try for seven," Annie suggested.

Joe grunted. Truthfully, it was the only response he could think of.

* * * * *

Joe's truck wasn't at the café at seven. Annie turned her rental around and drove to his office. Joe's truck, as well as four other vehicles, were parked in front. Shaking her head, she grabbed her purse and headed in.

Pushing open the front door, Annie nodded at the people waiting. This time, she really looked over Joe's place of business. A poster depicting every breed of dog known to man took up a whole wall. Shelves of medication and shampoo gathered dust. For the most part, the human patrons looked more miserable than their animal counterparts. Who knew how long they'd been waiting. Annie's fingers itched for a broom. Joe's place of business needed a woman's touch almost as much as his dad's house did. Helping Joe might actually give Annie insight into what was happening with her mother. Plus, it gave her something worthwhile to do.

Picking up the yellow pad, she asked, "Has Bridgett Doolittle been helped?"

"She went in an hour ago," a disgruntled cowboy said.

Annie crossed that name off the list and called out four more names, only to be told they'd come and gone. The cowboy finally set his wiggling Chihuahua down—Bonner Springs certainly had more than its share of Chihuahuas—and came over to show Annie who was in with the doc.

If the list was correct, Joe still needed to see three patients before he'd be ready to meet Annie for dinner. She smiled at the people waiting and went back to the examination room. Carefully opening the door, she asked, "Do you need anything?"

"You? Again?" Joe was clipping the toenails of a Dalmatian.

Black and white fur blurred against the black T-shirt and white pants of a woman who had dyed her hair an interesting shade of black. She looked somewhat familiar. A small girl was by her side. The woman popped her gum and smiled with interest at Annie. "You new?"

"No, old and desperate. I figured if I helped Joe out, he'd have no choice but to take me out to dinner."

Joe raised an eyebrow. "Just exactly what are you doing out there?"

"Figuring out where you are with your schedule. You have three people waiting."

"Was Jacko out there?" he asked, completely off topic.

"No."

He whistled. Immediately, Annie heard a bark from out back. After a moment Jacko joined them. Joe looked relieved and went back to working on the Dalmatian's nails. The dog's owner perused Annie.

A little disconcerted, Annie rubbed Jacko's ears. "We're not going to eat at seven. You do know that?"

"Last time I checked my watch, it was six thirty." Joe carefully finished the back paw he was working on. He placed his clippers on the counter and moved toward Annie. It took two steps to get from the dog to her. Annie wanted to back away, but his eyes held hers. They were deep brown, intelligent, and so challenging that she felt a shiver feather down her back.

"Lady, my father wants help. I don't."

"We can help each other." She tried to make her words sound brave, but instead she squeaked a bit like the dog lying on the examining table. His whimper earned him a quick kiss from his owner. Annie's whimper didn't even earn a halfhearted smile.

"We cannot work together." He said the words slowly.

Her mouth went dry. Whatever had she been thinking coming here on the spur of the moment? Working with the son probably wouldn't get her any closer to understanding what was going on in the Kelly home.

It was the *probably* that kept her determined.

"I need a good meal."

"Go back to Arizona."

"I'm not going without my mother."

"Take her."

"She won't leave. I tried common sense with her last night, as we searched the front porch for the coins. I tried wheedling this morning. My older sister's used every threat in the books. Mom says she has a job to do and she's not leaving until it's done."

"Well—"

Annie felt anger start to burn. "Joe Kelly, if you'd take the time to listen, you'd see that we are on the same side."

"Take a chance, Joe," the Dalmatian lady encouraged. "You need more excitement in your life. Plus, she's from Arizona. I happen to know great things happen there. My mom is there."

"Hush up, Marlee."

"I like Arizona, too," the little girl said. "Last time we went there, we visited the gland canyon."

One of Joe's eyelids twitched. Annie saw the beginning of a smile. She needed to act quickly. "I'm off work for two weeks, but I don't want to stay that long. If we meet tonight, maybe we can figure out how to cut that time in half. Maybe we can figure out a way to get my mother and your father to come to their senses. Believe me, I want to go home."

"Taking your mother?"

"The quicker we find the coins, the quicker that will happen."

Joe grunted.

"You guys pick at each other like you're married," Marlee said. "Take her up on it, Joe. It's long past time for those coins to turn up."

Joe picked the clippers back up and shook them at Marlee, who simply grinned.

A few moments later Annie stood at his front desk. Both Jacko and the little girl had followed her. "I'm Katie. I like your bracelets. See mine?"

She held up her arms. What looked like rubber bands circled her delicate wrists.

Annie bent down until she was eye level with Katie. "Yours are very pretty."

"Mommy bought them for me. Where did you get yours?"

"I made them."

Katie's eyes widened. "Really? I wonder if Mommy would let me make some bracelets."

Before Annie could respond, Katie twirled around and was gone, leaving her alone to consider Joe's reception area. It was a study in simplicity. The computer looked forlorn, a glass of pens and pencils waited for somebody to realize they were there, and a calendar advertising some sort of ringworm ointment hung on the wall. After determining which animal was next, Annie thumbed through an old banged-up cabinet and found the file. A quick glance showed small, precise handwriting and detailed accounts. She put it on the counter to give to Joe. On the yellow pad, a few people had written notes concerning when they wanted their next appointment. Annie put them next to the computer so they would be noticed and typed in. She even managed to convince one of the people waiting to reschedule. Then she started to clean. Jacko curled up on the floor and watched.

At eight o'clock she blew an errant, flying cluster of dog fur away from her mouth and went back to the examining room. The last patient was obviously one of Joe's favorites. Annie leaned against the wall and listened as he discussed with Agnes Miller what to do for the dog that must be at least as old as its owner.

"Are you buying the special Science Diet I told you about?" he asked.

"Now, that stuff is too fancy for Clarence here. He turns his nose up at it. He likes what I eat."

"But what you eat isn't good for him."

Mrs. Miller blushed, and Annie saw what a beauty the woman must have been in her prime. This was a side to Joe she'd not seen before. Yes, coming here had been a good idea. They were on the same side, and if they worked together, Annie could get her mother home much quicker.

A few minutes later, armed with a grocery bag full of free samples of the Science Diet dog food and a prescription for canine arthritis medicine, Mrs. Miller left.

"I'm going to head upstairs to my apartment," Joe said. "Give me a few minutes to shower and change, and I'll be ready."

"I don't think so," Annie said, looking down at her shirt decorated with so many animal hairs that she was tempted to consider shaving. "I'm not going out covered in fur if you're not."

"Go home and change…" He stopped, a pained look on his face.

Home? Yeah, right, thought Annie, disturbed that he felt as awkward about the word as she did. His aunt's house was not her home. "I bought some new clothes today. They're in my car. I'll get them and then use the restroom down here to get ready."

She should have tried on the jeans before buying them. They

were a bit tighter than she liked. Okay, no more candy bars. Ever. Sucking in her stomach, she managed to secure the snap. Okay, no more French vanilla creamer in her coffee. Ever. Then she brushed fur from who knows what or how many animals off the knees. She might as well be a magnet. Well, she wasn't out to impress anyone.

A moment later, Joe ushered her out the front door of the clinic. His jeans molded to perfect thighs, and his button-down shirt did little to hide firm muscles. He'd washed his hair, or at least dampened it, and tiny beads of water glimmered on the long brown strands. Usually, Annie liked clean-shaven men, but Joe Kelly could be the one to change that little preference. Jacko pranced at his side.

Annie stuffed her hands in her back pockets. He was tall. Too tall. She had always had a weakness for tall men. Tall meant she could add a little heel to her sandals. Surely the urge to touch his hair stemmed from her desire to straighten up his clinic, not straighten him up.

Yes, that was it. The need to clean up, to help mankind, the cluttered and the tall.

Only Joe wasn't looking for help.

She looked from him to his dog. "Are dogs allowed in the restaurant?"

"No, he'll wait out in the truck."

"Wouldn't it be better to leave him here?"

"My last dog would have stayed behind, but Jacko and me, well, we're a team. About the only time I leave him home is when I go to church."

"So, you even take him on dates?"

The corner of Joe's mouth twitched, and Annie had an uncomfortable feeling he was about to laugh.

"Why?" she persisted.

"What do you mean?"

"Why do you always take him with you? Isn't it an inconvenience?"

"He's good company. I don't call that inconvenient. Besides, he cries when I leave him behind."

"He cries? You're kidding!"

"No. I'm not sure who had him before me. I found him in the middle of the road during one of my early morning calls." As if remembering, Joe put his hand on top of Jacko's head. "He'd been hit by a car. I got him back here, examined him, and found out he had a couple of broken ribs. It didn't take but a couple of weeks to figure out that he didn't have an owner."

Annie looked at Jacko. The dog smiled at her.

Right, as if dogs could smile.

Joe continued. "He didn't know how to play. I'd never met a dog who didn't know how to play. And he was scared. He stayed scared for a long time."

Jacko sat at Joe's feet, still smiling but now with his head cocked. Annie just knew that if the dog could talk, he'd say, "Me, scared? Nah, never."

Joe chuckled as he walked to his truck, opened the door, and let his dog jump in. Quickly, Jacko settled in his spot by the passenger-side window and waited for Joe.

"He's not scared anymore," Joe said. "Why should he be?"

"And you taught him how to play?" Annie already knew the answer to that.

"Sometimes," Joe said as slid in beside his dog, "I think he's taught me more than I've taught him."

Annie slid behind the wheel of her rental and headed for the café. After Joe pulled in behind her and opened the window a bit for his dog, he exited the truck and she followed him inside the café. Not only did it have atmosphere, noise, and dead animal heads, but it was close to a train track. Marlee, the Dalmatian owner, was sitting at the counter along with her daughter, who pointed at Annie's wrists and gave a grin. What had to be Marlee's twin led them to a booth, and after a lengthy discussion with Joe about ear mites and how to get her cat to actually swallow the medicine, Missy, who looked more than tired, took their order, promising Annie a fresh cup of coffee.

Annie leaned forward and whispered, "Why does she look so sad?"

Keeping his voice low, Joe said, "The whole town wants to know the answer to that question. She moved back to town awhile back, came to work for her sister, and pretty much forgot how to smile."

Annie didn't have time to ask anything else, because a burly man in a police uniform plopped down next to Joe. Annie gave up all hope of bargaining with the enemy. She was clearly outnumbered.

Joe didn't look all that welcoming as he introduced the newcomer. "This is our sheriff. Steven Webber."

"Good to meet you finally, Annie Jamison," Sheriff Webber said. "That's quite an ad your mother put in our little newspaper. Everyone's talking about it. Has she been finding lost things all her life?"

Annie squirmed, looking around for Missy and wishing she

could get a shot of caffeine before being interrogated. "No, this is a fairly new adventure, perfectly harmless."

The sheriff looked quizzical, a look so purely cop that Annie wanted to laugh. But now wasn't the time or place. When she didn't say anything else, he leaned forward. "She's not really an armchair detective, by the way. If she were, she'd be back in…?"

"Arizona."

"Yes, that's where she said she was from."

"How did your mother wind up putting an ad in our paper here?" Joe asked.

The sheriff settled back, waiting.

The restaurant increased in temperature. The coffee appeared. Annie took a long drink that didn't make things any better. Her too tight pants pinched. Suddenly an errant pet hair made its presence known right next to her nose, and she needed to sneeze.

Joe didn't seem at all uncomfortable. Missy showed up at their table and gave Joe his salad. He looked at both the sheriff and Annie and then bowed his head in silent prayer.

"I'll have the chicken-fried steak special," the sheriff told Missy the next time she passed by.

"The order's already in," Missy said.

"I'm not sure," Annie admitted, taking the conversation back to her mother. "She has a couple of friends, classmates really, who formed the armchair detective business with her. They helped find this case, I'm sure."

"What friends? Are they calling themselves detectives, and are they licensed?" Joe's face once again showed the dark look from yesterday when he dropped her off all alone in front of the B&B.

The sheriff, too, looked like he was drawing his own dark conclusions. He leaned comfortably in the booth, but Annie wasn't fooled. This man, who appeared so jovial, wasn't as receptive to having an armchair detective in town as he'd sounded to be on the phone.

The meeting she'd arranged with Joe wasn't quite going the way she planned. Instead, it looked like it was two against one.

She didn't like the odds and suddenly felt hesitant to answer.

"And," Joe added, "why choose a town as small as Bonner Springs?"

Finally, something she could relate to. "The locale surprised me, too."

Missy placed a salad in front of the sheriff, who gave her a wink as he asked for more iced tea.

"Whereabouts in Arizona are you from?" the sheriff asked.

"I grew up in Tucson but was working in Casa Grande."

"Your sisters planning on coming down, too?"

Annie felt Joe's gaze. How this must look to him. If the sheriff was suspicious of Annie's family, no wonder Joe had booted her from his truck.

"Mr. Webber, I came here to get my mother and take her home. My father died recently, and she's just not recovering from it. She's not out to steal money or anything else. I can assure you of that."

"How recently?" the sheriff asked.

"Just over a year. We lost him to cancer."

"You got identification, Annie Jamison?" the sheriff wanted to know.

Annie reached for her purse.

Joe's hand stopped her. His palm felt warm on the top of her fingers. "Steve, it's all right. I'm taking care of this."

"You sure?" Sheriff Webber said.

Joe hesitated, just for a moment, before saying, "I'm sure."

The sheriff grinned. "Good. That means you'll be staying around for a while, Annie Jamison. We just might get to know each other a bit."

Joe answered before Annie had a chance.

"Annie's going to be busy helping her mother at my dad's place. I doubt she'll have time to get to know you."

Annie's mouth opened. If this were any other day, any other place, she'd have been annoyed at his medieval behavior, but today she was in the middle of a strange town where the only person she really knew was her mother.

Who was just as vulnerable as Annie.

Chapter Seven

....

The sheriff's phone chose that moment to beep. Joe and Annie barely had time to give each other a do-we-know-what-we're-doing, deer-in-the-headlight kind of look before both of their cell phones sounded, too.

Missy delivered their food just then. Great, everything would be cold when they finally got to eat.

"I know why Mom picked Sunflower, Kansas," Beth announced without so much as a hello.

"She didn't pick Sunflower, she's in Bonner Springs." Annie pushed her wilted salad aside, appetite gone. The last bit of her coffee was cold.

"Same thing, just next door. I'm on the college campus, standing right outside Mom's criminal justice class."

Annie checked her watch and calculated the time. The class should have started twenty-five minutes ago. She asked, "Why are you outside instead of inside?"

"The professor knows his stuff. He started with a 'You can't stay here because of insurance purposes' and ended with 'I'm going to call security.'"

"I take it he wasn't afraid of you."

"Not a bit. Luckily, the two ladies we met at Mom's were fashionably late. I got to talk to them before they went in."

"Okay," Annie said, "so how did Mom wind up in Bonner Springs?"

"Wendy and Alice are *from* Bonner Springs. Seems the Armchair Detectives decided to advertise on a small scale. They each chose one locale to focus on. The laptop guy is from Elkhorn, Nebraska. He advertised there. Mom, it appears, put an ad in one of the papers that goes out in Sun City."

"Mom's not from Sun City."

"I know that. It's a retirement community and she knows a lot of people there, but that's beside the point. The older sister, Alice, still gets the Bonner Springs newspaper. It's a weekly. All it took was a phone call to a personal friend and their ad was placed. I don't think they were expecting a client quite so quickly."

"Alice is from here? What's her last name?"

"Her last name is Hicks. And her sister Wendy's last name is St. Arnold."

"There are a lot of Hickses here." Annie closed her eyes, trying to think. Opening them again, she looked at the sheriff, who seemed to have no problem eating and talking at the same time. He now sat at an angle, turned away from her. But she could tell nothing got past him, certainly not her words. His phone conversation appeared interesting, too, at least the last tidbit. "I don't care if he's a hundred and two, tell him it's against the law."

Joe didn't sit at an angle and wasn't trying to hide his phone conversation. He had a perplexed look on his face, but Annie couldn't tell if it had to do with the problem he was solving—"The bluejay is attacking your window because he sees his reflection and thinks another male is in his territory"—or with what he could overhear from her end.

She lowered her voice. "Why didn't Alice and Wendy come instead of Mother? After all, they know all these people."

"Seems that's the problem. They know everybody. Wendy— the one we spoke to, the one who said Mom was in Sunflower, Kansas—wanted to come, said they'd have a great time visiting all their friends and family, including a grandchild. The more I talk to her the more I realize she only has one foot in the world of reality. Alice, the older sister, seems pretty coherent, agreed. They'd have a marvelous time, but that wasn't what the client paid for. She also said it would be a conflict of interest."

"Not very professional."

"No," Beth agreed, "and guess what else isn't professional?" She didn't wait for Annie's response. "They have a one-page, very vague contract—which they won't let me see—and payment is one-fourth the value of what is retrieved."

"Yes," Joe agreed, "male birds have just as many strange habits as do male humans."

"So, what have you discovered in the land of Oz?"

"I'm at a booth in a restaurant with Max Kelly's son and the sheriff."

"Are you in trouble?" Beth's voice went from businesslike to guarded. Annie might have been the sister who cleaned things up, but Beth was the sister who kept everyone safe. And if Beth knew how cute Joe Kelly was, she'd realize the trouble Annie was in might have more to do with the attraction factor than with the errant mother problem.

"No, but I can't talk now. I'll call you later."

"Are you sure?"

The sheriff was no longer on his phone. He watched Annie.

"I'm very sure." Ending the call, Annie tried to settle back, eat her food normally, act like nothing bothered her. But never before had she felt so alone. The sheriff didn't say a word. He, like Annie, waited for Joe to hang up. When Joe finally did, Annie took a deep breath, but before she could say a single word, the sheriff interrupted. "So, you're acquainted with Alice Hicks. How is that?"

If Beth were here, she'd advise to *say nothing*.

But Beth wasn't here, and Annie was of the mind to be honest but only say what she had to. "I'm not acquainted with Alice, not really, or her sister. They're the classmates I was talking about. I've only met them once."

"Where was that?"

"At my mother's house."

"What kind of class were they taking?"

"A criminal justice class, forensics I think, at the local community college. And from that class, they started a business called the Armchair Detectives." Annie's voice rose as she started to get a bit excited. "And involved my mother!"

The sheriff handed the waitress his check and money, put his hat back on his head, stood, and sauntered away. Before he got to the front door he turned and added, "Say no more, Miss Annie Jamison. I understand now. Joe, I wish you luck. If Alice and Wendy are connected with this venture, it's not a con job. But that doesn't mean it's going to end pretty."

The café's door slammed behind him.

The other customers halfheartedly went back to their meals, and Annie wondered just how much they'd heard. Based on Marlee's smile, everything.

Leaning forward and keeping her voice low, Annie said, "Just when I think I'm making sense of this, something new happens. My mom is not a detective. She reads cozy mysteries and, yes, a bit of Edgar Allan Poe, I'll say that, but if she loses something, she's more likely to go out and buy a new one instead of looking for the old one."

"Which is probably why she needs money," Joe stated.

"She doesn't need money."

"Then why is she here?"

"To find your dad's stupid coins."

"They're not stupid, and Alice should have told you that."

"I repeat, I've only met Alice once."

They sat in silence for a while, Annie eating the crackers that came with her wilted, neglected salad and Joe eating a hamburger that had to be cold. He didn't seem inclined to finish his fries.

Finally, Annie said, "Tell me about Alice, Wendy, and what the sheriff meant by 'that doesn't mean it's going to end pretty.'"

Joe wiped ketchup from the side of his cheek. "What do you already know about the girls?"

"Girls?"

Joe chuckled and visibly relaxed. It was the first time since he'd figured out who she was that he'd let his guard down—at least in her presence. "That's how my dad, and just about everybody in town who knows them, refers to them. Of course, they left town more than twenty years ago." He pushed his plate away. The pinched look he'd worn while interrogating her disappeared, replaced with a smile that made him look a bit rascally.

"Alice taught fourth grade at my school. I remember when she took our class to the old one-room school on the outskirts of town. The town had just started expanding it, turning it into a tourist attraction. You should see it now. It has a fake western town and everything. Back then, though, it was just the historic school and an old outdoor bandstand no one was allowed on because it was falling apart. The town was planning to tear it down and build a new one. Apparently, Alice had some fond memories of the bandstand. She decided she wanted a picture with all of us in it. We climbed in, it collapsed."

"Was anyone hurt?"

"My friend Kyle got a good-sized bruise on his cheek. Other than that, nothing more than a few splinters."

"That's funny, but not enough to make history," Annie said.

Joe leaned forward. "Instead of telling someone in authority, she got some of the dads—mine included—to go out the next day and rebuild the bandstand. I didn't get a scratch when the thing fell, but you should have seen what I did to my finger with a hammer."

"How did the dads do with the rebuilding?"

"Good enough to fool people into thinking that nothing had happened. That weekend, however, the mayor came out to the old school to give a talk. He positioned himself dead center in that old bandstand. It collapsed right as the newspaper photographer took the picture."

"Did Alice get in trouble?"

"Luckily, the mayor was Wendy's husband. He was a single male in a household of females—he had daughters and granddaughters.

He had a sister-in-law but no brother-in-law. Even their dog was a female. He knew when he was outnumbered."

Annie decided to look up the picture next time she was in the library. Any event that was remembered for this long was worth investigating.

"That's not enough to make the sheriff think something's going to go wrong."

"All the kids wanted to be in her class. Every year there was something new. She retired the year I had her."

A man from across the aisle leaned over and said, "The year I was in Miss Alice's class, she had everyone bring their bikes to school. She took us out to the playground and we had to ride around and around. When we finished a lap, we had to get off our bike and jump on someone else's. We did it all morning, always changing bikes and not allowed to ride any of them twice. I rode bikes that were too big for me, too little for me, and one that didn't have brakes. Then we wrote papers on which bike we thought was the best and why, how much we would pay for it, and who it belonged to, plus how they got it. It's my favorite school memory."

Annie didn't have time to even consider whether this story ended pretty or not. Marlee, two coffees in hand—a fresh one for Annie and one for herself plus some milk for her daughter—joined them and said, "My grandmother and her sister actually burned down a shed."

"I don't remember that story," Joe said.

"I do," the man across the aisle said. "It was while they were kids."

"So, Wendy is your grandmother?" Annie scooted over so Katie could sit next to her.

"Yes, and Alice is my great-aunt. I wish I'd known them when they were young. They knew how to have fun."

Missy came with more coffee. "It was easier to have fun back then, not so much pressure."

"Ah, sis, we have plenty of fun."

Missy didn't look like she agreed, but Marlee didn't lose her smile as she turned to look at Annie. "My grandma and her sister liked going to the shows, especially westerns. I think Grandma liked Audie Murphy the best. At least she used to talk about him the most. Alice preferred John Wayne. I think she met him once. But never mind that. Apparently, in one of the movies, they watched the Indians shoot flame arrows."

"Oh no," Annie breathed. "How did Alice and Wendy get flame arrows?"

"They didn't, not exactly—they had to make them. They took rubber bands and sticks for bows, and then they took Q-tips, dipped the cotton end in rubbing alcohol, lit them on fire, and shot them at each other." Marlee gave Katie a stern look. "You don't get to try this."

Then she continued, "Apparently, Alice caught Wendy's shirt on fire. Wendy took it off and threw it on some newspapers. When they ran out of the shed, the only thing they thought to save was the rest of the bows and arrows. Needless to say, soon there was no more shed. Wendy wasn't even wearing her shirt—"

Annie held up her hand. "Stop. I see what the sheriff was talking about." Leaning in again, she said, "But really, I only met them the one time, and aside from their really big wigs and addiction to rhinestones, nothing seemed too unusual about them."

"My grandma's a lot calmer since they moved to Arizona," Marlee said, standing and heading back to the counter. "But it's not near as exciting around here."

"I don't want this much excitement," Annie admitted. "Just taking a leave of absence from my business and coming here to get my mother is excitement enough."

"I don't want more excitement, either," Joe agreed as Missy set a piece of apple pie in front of him. Missy raised an eyebrow, Annie nodded, and soon another piece of pie was dropped off. Over dessert, she filled Joe in on what had happened from the time Burt called until they'd found the Bonner Springs *Chieftain* in her mom's dresser drawer.

When she finished, he said, "It's going to take longer than apple pie to tell you about the problem between my family and the Hickses."

"That's the truth," Missy said, picking up their plates and clearing the table. She dropped off the check a moment later. Joe grabbed it before Annie could.

"Let's finish up and I'll tell you what you want to know back at Dad's house. We won't have quite the audience there."

"Our audience will be your father and my mother. And I can pay my half of the bill."

"It's Tuesday night. Dad's at the elder/deacon meeting at church. It never gets over before ten. I'm not sure about your mom. She's been watching lots of television over at Aunt Margaret's, and Aunt Margaret won't think to move from her seat until Jay Leno starts. We'll figure out who owes what then."

Annie still wasn't convinced. "I thought your dad had retired."

"From preaching. Actually, I think being an elder is more work."

Annie opened her mouth to protest again but stopped. What was really bothering her?

The thought of being alone with Joe?

Chapter Eight
....

He was right, Annie realized twenty minutes later as she settled in one of the rocking chairs on Joe's dad's porch. Max's car wasn't in the driveway. Next door, the living room light was on, but only Margaret was visible in the window. Annie could hear the drone of her overloud television. Jacko, deciding he liked her best at the moment, settled at her feet, unconcerned about the possibility of getting nailed while she rocked.

Joe went inside to pop some popcorn. How he could even think about food after that apple pie was beyond Annie. She took the time to text a quick message to her sisters. She'd barely hit the SEND button before Joe handed her a bowl of popcorn and a bottled water. He settled down in the rocker next to her.

Bonner Springs was beautiful in the evening. The trees were twice the size of the ones in Tucson, in both height and width. The sky was an amazing blue with streaks of gray clouds adding contour.

"There was a time when practically the whole town could trace their ancestors back to either a Hicks or a Kelly," Joe began.

Arizona was a migratory place. Annie didn't even know her cousins. Her father had wound up in Tucson because he was stationed at Davis-Monthan in the Air Force. He'd met Mom, who'd been going to school at U of A. Annie and her sisters only knew their paternal grandparents from five measly visits. Her mom's parents lived in assisted living in Scottsdale, and her only sister was in New York.

With a tinge of guilt, Annie remembered the words her mother had said earlier: *"Days go by without phone calls from any of my daughters...."*

Without proximity, it was easy to neglect family.

"Is the sheriff a Hicks or a Kelly?" Annie asked.

"He's neither, although there are a couple of Hicks girls who've let him know they're available. He's fairly new. I think he moved here about fifteen years ago."

Fifteen years practically meant original owner in the area of Casa Grande Annie lived in.

"So," she said, after opening her water bottle and taking a drink, "now that you know Alice and Wendy are involved, and that my mom is not a crook, can we work together? I took a two-week vacation, but I'd rather go back sooner. My partner's great with computer software and accounting but not so much at managing people. Plus, I have a show I'd like to work this weekend."

"We've torn the house apart a dozen times. The coins are gone."

"Why does your dad suddenly want to look again?"

"One, he's thinking of selling the place, and I wish that were the only reason."

"What's the other reason?"

"Lydia and Robert Hicks, and their son Kyle. It was their land you ran out of gas on."

"I remember. This morning your dad told me you'd shown his coins to someone. I guess that would be Kyle."

"Yeah, that would be Kyle. His parents call me whenever they need a veterinarian. I'm pretty sure it's their way of insinuating that nothing's wrong. Truly, though, I am the closest, and for them, I'm definitely the cheapest. I can't bring myself to charge them full price. I keep thinking I'm repaying a debt I don't owe."

"There's a song like that," Annie said.

"Yes, and my dad definitely feels like finding those coins is something he needs to do to take some sins away."

* * * * *

His opinion of her went up a notch when she didn't ask about those sins. Those sins that weren't really his father's. Instead, she rocked for a moment, and the chair made a creaking noise. It was a comforting sound, reminding him of the many evenings his parents sat on the front porch watching him and Kyle and some of their other friends play in the front yard. Annie sat in the one his mother preferred.

Mom had been sitting in that chair the first time Joe brought home a wounded bird. She'd nestled it in her lap, not minding how the feathers fell onto her clothes.

He shook away the memory. "Kyle Hicks and I are pretty much the same age. We went through school together. Best friends from cradle roll through almost the end of our senior year."

"A long time," she said softly.

"We had a youth gathering here, a celebration in honor of the graduates. Our little church had five kids in the senior class that year. Dad said it was some kind of record. Usually we only had one or two, sometimes none. Most years, our whole youth group was made up of five kids from ninth through senior. But when I was in high school, there were quite a few of us, especially in my grade. There was me, Kyle, and Billy Whittaker. His dad was one of the chaperones. Then, too, there were the twins."

"Would that be Marlee and Missy?"

He remembered them like it was yesterday. They'd both had blond hair and blue eyes. He missed that look. Dalmatian wasn't the best choice for Marlee. Tired and sad wasn't the best look for Missy. "Yes, they were really a year older than the rest of us, because their mom heard that school valedictorians were always in the oldest twenty-five percent of a class. She decided to make her girls the oldest in the class, so she started them in kindergarten when they were six."

"Two girls, one valedictorian slot. That must have caused some problems."

"Not as much as the fact that neither girl wanted to be valedictorian."

"Missy's a waitress. What does Marlee do?"

"She and her husband own the diner. She manages the front, he the back."

Annie nodded. Joe got the idea that she was filing that information away somewhere. It reminded him that although Alice and Wendy were involved, which gave him some peace of mind, he really didn't know much about Annie, not really. Or her mother. Or what their home life had been like. He started to worry again, about what brought her here, how much he should share.

"You a believer?"

She started. "In God? Of course."

"You go to church?"

She squirmed. "What does that have to do with anything?"

"Just curious."

For a moment, he thought she wasn't going to answer. Then she sighed. "I was raised in the church. Every Sunday morning, Sunday evening, and Wednesday night, we were there. We did church camp in the summer, Leadership Training for Christ during the school year. You name it, we were there. After I got out of high school, I went off and on for about a year, but quite honestly, if you're not in the youth group and you're not in the college-age group, you kind of feel misplaced. When I moved to Casa Grande, it was too easy to stop attending."

He'd heard this before but never understood it. Maybe it was the preacher kid in him. He felt at home with just about any age.

"Where do you go when you need help?"

She looked surprised at the question. "I go to my sisters."

From the time Joe was old enough to understand, he realized that mealtime at the Kellys' house was a bit different from most people's. They'd sit down. His dad would say the prayer, and almost without fail, the minute Dad took a bite of his meal, the phone would ring.

Joe and his mother would finish dinner while Dad guided someone from the congregation. Then, when Dad hung up, Mom would warm up his meal.

Joe had heard many a one-sided conversation and knew just how important God was. Without God, eternity was blacker than the Kansas sky without stars.

He thought it best not to point this out to Annie.

She started rocking faster. "When I moved to Casa Grande with my best friend, I meant to find a home congregation, but none of them felt right, and pretty soon I got in the habit of not going."

"Your best friend a Christian?"

"She is. And she found a congregation. But we're off topic and it's getting late. Tell me about the coins and Kyle Hicks."

She'd traveled three states, slept alone in a cornfield, talked him into meeting her for supper, and held her own with the sheriff, but talk about the state of her soul and she suddenly acted both uncomfortable and vulnerable. He wanted to probe deeper, but that wasn't why she was here.

"We had a party."

"You already said that."

"It was here. Dad arranged everything. Mom was still alive, but she was visiting a friend in Nebraska. Billy's dad was helping, but Billy got sick and they had to leave."

"You remember a lot."

"I remember everything because after that day, everything changed, and not for the better. I lost my best friend and blame myself."

"Why?"

"Because Dad told me not to ever mess with his coin collection, and I usually didn't because there was no opportunity. He always had them in his bedroom closet, locked in the safe. But the day of the party, he had them out. He was actually planning on using them for Sunday's sermon. He liked visuals, and I think he'd been thinking about the lost coin parable or something. Instead of in his closet, locked in his safe, they were in his office on top of his desk, which wasn't exactly off limits, but not where the party was."

"Why did you go in there?"

"I pulled Kyle into Dad's office because I was going to ask Missy out."

"The sad waitress? Why would you need to ask Kyle?"

"He'd been dating her off and on for the previous six months. They'd just broken up, but I wanted to make sure he didn't still like her."

"So, how did the coins come into play? Your dad said you wanted to show them to Kyle."

Joe swept the last bit of popcorn off the plate, into his hand, and then into his mouth. "That's what I told Dad all those years ago. I was too embarrassed to tell him that I had a crush on Missy. I should probably come clean now that a decade's gone by."

"Wait." Annie stopped rocking. "If Kyle is a Hicks and Wendy is Missy's grandmother, aren't they related?"

"Only by marriage."

Sometimes Joe thought he needed a family tree for the whole town.

"The coins were on Dad's desk, by the computer. I was busy looking behind me to make sure Missy wouldn't overhear. Plus, I was worrying that he still had feelings for her. I wasn't paying attention and before I could stop him, he'd taken some of them out of the case."

"That seems a little cheeky on Kyle's part. Why would he do that?"

"Kyle was a collector himself. Granted, he didn't know a rare coin from a minted-two-minutes-ago coin. But he'd started collecting the state quarters. He kept his in a special cardboard poster. He was fascinated by what my dad had."

"Did he take them all out?"

"If you'd asked me five minutes after we left the room, I'd have said no. I know for sure he took two out, but then my dad called me. I told Kyle to put them back and then went to help in the kitchen. When I went back later, to make sure he had put them away properly, three were missing."

"Did your dad suspect Kyle from the beginning?"

"No, he's always thought they rolled off the desk, accidentally got in someone's pant cuff or something."

"People would have really searched. Who called the police?"

"I don't remember. Everybody was so upset. Kyle just kept saying he was sorry and that he hadn't taken them."

"And your dad absolutely believed him?"

"Absolutely. Dad even went so far as to say someone probably slipped into our house. After all, the front door was unlocked."

"But they would have taken all the coins."

"I know that, but we were grasping at straws. And when all the straws hit the floor, they were in a straight line dividing the room. On one side were the people who believed Kyle took the coins. On the other side were the people who didn't know what to believe."

"What all did Kyle say?"

"He felt awful. He said he started to put them back, but something distracted him."

"And this ended your friendship with Kyle?"

"Worse than that. After a month of hurt feelings and no one being able to forgive and forget, his whole family stopped coming to church."

"Your dad's church or church altogether?"

"Church altogether. They'd already been going through a hard time. Kyle's older brother had gotten his girlfriend pregnant a couple of years before. He'd been awarded a football scholarship and all the kids at church looked at him as a role model. So, although having a baby out of wedlock is nothing new, this one pitted family against family. He married Susan and moved to Kansas City. He didn't attend college, and Susan's parents—who used to attend our church—took it pretty hard. She'd been set on college, too. Her family didn't treat the Hickses right. They acted as if the Hickses were beneath them and that everything was Kyle's brother's fault."

"That's not fair."

"No, it's not, but Susan's family was new to town and had lots of money, lots of material belongings. Kyle's family isn't into the newest car or biggest house."

"So they stopped attending because it was easier."

"They stopped attending because they felt they lost both their sons. They felt they'd done everything right. Gone to church, been there for their kids, taught them, but both boys made decisions that broke the family."

"Broke the family? Interesting term."

Joe nodded. "At a time when the Hickses needed God the most, they turned their back on Him."

Annie could only nod.

"It's something many Christians decide to do. You did when you moved to Casa Grande."

"Mine was a personal decision, probably a bad decision, that had to do more with time and desire."

"No different for them," Joe said. "Although I doubt it's what they desired. They were great parents—involved—and yet both boys made mistakes."

"But Kyle didn't. You said your dad never believed he took the coins."

"Something happened. I'm not sure what. Kyle never acted the same after that party. I tried to keep things as they were. I mean, we'd been friends forever. How do you stop? But his family was so offended that he'd been accused. My dad wanted the whole thing to go away. He cared more about the Hickses than the coins, but once the police were called, there was no turning back. Two weeks later we graduated from high school. Kyle left. He's been back once that I know of."

"Were the other kids questioned? Could any of them have taken the coins?"

"The police didn't seem to think so."

"How about the dad who left?"

Joe smiled. "Maybe you should have been a cop. You ask just as many questions."

"I make more than cops."

"Cleaning houses?"

"Yes, but their retirement is better. Now, how about the other dad?"

"Cliff Whittaker left before the coins went missing. His son Billy went home with him. They had nothing to do with it."

"You sure?"

"Yes, and the cops seemed pretty sure, too."

Annie's cell beeped. While she took the call, he cleaned up the trash left from the popcorn. Jacko roused from sleep and followed Joe, herding him back out to the porch.

Joe hadn't talked about the missing coins for years.

When he headed back to the porch, he couldn't help but overhear

Annie telling someone, "You don't need to come. I have everything under control."

The words were barely out of her mouth when his aunt came walking up the path.

"Tell Willa I'm leaving the front door unlocked and to be sure and lock it."

Joe frowned. "I thought Mrs. Jamison was at your house."

"No, she's been gone all day. I thought she was here."

"Maybe she went with your dad to the elders and deacons meeting," Annie suggested.

"Not a chance." Joe took out his cell. "There'd be nothing for her to do but sit in a room and wait. She'd not be able to attend the meeting." Quickly, he dialed a number. After a moment, he cut it off. "Dad's not answering." He punched in another number. When a groggy voice answered, Joe said, "Hey Agnes, Frank home?"

Agnes turned the phone over to her husband, and Joe quickly asked, "Was my dad at the meeting tonight?"

When Frank said, "No," Joe felt his heart stop. He asked Frank a few more questions, but Frank hadn't seen Max at all. In Frank's words, "Since Willa arrived, he's been keeping busy."

Aunt Margaret came up on the porch. "I figured all this time she was with Max."

Joe told Frank he'd keep in touch, hung up the phone, and turned to Annie. "What time did they leave for the farmer's market?"

"Early this morning, about eight."

"I thought they were home," Aunt Margaret repeated. "When I heard you drive up, I thought the second car was Max's. It never occurred to me it was Annie's."

Fourteen hours, they'd been gone fourteen hours. Joe didn't know about Annie's mom, but his father was the type to call and let a body know, especially a body like Aunt Margaret who lived next door and expected them home *hours ago*.

Chapter Nine

It was just plain bad luck that Beth had been on the phone right when Annie realized their mother was missing.

"I'm flying out, call the police." Beth made plans and issued orders.

"We're not sure anything is wrong. They drove to the next town for some farmer's market. Maybe they ran into one of Max's friends."

"Mom would have called."

"Mom's falling down a bit on the keep-in-touch responsibilities," Annie argued. "Let me try to get a hold of her before you do anything rash. They might have had car trouble. Give me an hour, and I'll call you. If there's a problem, you can make plans to fly out and I'll have already called the police."

Margaret was pacing, her hands moving from clenched fists to flutters, to running through her hair, each action taking only a matter of moments before spurring the next. Jacko, excited, followed her. "This isn't like Max. Maybe you should call the police."

"I'm trying Dad again." Joe hit a button on his phone. Annie did the same. Her mother's phone rang and rang; no one answered. Someday, someone needed to invent a cell phone that was always charged.

Joe pushed a button and glanced at Annie. "No one answered. And believe me, once a minister, always a minister. My dad answers his phone."

Her mouth went dry. "Not my mother. She's the queen of forgetting to charge her phone. She's just in the last year gotten used to us texting her. Margaret's right, maybe you should call the police. Even if they can't do anything, it will let them know what we're concerned about and what we're doing."

"Then we better decide what we're doing," Joe said. "I'll be tracing my dad's movements, trying to find them, starting with the farmer's market."

"Was it an all-day event?"

"No, the farmer's market ended at noon, but it's put on by the Basehor Historical Museum Society. Dad knows all the people who work there. Chances are he took your mom through the museum and to some of the other historic sites. He thinks he knows more about De Soto than the volunteers."

"That's still not all day," Annie protested.

"With anyone but my dad, you'd be right. But put him next to an antique fire engine or a bunch of handmade farm tools, and you have a history buff willing to share everything. Even more, if he found someone who needed to hear the Word, he'd sit down and talk all day and night. What about your mother? What kind of things does she like to do?"

Annie thought hard. Everything that came to mind was lame. "She goes to the grocery store a lot because she likes to cook? She's artistic, but she stopped painting just after she married my dad. Sometimes she joins exercise groups. She loves antique shopping."

The expression on Joe's face told Annie what she already knew. She wasn't helping.

"Max would never forget the elders and deacons meeting," Margaret said.

"That's the worrisome part," Joe agreed.

"Let's get going," Annie suggested. "If I think of anything else, I'll let you know."

"I'll stay here in case Max shows up," said Margaret.

Annie quickly wrote down her cell phone number for Margaret and then followed Joe to his truck. He'd called another man, who also hadn't seen Max all day. Annie listened while Joe listed a few places Max and her mother might be. Soon, it sounded like Joe had Bonner Springs covered, leaving Annie and him free to head to De Soto. He even managed to squeeze in a call to the sheriff, to get and give an update. The sheriff had no new news. Finally, Joe was ready to go.

"Got a flashlight in—"

"Always," Joe interrupted.

"Food and water?"

"That's a good idea." Even though he was almost to the car, Joe pivoted, went back inside his dad's house, and after just a moment returned with a grocery sack. "I have four bottled waters and some granola bars. You're thinking they broke down somewhere?"

"I'm hoping that's the worst-case scenario."

He opened the truck door. Jacko jumped onto the seat, settled in the middle, and even scooted over a bit to make room for Annie.

"Have you ever been to this farmer's market?" Annie asked.

Joe started the truck. "Yes, but it's been awhile." He started to back out but only made it a few blocks before a Volkswagen Beetle pulled up directly behind him and a woman frantically waved for him to stop. Joe stuck his head out the window and said, "Have you heard from my dad?"

It was Carolyn Mayhew. She jumped from her car, sheltering something in her arms, and hurried toward Joe. "No, no, it's something else."

"Sorry, Carolyn, I'm on my way to De Soto, looking for my dad. If it's one of your animals, I'll have to take care of it later."

"It's not any of my pets," Carolyn shrilled. Annie watched as the woman who'd picked her up just two mornings ago hustled Joe's way, and she could see that Carolyn was carrying a shoe box that she promptly tried to hand over to him. "Rambo brought home this kitten. It's clearly just a few weeks old and I can't—"

"You'll have to watch it until I find my dad," Joe said. "I'll stop by your place the minute I know something."

"Your dad's missing? I didn't know." Carolyn looked perplexed, but that quickly turned to both thoughtful and determined. "Well, Max has never been one to get lost. I'm sure you'll find him safe and sound. In the meantime, you've got to take the kitten because I can't sleep with worrying. Rambo won't leave this precious thing alone. He might accidentally kill it."

Without further discussion, Carolyn shoved the box at Joe, headed back to her car, and backed out.

Joe didn't hesitate. He handed Annie the box, hit the gas, and they were on their way.

"What am I supposed to do with this?" Annie asked. Jacko sniffed at the tiny yellow kitten and then looked at Joe as if he had the same question.

Joe didn't slow down but said, "If we have a chance, we'll stop and get it some yogurt or baby formula or something. You'll have to feed it every three hours or so."

"Baby formula or yogurt? Why not milk?"

"I'm pretty sure it's hydrated, but I'm not taking the chance. Cow's milk, at best, will upset its stomach. At worst, well, let's just say I don't want to be dealing with what that baby's bowels might do just now. Look in the backseat in the brown bag. I know I have an eyedropper. You'll need it after we stop."

"Me? I don't know how to take care of anything this young and vulnerable."

"There's a first time for everything."

For the next half hour, they drove with the radio off, neither talking. Finally Joe turned the music on, so low the words couldn't be heard, but loud enough for the faint echoes of a melody. Annie and Jacko took turns studying the sleeping kitten, who didn't seem concerned about his orphan state.

Finally, Jacko decided to ignore the intruder. Annie was afraid to let go of the box. She held it tightly while she rolled down her window and watched for any sign of the unusual.

This was exactly like the night she arrived: the curving roads, the giant shadows of cornstalks marching in the wind, the gray-black night. Every once in a while Joe's phone sounded and Annie heard his worried voice. So far, there was no sign of their parents in Bonner Springs. It also seemed the sheriff had put a call in to his contemporaries in De Soto, and their police had a cruiser out look-ing. After he hung up from each call, Joe muttered to himself. Annie doubted he even realized he was doing it.

"Does your dad have any health problems?" she finally asked.

"Not really. He complains about his knees."

"Has he been in many accidents?"

"He's never even had a ticket." This time, Joe's voice sounded tight. Annie stopped asking questions and busied herself with the kitten.

Next to her, Joe leaned forward, gripping the steering wheel. Every once in a while, Annie noticed his lips moving. Finally, she had to ask. "Talking to yourself?"

"No, praying."

Annie didn't know how to respond. Praying was so obviously the thing to be doing, so why hadn't she been doing it?

Closing her eyes, she sought for words, but only two echoed over and over in her mind: *Please. Help.*

When had praying become so difficult?

They made it to De Soto and slowly drove around before stopping at the police station and learning nothing new. Yes, the officers were aware and yes, they were looking.

"Your dad have dementia?" the man on duty asked. "Because if he does, we can issue a Silver Alert. That might speed things up."

The question only intensified Joe's black mood. For the first hour, they drove through town looking at the cars parked on streets with names like Lexington Avenue and Sunflower Road.

Sunflower Road? From the start of Mom's adventure, the sunflower seemed destined to make an appearance. Most businesses were closed, and the few times Joe stopped, Annie busied herself by showing her mom's photo after checking ladies' restrooms.

"Yes, I've seen her," one clerk said as Joe paid way too much for a small tub of yogurt. "It was this afternoon. Maybe around four. She was all happy about some produce she'd purchased."

That was Mom, all right. She never thought the produce back in Tucson tasted like it should. She'd be all excited about what Kansas had to offer, even in May.

"At least now we know they made it to the market," Annie said.

The news provided a much-needed mood lifting. Annie called Beth, who still thought she should come. Joe called Sheriff Webber, who was now also out searching. So far each phone call, whether to a friend back in Bonner Springs or to the police, came back with the same message: Max and Annie's mom were still missing.

The night grew darker. Turning on the overhead light, Annie carefully dipped the eyedropper into the yogurt and drew it up. Jacko wanted to watch and managed to help her get more on her pant leg than in the eyedropper.

"What do I do?"

"Hold him on his back gently and nudge his mouth open. He'll take it from there."

"How do you know it's a he?"

"I don't at the moment. We'll just assume."

"You assume a lot of things," Annie grudged.

"Right now I'm assuming Dad left the main road." Joe drove through the empty field that hosted the farmers' market for the third time. He headed for the outskirts of town. "Otherwise, we'd have seen him."

"Are there any scenic destinations or landmarks around?"

"You know, there's the farm, our farm, as a matter of fact. It's in Sunflower, the town that is no more, the one you were so curious about the day you arrived. There's nothing there but a broken-down house. Still, it's worth a try."

It seemed that with each mile, the night got blacker and so did Joe's mood. Finally, Joe spoke, his words biting. "How many times has your mom disappeared?"

"What?"

"Well, you came out here to find her because she disappeared. Has it happened before? How often do you go out looking for her?"

"This is the first time. This has never happened, ever, not until she and her friends formed this company."

"Could she have talked my dad into taking her someplace else?"

"Like where? She doesn't know anything about Kansas. This is her first visit."

He exhaled, then leaned forward and slowed down. "There's someone on the road."

Annie saw the figure now, waving, and even from a distance she recognized her mother. Fear had been constant since Margaret first alerted her of Mom's failure to return. Now, the tears started.

Joe pulled over to the side of the road. "Hey, hey," he said gently. "Why are you crying now? We've found them."

Mom ran toward them. "What took you so long? Come on, hurry." She climbed in, scooting Annie over, and said, "It's straight ahead a ways. Then turn right."

"Why didn't you call?" Joe said, following her directions and glancing at Annie. She felt the tears sliding down her cheeks. "And where's my father? Is he at our property? What's wrong?"

Her mom was too out of breath to say much. She just nodded, put her arm around Annie, and said, "Yes, the farm. We're all right. Really, everything will be fine. We just had a bit of an accident."

Joe knew right where to go. After a moment Annie could see,

thanks to the truck's headlights, where Max's car had left the street, but she couldn't see the car. Hurrying behind Joe and her mother, she tripped once, righted herself, and caught up with them. The car wasn't visible from the road. It looked like Max had been aiming for the tall grass but instead had gone into a ditch. The front of the car had almost made it across. The back hadn't.

"There was a cow in the road. Your dad started to go around it and here came a calf. Next thing we know we're off the road, and then Max accidentally hit the gas instead of the brake."

Joe carefully picked his way into the ditch and opened the driver's side door. "You all right?" he asked.

"Fine, I'll be fine," came Max's voice.

"No," her mom said. "He's not all right. We didn't realize that we were over a ditch. He opened the door and fell out. I think he broke his leg. It took us forever to get him out of the water and mud and back into the car."

"Why didn't you call?" Joe repeated.

"It's not important," Max protested. He sounded like he was in pain. "You're here now."

"His phone went into the ditch and landed in water. By the time I found it, it no longer worked." Mom hovered by Joe's side. "My phone's battery died earlier today."

Joe turned to Annie. "I left my phone in the car. I have the sheriff and Frank both on speed dial, plus they'd be the last calls I made. See if you can get a hold of them and tell them what's happening."

Annie headed back to Joe's truck and did as she was told, guessing that the hospital would be their next destination. Then she hurried back to Joe and watched as he reached up to his father. She couldn't hear his words, but she caught the tone. He spoke to Max the way he did to Agnes Miller and her cat. Calm and reassuring.

She moved past her mother so she could crowd next to Joe.

"Did you take off your shoe?" he asked.

Max shook his head, his expression half-pained, half-pleased. "No, Willa wouldn't let me."

"Smart woman. Is your ankle the only thing that hurts?"

"A few hours ago I'd have said yes, but right now the whole leg hurts."

"Can you put weight on it?"

"Do we need an ambulance?" Annie asked. "Should I call 911?"

"City girl," Joe chided, looking at her hard, glad the tears were gone. "There's no 911 out here."

"No ambulance, either," Max said. "The nearest hospital is in Kansas City, Missouri. It would cost too much."

"Worth it," Joe responded.

"Not for over forty miles. Just get me to your truck. I can put some weight on it, I think."

Joe spent the next half hour binding his dad's ankle and scrounging for items to help Max climb from the car to the side of the ditch without stepping in water and mud. Annie's job was covering the mud with the tarp from Joe's truck.

Mud that oozed over her sandals and between her toes. Cold mud.

Following Joe's directions, Annie drove his truck to the edge of the ditch, with the passenger side door as close to Max's driver's side door as possible.

"We'll stop whenever you say," Joe said. "I don't care what you think—don't you dare put weight on it. If you feel yourself about to fall, holler. I'll support you."

"I'm fine," Max insisted.

"He was better earlier when I helped him back into the car," Willa said.

"I have no idea where you got the strength to do that." Joe was on a box, edging his dad forward. Her mom was behind, ready to hold on in case Max slipped. Annie was at Joe's side, ready to assist once Max got within reach.

Slowly, Max slid from the car, good leg first, and then all three of them—Joe, Annie, and her mom—carried him over the mud and up the side of the ditch.

Jacko stood guard at the top of the ditch and barked advice.

It wasn't a graceful rescue, but it was a rescue nonetheless.

Annie's mom got her second wind. "I started to walk back to town, but we'd turned this way and that, and I didn't know which way to go. I was so afraid I wouldn't remember where we'd left the road that I put some of the tools Max had in the trunk by the road as a marker. Then I kept worrying someone would come steal them. I walked until I came to a divided road. It didn't have any signs and it was starting to get dark. I knew then that I'd be taking a chance if I kept going."

"Mom, you did fine. You stayed by the road and waited."

"I should have kept walking. I'd have found a farmhouse. Those cows had to belong to someone."

"Your daughter's right, Willa." Max was breathing hard as they helped him into the passenger side of the truck. "You did fine. If someone hadn't driven by tonight, I'd have sent you out in the morning. That way I wouldn't be worried about you walking in the dark."

"I've never been so scared in my life," Willa said.

"I wasn't scared," Max said. Even in pain, he put on his seat belt and gave Jacko a pat. "Once Willa got me back in the car, I said a prayer. That's all I needed."

Joe and Annie quickly cleaned out the back of the extended cab so there would be room for both women. Once Joe had the vehicle started, Annie reached over and took her mother's hand. "Mom, are you sure you're all right?"

"I'm fine," Mom said, "but I'm a little angry at the cows."

"Me, too," agreed Max. "They wouldn't mooove out of the way fast enough."

Joe was the only one who didn't laugh.

* * * * *

Annie's mother had kept up a steady dialogue the whole way to Kansas City. Not just to those in the car, but on the phone, too. During the calls to her daughters back in Arizona, Joe noticed she got a little testy with the oldest one, just the way Annie did. The youngest daughter kept Willa on the phone the longest. In the back, sitting next to her mother, Annie was quiet, and once again was feeding the kitten. Joe wondered what she was thinking.

If they were alone, he'd ask.

It wasn't Joe's first time to Kansas City's big hospital, but that didn't mean he knew the way. Max, who'd preached for almost forty years, had been there often—visiting not only members of the church but anyone else on his preacher radar. Sometimes on those long ago days, his father's absence had bothered Joe. After all, a drive to Kansas City to visit someone in the hospital took time away from playing Legos with Joe, took time away from taking Joe to the park, and took time away from watching Joe play baseball in high school.

He understood a bit more today, a bit more right this minute, because to Joe's surprise, the sheriff and Frank Miller, the elder Joe had spoken with earlier, were sitting on a bench outside the emergency room door. Seeing the people who loved his father enough to drive dark roads and then come all the way to Kansas City, Joe suddenly understood his father and what he'd been doing all those years.

As two orderlies helped Max onto the stretcher, Willa confided in Joe, "I kept talking because it seemed to take his mind off the pain."

Joe nodded and followed his dad through the doors and into a big lobby. Behind him he could hear Willa talking to the sheriff and Frank. Her voice, reassuring, probably did more to comfort Joe than it did the two men. It took a minute at the nurses' station, but soon Dad was in a private room with a nurse taking his blood pressure.

When they were finally alone and Joe had helped his father into a hospital gown, he divulged, "I kept Willa talking because it seemed to calm her down."

"Dad, what were you thinking?"

"That I wanted to go on a nice, leisurely drive. If it weren't for those stupid cows, we'd have been fine."

"You've been driving around cows and kids and tractors your whole life."

"And until today I didn't realize how much I hated driving around those cows and kids and tractors all alone. I was with a charming woman and I wanted it to last longer, so I thought I'd show her some scenery and even a little of my family's history."

"You hired her to do a job. That's all."

"She's doing her job."

"She hasn't found the coins."

"You can't expect her to accomplish in one week what we haven't accomplished in ten years."

The doctor came in just then and Joe scooted to the wall to give the man room.

The routine wasn't all that different from what Joe had gone through last week setting a collie's broken leg, except that the patient could answer the questions posed without the help of a third party. It made it much easier to ascertain exactly where the break was, gently explore the area with fingers, take an X-ray, and finally bandage.

The collie had whimpered. Max grumbled, insisting repeatedly that his leg wasn't broken. The collie hadn't even bared his teeth at Joe's probing fingers. Max didn't bare his teeth, although he'd practically come out of the hospital bed when the doctor's capable fingers assessed the damage.

Once they'd wheeled Max out of the room and to X-ray, Joe headed for the waiting room.

"The sheriff wasn't able to stay," Willa said. She didn't even look tired. "He got a call and said to contact him when you have something to report."

Joe looked around. "Where's Annie?"

"She went to the restroom to clean up," Willa said.

"Max going to be all right?" Frank Miller stood, yawned, and stretched. Frank had been his father's best friend for decades. Funny, Joe just now noticed how gray Frank was getting and how much smaller he looked. The man also looked tired, but thanks to Max, they all did.

"He'll be fine," Joe said. "Thanks so much for sticking around. I can't believe you came here knowing it was probably just a break."

"I was already up, and I was already somewhat in the neighborhood. Agnes will appreciate that she gets to pass on firsthand news. So, tell me, how's the old man doing?"

Joe gave him a quick summary, finishing with, "They'll probably dope him up and keep him for a few hours. He'll have something to talk about for the next month."

"He's already given us plenty to talk about," Frank said, reaching for his hat and looking at Willa. She was too worried about Max to notice.

Joe agreed. Not only had his father given the town of Bonner Springs something to talk about, but Annie's mother—such a colorful bird—had also.

Yes, their parents had certainly given the town something to talk about. They'd given Annie and Joe something else. Something to worry about.

Chapter Ten

. . . .

It could have been an uncomplicated simple fracture. However, since it had remained untreated for hours, the swelling had made merely refitting the bones nearly impossible. So, after all the X-rays, Max went into a cast and would remain in the emergency room under observation for a while longer. He was also dehydrated and his blood pressure was up, thanks to choosing to break his ankle in the middle of nowhere and without the means of getting help.

"What would you like me to do?" Willa sat in the chair next to Max's hospital bed and looked at Joe. "Do you want me to stay here and keep him company while you go home and do what you have to do? It could be hours."

"Pshaw," Max said to Willa. "You go to Margaret's and get some rest. You're the one who walked miles trying to find help. You're the one who had to lift me back into the car."

"I needed the exercise."

"I can't believe I fell out of the car and broke my ankle," Max complained, albeit good-naturedly.

"I can't believe between the two of you, you didn't have a phone to call for help," Joe grumbled.

"Could have been worse," Willa quipped and cited another

statistic. "Did you know that eight hundred adults go missing in Texas every year? At least you found us."

"Mom, how do you know how many adults go missing in Texas?"

"It was on some handout I had to read for my criminal justice class."

Joe shook his head. "Kansas is not as big as Texas."

"That's beside the point," Max said.

Joe looked at Annie. The expression on her face mirrored his. *Who are these people and what have they done with our parents?* Joe had never seen his dad this sappy. He had no idea about Willa. Maybe she acted like this all the time.

"I'll go get Aunt Margaret's car. It will be easier to get you and your cast inside."

"Your truck's fine," Max insisted.

"But you're not fine," Joe replied as he checked the time on his cell phone. "Look, I've got to check on a few things, and then I'll be back." Before his dad could protest again, Joe gave him a hug and headed for the door.

Annie followed. "Just take me back to your dad's house. I'll get my car and come back for Mom. You can do whatever you need to do without worrying about us."

"I don't think those two plan on separating."

Her silence as they walked to the parking lot was all the answer he needed. She saw it, too.

Opening the truck door to help Annie in, Joe saw that Jacko was the only sane being—snoring comfortably on his blanket in the middle of the seat. The kitten was awake and mewing for sustenance. Annie didn't hesitate, just got busy taking care of the tiny creature.

"I'll make sure your mother gets back to Margaret's later on today," Joe said. "You don't need to worry about her or my dad, just get some sleep."

"I'm fine."

She didn't look fine. She looked tired. She'd washed her face, and he could no longer see any evidence of tears. He started the truck, turning on the lights and heading out onto a deserted street. "The sun's already rising. You might want—"

"I'm fine. I just need some coffee, lots of coffee."

"You need some sleep, lots of sleep, and you'll be feeding that baby every three hours. A schedule like that gets old fast, believe me."

"Do you always tell people what to do?"

He deserved that. He'd pretty much run the show during the search, deciding when and where to stop. Maybe he'd been a little hard on her, but he'd been worried. "No, I don't always tell people what to do. Animals yes, people no."

"You might be saying no, but I'm hearing yes."

"You have to remember I'm an only child. We do pretty much run the show."

"Well, I'm a middle child, put on this earth to make sure my big sister knew she only 'thought' she ran the show. You take care of your father and I'll take care of my mother."

He started to protest, then realized that was exactly how he wanted it.

Really, it was.

Only, if all the other stuff disappeared, Joe wouldn't mind taking care of Annie.

Whoa. Stop. Obviously, he needed sleep. It was a murky mind that had him turning as sappy as his dad. Yes, sleep deprivation was to blame. This was going to be night number two without much sleep, and besides transporting his father from the Kansas City hospital to Bonner Springs, he had plenty of things to do.

What did he have planned for today, a today that was already making its presence known as the sun grandly peeked over the horizon?

First, take care of the kitten. Convenience stores were a dime a dozen in Kansas City. Joe pulled into the parking lot of the first one he saw.

"Coffee." Annie's eyes lit up. "Real coffee."

"The hospital had real coffee," Joe said.

Annie just made a face and exited the truck. She'd only gone a few steps when she stopped suddenly.

"What?" Joe asked.

"I just realized how I look."

"You look fine. A little muddy, but fine."

Ten minutes later they were back in the truck. Joe turned in the direction of home, and next to him, Annie carefully measured yogurt into the warm water she'd filled the bottle with. Then, she took a big sip of coffee and settled back, looking quite comfortable in his truck.

It didn't feel like a Wednesday. It felt like a surreal Saturday. For Joe, Wednesdays were farm days again. He was supposed to be on the road. Then, too, he needed to start looking for someone to hire permanently. He thought about asking Annie to man the office, just field phone calls and direct walk-ins, but, he reminded himself, she was neither friend nor family.

He smiled. Too bad, because he already knew enough about her to realize she'd clean the place up—in more ways than one.

But he didn't need to worry about any of that today, not really. If a pet owner really needed him, they had his cell. And he'd put notes on his door before, explaining absences. The woman next to him needed a good night's sleep. At worst, Annie would scare his patients. Her hair, once again, was flat on the side. At best, she'd fall asleep at the front desk.

Unbidden came the memory of finding her asleep in her car early Monday morning, just two days ago, about this same time. If he remembered correctly, he'd wanted her—no, not her, but someone like her—under his Christmas tree, all wrapped up and just for him.

Forever.

Before he had time to really consider the directions his thoughts were heading, his phone sounded. He didn't even look at caller ID—he figured it would be someone asking about Dad.

It wasn't.

"Sorry to bother you," Cliff Whittaker said, "but something happened to Dot. Something either got to her or the fool horse has gone and run into something sharp. I don't know. But she's got at least two jagged wounds on the pastern of her left front leg. They're deep, deeper than I'm able to deal with. I can't stop the blood."

"You think it's an artery?"

Cliff hesitated, but only a moment. "No, not an artery. Still, it's more blood than usual."

"She able to walk?"

"Not what I'd call a walk."

"Was she in the pasture when this happened? Did she get near a fence?"

"She was pastured, but I can't imagine the fence doing this."

"I'm on my way," Joe promised. Before ending the call, he asked what Cliff had done as far as ice and wrapping. Then Joe looked at the woman next to him.

Her eyes were weary but her smile wasn't. "So, where are we going?"

"Blue Sunflower Farm. Friend of mine, Billy Whittaker's place, well, his dad's place. They have a few quarter horses and his favorite mare's hurt. I'd take you home first, but then I'd have to backtrack. Dot might have damaged her tendon, so I'd like to get out there as soon as possible. Billy and I go way back. "

"Let's go," Annie said.

"Call the hospital—you remember dad's room number? See if they know what time he'll be released."

Annie obeyed, finding out that two in the afternoon was the best estimate. Then she called her sisters. Joe listened as she spoke to Beth, who must have answered on the first ring and, judging by the one-sided conversation he was privy to, was annoyed at being out of the loop—if there was a loop—for so long.

Cathy didn't answer, so Annie left a message, not only giving her a brief update but adding, "Remember to make note cards for your Spanish class and read them aloud to yourself."

Then she called her assistant, someone named Rachel, who had a cold and wasn't going to work today. Watching Annie's face, he realized that her being here in Bonner Springs to retrieve her mother meant a real sacrifice.

"Everything all right?" he asked.

"No, not really," she answered softly.

Joe swerved to miss a squirrel running across the road, and

Annie cradled the box, making sure the kitten didn't get spooked. The squirrel stopped, stood on its tiny back legs, and stared as Joe's truck left the pavement, skidded on the dirt, and then scrambled for pavement again. Thanks to the bumpy detour, Jacko woke up, stood, stretched, and then turned so he could sleep with his muzzle on Annie's leg.

"It's just one thing after another out here, isn't it?" she noted.

"What do you mean?"

"Well, I've known you two days and so far you've been involved in two cornfield rescues, first me and then your dad. That has to be some kind of record. Then you've managed to lose a receptionist, gain a kitten, and now you're going to help a horse. All on little or no sleep."

"With the exception of cornfield rescues, everything else is par for the course. And I didn't gain a kitten, I think you did. But, yes, things were a lot easier before your mother and you showed up," he agreed.

"Which is why I need to get busy helping my mom find those coins so I can get her home before something else goes wrong."

Joe shook his head. "Finding those coins comes with a price, one my dad hasn't considered. What if Kyle did take them? What if somehow one of you stumbles onto proof—not that I think you will, mind you, but what if you do? All these years there's been a debate. Ending this debate and solving the mystery might not make things better."

"Whatever we find, we'll tell your father and he gets to decide. It doesn't have to be announced."

"There are no secrets in a small town," Joe said.

"What made you think of this now?"

"I've always thought about it." Not a chance did Joe want to tell her the real reason, that he was—in just a few short days, two to be exact—getting used to seeing her. Finding the coins meant she'd leave for good and he'd know for sure there was no Santa Claus, nothing under the tree for him.

She was good company, she was entertaining, and he enjoyed being with her.

"What made you think of this now?" Annie repeated. Apparently, she didn't like his first answer.

"I'm just playing the devil's advocate," Joe went on. "What if we find out who really took them and it's not Kyle, it's someone else who was at the party?"

"Like Missy or Marlee? Could they be guilty?"

"No, I really don't think so. Marlee married Dwayne right after high school. They were pretty much a couple from the time she was in eighth grade and he was in tenth. She and her husband own the restaurant. They're two of the happiest people I know. Actually, three of the happiest people. Their daughter, Katie, is full of spit and vinegar. Good with animals, too. They have money because of the restaurant. No, she wouldn't have taken them. Missy left after high school, but all I ever heard was how tough a time she was having. If she'd have taken the coins and sold them, she would've had some fun, don't you think?"

"But there are two others, right? You told me about a father and son who were there. You said they left before the coins went missing."

"That's why I'm bringing this up now," Joe answered. "There's not a chance the dad who acted as a chaperone took the coins—

not a chance, nor his son. They're Billy and Cliff Whittaker, and you're about to meet them."

* * * * *

Blue Sunflower Farm was so much more than the rustic farm—like all the others they'd passed this morning—that Annie expected to see. It was a Norman Rockwell painting that somehow collaborated with a creative ten-year-old girl armed with a paintbrush. Annie rolled down the window and leaned out. The fresh air whipped her blond hair and rushed against her cheeks. Not quite as good as coffee, but close enough. She just might manage to stay awake long enough to help. "It looks more like something from a kid's movie than a farm."

"Clifford's family is one of a kind."

The fence was fairly close to the road. Someone had attached bright blue wooden sunflowers, complete with yellow centers, on every post.

"Mona, that's Clifford's wife, paints them every year. She sells them, too. I guarantee she has a booth at the farmer's market our parents went to. The dirt you see behind the fence, that's the acre she's using for the real thing."

"Sunflowers."

"Yes, she probably planted a few weeks ago, and if we were a bit closer we could see some of the seedlings emerging."

Annie sat up. "How cute is that!"

"What? The acre?"

"No, over there, the cows!" A line of cows—all standing at attention—obviously took guard duty seriously. If not for an occasional swish of a tail or a baby nudging at a mama, Annie would have thought they were sculptures.

"Haven't you seen cows before?" Joe sounded amazed.

"Of course I've seen cows. I've just never seen them stand like that."

"Here in Kansas, the cows care about and protect their owners."

"Oh, hush."

He was teasing, and had he been anyone else, she'd have hit him playfully or stuck out her tongue. As he turned into a long driveway leading to a white clapboard farmhouse, he said, "Cliff has a grazing herd of Ayrshires with a few Milking Shorthorns thrown in."

"I have no idea which cows are Jimmy Choo caliber and which cows are Payless, so tossing out their brand names does nothing for me."

Joe started to laugh but quickly stopped. The cows had been stationary. The hogs were not. He slammed on the brakes to avoid hitting one that ran right in front of the truck. "Cliff's hogs break out of their pens on a regular basis. He'll also tell you they're docile, but when you're chasing them, they're anything but."

"More trouble than they're worth?" Annie asked.

"These are purebred Hereford Hogs, quite a few of them pregnant. They need a closed pasture, but outside of chasing them down every day or so, they aren't much trouble. Actually, if you look closely, you'll see that Cliff's grandkids—the ones chasing them right now—don't seem to mind too much."

"They chase them down every day or so?"

Joe paused a moment before answering, "Pretty much."

Jacko suddenly sat up, barked, and scrambled across Annie's lap so he could see out the window better. The jiggled kitten let out a tiny sound, and tiny paws stretched and curled, kneading for comfort that wasn't there.

Jacko barked again. Annie wasn't sure if he was saying, "Dad, let me out of the truck now!" or if he simply wanted to remind his owner "I'm awake and on the job!"

Joe parked by a barn, got his brown bag from the backseat, and headed inside the blue structure dotted with sunflowers. Jacko, without a backward look or bark of farewell, ran to join the pig chase.

Annie followed Joe, carrying the kitten box and wrinkling her nose at the strong odors while trying to keep an eye on where she stepped. If she stayed longer than a week, she was buying boots. Oz was no place for the sandals both she and her mother preferred.

"Thought you'd never get here," said a voice from inside a stall.

Annie jumped, but Joe merely turned to his left and entered an enclosed area. When Annie started to follow, he said, "Wait out there."

"I've already cleaned the wound with a saline solution," a large man wearing blue cambric said. "I still have no idea how this happened. We don't have any barbed wire in the pasture. I had Billy look to see if anything glass or metal somehow got into the field. He walked around for an hour but didn't find anything. Of course, he's not nearly as good at finding trouble as our horses."

Joe took a small computer out of the bag he'd retrieved from his truck. After a moment, he said, "Dot had her tetanus shot two months ago." He rubbed his hand over a big, dark brown horse's head and the beast closed her eyes. "Yes, little girl, that's right. This isn't the first time I've stitched you up."

Annie found a spot where she could see better, put the box with the kitten on a shelf, and leaned against the pen. The horse, one leg bent so it wasn't touching the ground, stood trembling. A makeshift bandage bound the wound. Joe carefully unwrapped the binding.

"It looks awful," the man observed. "Her skin's just hanging there."

Annie agreed.

Joe had something in his hand and was guiding it ever so slowly into the wound. Annie thought about looking away, but she was fascinated.

"Judging by how Dot's taking this all in stride and the wound isn't as deep as it looks, I think she's going to be just fine. I'll flush the wound, stitch her up, and bandage it. You remember what to do?"

"I own stock in petroleum jelly," the man said. Now that his horse was no longer in danger, Cliff turned his attention to Annie. "Who's this?"

"Annie Jamison," Joe introduced, "meet Cliff Whittaker."

"Ah, Willa's girl. You find them coins yet? I've always wondered where they got off to." He didn't wait for an answer; instead, he turned back to Joe. "I hear your latest receptionist headed on up to Denver, Omaha, or some such place. Why would she want to do that?"

"Makes no sense to me," Joe said.

Cliff turned again to Annie, looked her over, and then looked back at Joe. "You both fall in a mud puddle?"

"You could say that." Joe filled Cliff in on what had happened the night before.

"Sorry to hear that. I'll put your dad in my prayers." Cliff went from serious to curious, looking from Joe to Annie. "I'm amazed that your daddy's got one working for him and now you seem to be carting around the other."

Joe took a moment to consider, then finally said, "She's helping with the search, too. It's temporary and unexpected."

Cliff looked like he understood perfectly.

"By the way," Joe said, "I missed you at church Sunday night. Everything okay?"

"We had some things to take care of in Kansas City," Cliff said. "We stayed and attended services there." About that time, he noticed the box Annie had put on the shelf. "What's in the box?"

"A kitten I'm taking care of."

At that, Cliff chuckled. "Oh, Dr. Joe, she's going to work out just fine."

Annie felt like she'd passed a test she'd not been aware she was taking.

"Can I come in now?" She didn't wait for an answer but took one step through the half-open gate and into the stall. Then she stopped. The horse was bigger than she expected.

"You afraid of horses?" Cliff asked.

"Not sure. I've never really been near any."

"City girl," Joe explained.

"I'm from Tucson, Arizona," Annie protested. "We're more the Wild West than a metropolis."

"You look like your mama," Cliff observed. "I can see why Joe's carting you around with him, and if you represent the Wild West, maybe you can keep him in line. None of our local girls seem able to."

Behind him, the horse let out a snort. Cliff grinned. "Dot here's not feeling too good, so maybe we need to give her some space. You want me to introduce you to some of the other horses?"

"No, I'm good," Annie said.

Cliff didn't appear to be a man who took no for an answer—a trait most of the men she'd met in Kansas shared. Next thing Annie knew, Cliff had handed off the kitten to Joe, and while Joe cleaned up, she was being shown both land and livestock and hearing about the benefits of green grass, fresh air, and sunshine.

An hour later, after at least two miles of walking and one twisted ankle thanks to her stupid sandals, Annie joined the Whittakers for breakfast. She'd not managed to get a word in edgewise so hadn't brought up the missing coins even once. She hoped to do it when they rejoined Joe at the main house, but before she knew it, she was standing in a kitchen bigger than her entire apartment.

Cliff's two sons were at the table and introductions were made. Billy looked a lot like his dad and merely nodded his head while shaking Annie's hand. He was a gentle giant. No wonder no one accused him. He was painfully shy. Nothing at all like his dad when it came to conversation. No way would he do anything to bring attention to himself. He and Joe talked animals and family and then fell silent.

Joe leaned over and whispered, "Billy's always been the quietest of my friends, but he's great fun. He's always trying to figure out how something works, why something doesn't work, and he's always looking in corners expecting to find a surprise."

"Has he ever found anything?"

"He has a collection of old bullets, a pair of spectacles, and lots of antique bottles, all found because he saw something unusual and had to investigate."

Both the Whittaker sons had adjacent homes and worked for their dad. This added two wives, both friendly, to the already crowded table. In order to fit Annie and Joe, Cliff's wife, Mona, set up a child-sized folding table for the five grandkids. Nobody asked if Annie wanted breakfast, they just assumed.

"So, Annie," Cliff said after the prayer, "what did you enjoy the most? I'm thinking it wasn't the cows."

Joe, sitting next to her, laughed. "She liked them when we drove up. Thought they were cute."

"They aren't so cute up close," Annie said. "One of them got me with her tail."

And to think she'd been worried that Jacko would drool. "Eww" came squeals and snickers from the kids' table. "We know what's on a cow's tail."

"I know what I like best," a little girl piped up. "It's the kitten you brought. It's bootiful."

"We have a litter in the barn," Mrs. Whittaker added. "We always seem to have a newborn or two in the vicinity."

"So what did you like?" Joe encouraged, steering the conversation back to Annie.

"I liked the chickens."

Cliff took over. "We have almost a hundred hatchlings and more eggs than we know what to do with. Annie helped me rearrange a few eggs so they'd be under a brooder."

"It was interesting," Annie said. "He has what he called a chicken condo. It's divided in half and there's a door in-between, and on..." Her voice tapered off. "You know this already?"

Joe nodded. "I know of at least a hundred chicken condos around here."

"Tell them what you did next," Cliff suggested.

Annie really didn't want to tell them, didn't want to admit how out of her element she was. Most of her animal knowledge came from books and was obviously wrong.

"Go ahead," Cliff urged.

"A few years ago, I read that with baby chicks, the way you tell their gender is to hold them upside down by one leg. If it's a boy, he'll twist his head and peck at you with his beak."

"I've never heard that," said a daughter-in-law.

Both sons looked perplexed.

"It gets funnier," Cliff said. "I about fell over when she shared it with me."

"And if it's a girl chick?" Joe encouraged.

"Then she just hangs there, doesn't do anything."

"All my chicks are girls," Cliff complained.

"Impossible," his wife said, slapping him playfully on the arm. "The word 'henpecked' proves that we women know when and where to strike."

"My books are wrong," Annie said woefully.

"How many did you let her test before you stopped her?" Joe asked.

"Oh, about a dozen or so. I was having a good time watching."

She felt it then, bubbling in her chest and rising to escape. Laughter, the good kind, the kind she hadn't experienced since Burt had called her almost two weeks ago and said, "Something's going on with your mother. You might want to come home."

Home.

Annie couldn't stop the laughter; it spilled out. Sitting next to her, Joe laughed, too. And she suddenly noticed, again, how big he was, how strong, and how much she liked the hint of a beard at his chin. The man needed to get home and shave.

Home.

She needed to get home where all her jewelry supplies were and she could spread out. She needed to get home and help with the business. Rachel wasn't up to the task. She needed to get home and figure out what was going wrong with Beth and Charles. And then there was Cathy. She always acted like she was on top of things, but although it seemed that the youngest Jamison sister always landed on her feet, she needed encouragement, and not the kind that came over the phone. The kind that came with a girls' night out and some serious cheerleading.

Home wasn't Bonner Springs, Kansas, but Casa Grande, Arizona. And, for that matter, the sooner she and Joe headed back to Bonner Springs, the sooner she could really get to work. Not just for Joe, either. She could tear Max's house apart, find the coins, and leave Kansas before whatever it was calling her—green grass, fresh air, sunshine, laughter, handsome vet—needed some serious thought and an answer straight from the heart.

Chapter Eleven

....

When they left the Whittakers, Annie was the proud owner of not one but two wooden blue sunflowers. After a bit of back-and-forth with Mrs. Whittaker and the grandchildren, Annie had also found herself the proud owner of a dozen funny-colored eggs in various sizes.

"She should have let me pay."

"I'm surprised Cliff's wife didn't ask for payment or at least barter," Joe said. "She's usually quite a businesswoman. What were you talking about over by the sink?"

"My mother mentioned that I clean houses for a living. Mona said she'd been using a pumice stone, but it wasn't working on the old bathtub in their bathroom."

"What did you tell her?"

"To use a carburetor cleaner."

"You're kidding. Hmmm, how much would you charge me to clean my apartment?"

She thought maybe he was joking, but so far, in their brief partnership, he'd not shown much of a sense of humor, unless it involved sarcasm. "How dirty is it?"

"I'm a bachelor, not home much, and have lots of animals to take care of."

This made Annie's answer easy. "You can't afford me. Besides, you're the enemy. I'll probably clean your dad's place, but that's because I can clean and look for the coins at the same time. It's easier."

"I'm not the enemy."

But he was, in more ways than one, just not the typical enemy who threatened a person's well-being. Joe was more a threat to Annie's way of life. First, he was the son of the man who'd hired her mother for a job but instead seemed to be wooing her. Second, he was very much like his father, and for the first time in a long time, Annie felt in the mood to be wooed.

That was the third reason why Oz wasn't working out so well. The son of the enemy was turning out to be the nicest guy Annie had met in a long time.

"I'm just glad they were safe," Annie said.

"Who?"

"Our parents."

"Oh, funny. For a moment I'd almost forgotten what started this adventure."

"I can't forget. I'm still amazed that my mother came all this way just to look for coins."

"She's really not doing much looking," Joe pointed out.

"No, but I'm going to look some today. But first, you need to take me to Margaret's. You're right. I've got to get some sleep." She took out her cell phone and checked the time. "One o'clock. Wow, I can't believe I'm still functioning. I can't remember the last all-nighter I pulled."

"I can. It was the night you arrived. I was at the Hickses' place."

Annie gave a slight smile. "Not my fault. And I did get some sleep that night, scrunched up in the back of my rental car. Not comfortable at all. So, are you going to work at all today?"

"No. While you were exploring with Cliff, I called my appointments and rescheduled. None of them were emergencies. Almost all of them knew about Dad and weren't surprised. I'm going to do the same thing as you. Get some shut-eye. More shut-eye than you, actually, since you're feeding the kitten. Or, do you want me to take it?"

"Not a chance. I'm starting to like the little guy."

"Don't give him a name," Joe advised. "If you do, you'll want to keep him."

"Too late. One of the little girls back there named him Boot because he's bootiful. She didn't ask permission. I like it, although I'm sure I'll change it to Boots."

Joe was silent for a moment, and just when she was about to nudge him so he wouldn't fall asleep at the wheel, he said, "I am not the enemy."

He must really have been tired, because he'd indicated he was just as vulnerable as she when it came to dealing with their out-of-whack parents.

"You're right, you're not the enemy. I'm the one who said we should work together, so deep down I know that. It's just so weird."

"What?"

"Our parents acting so comfortable together, like they've known each other forever, like they're a couple. I about fainted when my mom opened your dad's front door for the morning paper the day I arrived. She looked like she belonged here."

"It's been like that since the evening she arrived."

"You were there?"

"Of course. I knew when your mom's plane was due in. I knew when he left to go pick her up. I was right here, sitting on the porch, waiting for their return. Margaret was next door pacing. I think it was the first time in years she'd missed her evening shows. Dad had convinced her to let Willa stay over there. Margaret started imagining some six-foot-tall, tattooed villainess."

Annie giggled. "My mom threatened to disown me if I so much as dared get a tiny rose tattoo on my ankle."

"So, no tattoos for you?"

"Not even a temporary one."

He pulled into his dad's driveway and turned off the engine. Jacko stood, tongue out and tail wagging, waiting patiently for freedom.

"When my dad drove up with your mother, he whipped in the driveway and got out of the car with this big grin on his face. I hadn't seen that expression in years. He hurried around the car—like a teenager—and opened the door for her. As she got out of the car, he bowed! I almost fell off the rocking chair."

"Because he bowed?"

"Not just because he bowed, but because I recognized what he was doing. He was flirting." Joe wasn't finished. "And it has only gotten worse."

He opened the driver's side door and he and Jacko got out. Annie gathered her purse and straightened the front seat up as much as she could. Before she finished, her door opened. Joe waited.

She climbed out.

He bowed.

* * * * *

Luckily, Margaret was so focused on putting the eggs in the refrigerator and cooing over the kitten that she didn't notice Annie's distraction.

The man had bowed. Then, before she had time to wrap her mind around his actions or what they meant or react herself, he'd walked her to the door. Then, checking his watch, he'd mumbled something about going to fetch his dad and how late it was, and having "places to go, things to do, people to see," and he'd left.

She'd had the most ridiculous urge to chase his truck.

Lately, she'd done a lot of chasing, mostly after her mother. But maybe it was time for a change.

Was he trying to be funny? No, not a chance, not after a whole night with no sleep. He'd talked about his father flirting, and then he'd mimicked his father. Why? What did it mean?

Why did it matter so much?

Margaret stared into the shoe box containing Annie's kitten. "Didn't take long for Joe to convert you," she commented.

"I'm not in the market for a cat; I'm just taking care of Boots."

"Boots?"

"Because he's bootiful."

"Indeed," Margaret said. "So, you've already named him, but you're not in the market for a cat."

"I didn't name him—one of the Whittakers' granddaughters named him. I just went along because the name is perfect. And I'm just taking care of him temporarily."

"I believe you." Margaret said the words but her tone indicated otherwise.

Back in the pink bedroom, Annie quickly checked her messages and responded to her sisters'. Beth was still assuming everything was wrong and that she needed to be in Bonner Springs. Not that she had time, mind you.

"So, tell me why our mother was lost in the middle of nowhere," Beth demanded. "I want to know everything, not just what Mom decided I should know."

Annie related that Max's family owned property in the area and that he'd been showing it to Mom. She also very carefully blamed the cow, four times. Cow, cow, cow, cow.

Something was going on with Beth, and it had nothing to do with their mother. Unfortunately, Annie was too tired to tackle Beth and her problems right now.

Annie's phone call to Cathy was easier. Cathy picked up on everything pretty much being all right—and that it might be fun to be in Bonner Springs.

"So tell me about this vet," Cathy demanded cheerfully.

All Annie could think about was the last moment she'd seen him, how he'd smiled, and the exaggerated bow.

What did it mean?

Knowing Cathy was a hopeless romantic and would start imagining emotions that didn't, *couldn't*, exist, Annie filled Cathy in about hunting for their mom and the visit to the Blue Sunflower Farm, and asked about school.

Annie noted how Cathy sidestepped the question and guided the conversation back to Bonner Springs and their mother. Annie redirected it back to school, especially the Spanish class Cathy was struggling in.

The next phone call, to Rachel, was a different kind of problem.

"Tell me from the beginning," Annie said when Rachel picked up the phone. "Your text message felt a little frantic."

"I do have one piece of good news," Rachel said. "Dad fixed the air conditioner. The rest, however, is not so good. With you out of town, it's like a free-for-all. I had two girls call in sick. Then, I had both of Suzette's customers call me yesterday to complain about her arriving late and then leaving early."

Suzette was a good worker, when prodded. Rachel was not a prodder. Annie was human relations, in charge of dealing with the employees. She was the heavy. Rachel was behind the scenes, not a taskmaster.

"Who called in and why?"

Rachel gave the names and added, "They didn't say why, and they both just left messages on the phone."

"Did you reschedule the houses?"

"No, I called and explained that you were out of town and that we had a sick employee."

Annie closed her eyes. On one hand, Rachel had done the right thing, but from a business point of view, one had to think of the money. Not rescheduling immediately meant the home owner could decide to skip a week. It saved them money. However, it *cost* OhSoClean money. They were in the black, but not enough to swallow many losses—especially not in this economy.

"First, call Suzette's clients and tell them you're sending them a holiday gift card. Short term, we lose money, but maybe in the long run we'll recoup. I'll call Suzette when, hopefully soon, I'm in town next. Then start looking through applications."

Rachel was silent for a moment, then muttered, "I'm trying so hard. I don't know how to talk to these people. Maybe I should just stick with marketing and numbers."

Some of Annie's annoyance fled. She'd been unfair to Rachel. Rachel had never signed on for the human resources end. She'd signed on as marketing, website upkeep, and accounting. Those were her gifts.

"You're doing fine," Annie assured her. "When a management change happens last minute, people feel displaced and can take advantage. I completely understand. And I want to be there so I'm not trying to troubleshoot long distance."

Rachel's responding laugh was on the wry side. "So, have you just about got everything sorted out with your mother? Will you, will both of you, be home soon for good?"

"I wish I knew," Annie admitted. "Nothing here is what I expected."

"Just like here. I expected I could take over your end, successfully, at least for two measly weeks. I'll tell what I did take over with some success. I'm keeping up on your jewelry website. You've sold five pieces in the last two days. I've mailed them out already."

"I repeat: You're doing fine. You can't control what others do."

Even after hanging up, Annie's final words to Rachel echoed through the bedroom.

You can't control what others do.

"We all have our gifts," Annie informed Boots. "I'm not trying to control my mother. My gift is keeping things running smoothly while keeping tabs on her. Your gift is being cute and staying alive."

With that in mind, Annie went to make Boots a new bottle. Once that was accomplished, she lay on her bed, holding the kitten in her lap. She'd never held anything so tiny, so vulnerable, so unbelievably soft. Funny how this tiny being, eyes seared shut and delicate paws reaching out for a mama that wasn't there, made Annie feel content in a way she'd not felt for a long time. Like she had time to breathe, had time to sit back and just enjoy.

No wonder Joe took Jacko everywhere with him.

"I think I'm going to have to keep you," she confided.

Boots was too busy enjoying his bottle to respond. Annie positioned the kitten on her stomach—carefully angling the bottle the way Joe showed her—and closed her eyes.

"You coming to church?"

Annie's eyes flew open. Margaret stood in the doorway.

"Uh, no, not tonight. How long have I been sleeping?"

"Just over four hours. It's six now. I almost didn't wake you up, but Joe called and asked about the kitten."

Asked about the kitten? For some reason, while Annie was glad Joe asked about the kitten, she was a bit perturbed that he hadn't asked about her.

Very unrealistic.

She blamed it on that stupid bow.

"There's meat loaf and some other stuff covered in the fridge. Feel free to warm it up and take some over to Max," Margaret said. "He'll have to take medicine tonight, and he'll need a full stomach."

"When did he get home? Did Joe bring him? Where is my mother?"

"Max and your mother got home about three. Yes, Joe brought them. Right now, Willa's at the drugstore picking up Max's medication. She's meeting me at church. We'll be back a little after eight. Your mother left Max's front door unlocked," Margaret continued. "Go on over when you're fully awake. He'll be glad for the company."

"I'm not sure I'll be much help. I'm not a nurse."

"He doesn't need a nurse. Right now he's asleep in his favorite chair. Just help him up if he needs it and make sure he eats." Margaret glanced at the clock. "I need to run."

Annie looked at the clock on the dresser, too. Six. She'd been asleep only four hours. It felt like just a few minutes, and the brief snooze barely took the edge off her fatigue and left a fuzziness she wasn't comfortable with. She could only imagine what Joe must be feeling. He'd not gotten any sleep at all.

As Annie listened to Margaret's footsteps heading for the front door, she gently nudged the kitten off her stomach and positioned him between pillows so there was no chance he could make it to the edge of the bed.

"Looks like I'll be taking care of both a big guy and a little guy," she whispered. "At least I hope you're a guy, since I named you Boots. If you're a girl, I'll have to call you Bootsette." The cat didn't so much as move when Annie rolled him over to see if he was indeed a Boots.

She had no clue.

Because Boots was sleeping so soundly, she decided to wait on the next feeding. Joe said the kitten would let her know when he was hungry. A quick shower and change of clothes later, Annie headed out the front door, kitten box in one hand, leftovers in the other.

It felt strange entering Max's quiet house. Since her arrival, it had been full of his come-into-my-fold personality and her mother's constant good mood. Her mother had always been cheerful, but it had been in a muted way, never boisterous like this.

"Cathy," Annie said suddenly to herself. "Right now, Mom reminds me of Cathy."

Too hungry to wait for Max to wake up, Annie found a plate in the cupboard, divided the food in half, warmed her share in the microwave, and sat down at the table to eat while checking her phone. Good news was, no calls from her sisters. Bad news was, Rachel didn't like the way any of the applications read.

Even as she texted Rachel with a "Do what you can I'll be home soon," Annie battled the desire to fly home right away. It had taken years to build the business. And she was good at it. But then, if one week away meant make or break with the company, just how firm a foundation did their company have?

After washing her dishes, Annie started cleaning. She wasn't sure whose peace she was keeping—her own or Max's—but doing something helped her not to worry. Since she was in the kitchen already, it was a perfect place to start.

As she bent down and opened the first cupboard door, she started analyzing what she'd accomplished since arriving in Bonner Springs. Hours spent looking for the coins: three. Hours spent not looking for the coins: fifty-four. Hours spent looking for the coins: three. Hours spent alongside a handsome veterinarian: twenty-one.

It was time to put things in perspective. Clearly Bonner Springs was an Oz of a place. Both Annie and her mother needed to remember it was a temporary place and they needed to get home.

She was on her knees, pots and pans circling her, with her head inside a bottom cupboard, busy running her gloved hand along the baseboards—coins rolled after all—when Max groggily called, "Willa?"

Annie was almost glad for the interruption. Besides dust and a greasy film, there was evidence that at one time an animal had made a home in the way back. "Mom went to church," Annie hollered. Right, like anyone could hear the muted words coming from the dark recesses of a dusty old cupboard. She backed out, managing to bump her head, stood, took off the gloves, wiped the dust from her brow, and blew an errant strand of hair from in front of her face. Then, in a calm voice, she shouted, "I'm coming."

First, Annie did what every good cleaning service employee did. She quickly looked around the kitchen and assessed her progress. It was a mess. She'd emptied three entire cupboards. Her assessment took too long, and Max obviously was not in a mood to be patient.

"Willa, I need a little help."

Right now the mess didn't matter. Annie quickly traversed a field of frying pans, various-sized pots, and Dutch ovens, and headed for Max. She got there right as he was trying to get up.

"Wait a minute." Annie offered an arm. For a moment, she thought he wouldn't take it, but then he seemed to think better of it.

"I'm a little weak."

She got him to his feet and handed him his cane. "You've had a tough twenty-four hours. Plus, your painkiller is wearing off. Mom picked up a prescription on her way to church in case you need more."

"Willa went to church? Good. I told her to go on without me." Max smiled and let her steady him. He slowly headed down the hall. "I'm all right, really. You should have gone with her."

Instead of coming up with an excuse that sounded weak, because it was weak, Annie headed back to the kitchen, warmed up the rest of the meat loaf, and carried it out and put it on the TV tray someone had placed nearby. While she waited for him to return—hopefully his food wouldn't get too cold—she headed to the kitchen again and stacked the pots and pans in the sink and started washing them. Most had a fine mist of aged dust attached and really needed scrubbing. Truthfully, after three cupboards, Annie had the same splattering of dust attached to her. She'd be taking yet another shower tonight.

She loaded the dishwasher with some things and hand-dried the rest. Cathy always said Annie was crazy to wash dishes and then put them in the dishwasher. After starting the cycle, she went to check on Max. He was back in his chair, looking exhausted. His food was untouched.

"I can scoot the tray closer if that helps." She started toward him, but he motioned her away.

"I'm really not hungry."

"My mother will kill me if you don't eat. That's one of the Jamison rules. We feed people."

Max smiled. "If what your mother says is true, then the only people you ever fed was your own family."

Feeling a bit uncomfortable, Annie started to protest, but then realized it was true. The Jamison house wasn't really a beacon for friends from work, social events, or the like, whether male or female. Not from Dad's side or Mom's side. Not once had Willa hosted a Pampered Chef or Avon party. Dad liked his privacy and didn't enjoy noise or clutter.

Mom catered to him, so the girls tended to either bring kids home before he got off from work—then they had to make sure to clean up after them—or not bring them home at all. Even Cathy, the social butterfly, didn't want to chance Dad's comments. All too well, Annie remembered her dad once asking, loud enough so the friend could hear, "Doesn't she have a home?"

Still, Annie was surprised that her mother would tell Max, a stranger, about how her husband liked peace and quiet and everything in its place.

It felt wrong talking about her father, especially about his faults, with someone who wasn't family. Come to think of it, though, she and Beth and Cathy never talked about Dad, either.

"Well, it's the thought that counts," Annie said, trying hard to sound upbeat.

"I could hear you doing dishes. Were there that many? I thought Willa did ours yesterday."

"She did. I thought I'd clean out your cupboards and search for the coins. You'd be amazed how often items turn up in the places you least expect them. Some of your pots and pans were pretty dusty, so I washed them."

"You think the coins could be in a kitchen cupboard? That's a long shot."

"You've probably looked in the obvious places. I'll look in the not so obvious."

He nodded. "Life's always a bit more interesting when things and people aren't where they belong. Don't you think?"

Chapter Twelve
....

Annie didn't want to touch that comment. Just the thought of him bowing to her mother, making her mother feel the way Joe had made Annie feel when he bowed, told Annie she no longer knew where things belonged. It more than told Annie that *home* didn't always mean the four-bedroom structure of childhood memories, but that home could be anywhere. Home wasn't always literal. Home could change, from just a look in a man's eye and the touch of his hand.

Suddenly, Annie missed the home of her childhood, having her sisters near and always knowing that Mom and Dad were nearby. She wanted *that* home back.

She headed for the kitchen and retrieved Boots. When she returned to the living room, Max hadn't moved, except to lean back in the chair and close his eyes halfway. She pushed the TV tray closer to him, put the fork in his hand, and made herself comfortable on the couch—comfortable meaning she took Boots out of the box and set him on her lap. Maybe if she stayed in the living room, Max would eat.

For a full minute, silence reigned and the fork didn't move. Could the man fall asleep holding the fork? Annie wasn't sure. Nervously, she looked around the room, noting the portraits on the wall. Joe had certainly inherited his father's build—although right now Max looked thin and tired—but his mother's dark coloring. Max was light-skinned, his hair mostly gray with just a bit of brown showing.

The largest family portrait in the room showed a tall, lanky, much younger Max. Joe and his mother had a little more padding. Joe, in all the right places.

"Black Irish," Max said, sitting up, eyes no longer half-closed, and scooting forward. "Joe's mom came with both excitement and temper. Joe, now, he likes adventure, but he didn't get the temper."

"That's good," Annie said.

"I always wondered," Max said, "what would have happened if Elizabeth hadn't gotten so angry when the coins went missing."

"Elizabeth was your wife?"

"Yes. She was in Nebraska visiting a friend. She got back the next day."

"She thought Kyle took the coins."

"Actually, no. She thought Missy Hicks took them. Missy was a wee bit wild and had already gotten into some trouble. She tended to follow Kyle around and try to get his attention."

No wonder the coins had never been found. There were too many suspects to narrow down.

"Where did you get the coins in the first place?" Annie asked.

"My father died in World War II. When they shipped his belongings home, the coins arrived. We were all surprised when we found out how much they were worth."

"If we find them, what will you do with them?"

He looked a little dazed at her question and pointed at her with the fork. "They'll be handed down to Joe. He can do with them what he wants. They're worth about fourteen thousand each."

"I'm sure Joe will appreciate them."

Max nodded and slowly picked up his fork. "I want to thank you for all you did this morning, helping Joe to get me out of the car and to the hospital. I know Willa ruined her shoes in the mud. I imagine you did, too."

"Silly shoes," Annie said. "Tennis shoes are more comfortable. I don't know why I was wearing sandals. Habit, I guess. I think living in my part of Arizona just trains us to think 'wear less' instead of 'dress sensible.'"

"I can buy you a new pair."

"Now you're worrying too much."

Max took a bite, savored it for a moment, and started eating. After a few more bites, he asked, "How's the kitten doing?"

Annie looked down at the tiny bundle she sheltered in her lap. He'd been exploring a bit, doing a kind of push-and-pull maneuver that allowed him to roll from one side to the next. "Boots seems to be doing okay. His stomach's fat enough. I think I'm going to keep him. I've never had a pet."

"Be careful," Max warned. "Once you start taking in strays, it goes out on the pet grapevine and soon other animals will start seeking you out."

"You're kidding."

Max chuckled. "I'm only half kidding. I help Joe sometimes when he gets in over his head and has too many animals to care for. I think my favorite was a squirrel Joe's mama cared for. Joe says not to get attached to the wild ones, but I sure hated when we let that one go. For years, I was out there throwing food to the squirrels and looking for Charlie. That's what I named him."

"I take it the animals Joe treats usually get better."

Max frowned. "I can't remember many that didn't get better, if they could. He gets his way with animals from Elizabeth." He looked at the portrait Annie had been studying earlier. A smiling dark-haired woman seemed to look approvingly at Annie.

"When Joe's mother was alive," Max continued, "it seemed we always had a dog and a couple of cats. She couldn't walk away from a sick animal, either. One time someone brought over a blue jay. What a scrawny little fellow. I thought it had deformed legs and that the kindest thing to do would be destroy it."

He was silent for a moment, a half smile on his face, and Annie knew he was remembering his late wife, the good times—the look in the eye and the touch of the hand. Memories were like that. Sometimes they were so strong it seemed as if you could wish yourself back.

"She coddled that bird, did something to make those legs harden. After a while, that blue jay was starting to fly and landing on her shoulder."

"Did you keep it?"

"No, Elizabeth said letting go was a gift, both to you and to the animal. Still, every day for a month, she stood at the back door and searched for the bird."

"You still miss her." It was a statement, not a question.

"Every day, but in a good way, and she'd taught me to let go. I know I'll see her again. I think her death affected Joe more than me."

"How so?" Annie thought back to the raw wound that still

lingered from her father's death. The early morning call, the rush to the hospital, finding out it was too late.

"He was just one year shy of graduating with his vet degree. He came home, supposed to only be for a week, but I practically had to force him to go back. Oh, not that he didn't want to finish, but his heart was breaking and he couldn't decide what to do."

"Some people, when they're hurting, bury themselves in work." Even as she said it, she knew she was talking about herself, and also Beth to some degree.

"Not my Joe. He wears his heart on his sleeve, always has. He was worried about me, about money, and all kinds of things that the Good Book says not to worry about."

"We're back to the worry conversation," Annie noted.

"Not sure we ever left it." He leaned forward. "Are you still worried about your mother?"

Annie thought about it. "Yes and no."

"Can't be both," Max said.

"Sure it can. But, relax, I'm no longer worried that you're some con man out to take advantage of her."

Max laughed. "Good. Although I must say, it's the first time I got to be cast as a villain. I almost enjoyed it."

"Now you're a different kind of villain. I'm worried that Mom will like it here and want to stay." She said it half in jest, but Max's answer sobered her up.

"And would that be so bad?"

"After not even a week, yes. You hardly know each other. I'd worry—"

"Ah," Max interrupted. "We're back to worrying. The Bible says, in the book of Matthew, not to worry, not about life or what to—"

"—what to wear, etc. Yet, we all worry. Do you think there's a person alive who doesn't worry? I mean, I was raised in the church. I'm pretty sure Mary worried when she found out she was pregnant with Jesus. Certainly, Peter worried when he denied knowing Jesus. Then, too, Matthew had plenty of things to worry about. He started out as a tax collector. He was hated. I'd sure worry if almost everybody hated me."

"I think—" Max tried to interrupt, but Annie was on a roll. All the Sunday school lessons of the past were finally going to be put to good use. She'd use them to champion worrying.

"And, although he redeemed himself when he became one of Jesus' followers, Matthew had plenty to worry about at the end. Didn't he die a martyr?"

"I doubt the way he died concerned him much, as he knew his heavenly reward," Max said calmly. "Most people don't understand that there are two categories of worry."

Annie shook her head. "Worry is worry. I've always been a worrier. I don't know how to change."

"Your mom says you're the daughter who tries to carry the world on your shoulders."

"Hmm," Annie said. "So, according to you, Joe wears his heart on his sleeve and now I carry the weight of the world on my shoulders."

"And both are burdens I'd like to help ease."

Yup, here was the preacher, finally showing up. Max was so engaged, he actually started eating. After a few bites, he said, "There's the worry that leads to anxiety—anxiety so crippling that one ceases to function in a healthy manner. Then, there's worry that inspires one to action. That's the kind of worry that had you and my son out looking for us last night. That worry might best be called concern."

"I'd call last night downright fear."

"I was never afraid. I knew somebody would find us and help."

"I think it would be easier for you not to worry, because you're from here and know everybody. My mom and I don't know anyone, not really."

"If you know God, then it doesn't matter where you are. He is there and He's all you need. Have you been praying?"

Annie opened her mouth and slowly shook her head. "Praying hasn't been easy for me, lately," she admitted. Then, she tried to think about how to steer the conversation back to something safe. Even talking about worry would be better than talking about why she wasn't comfortable praying.

She needn't have worried. The flash of headlight beams momentarily lit up the living room, saving her from having to say anything except, "I think Mom's back."

"No, it's the neighbors across the street. They attend church but leave the minute the last amen is said. They're just in time though," Max said. "You were worried about how to respond. Now you don't have to."

"Oh, finish your meat loaf."

Max chuckled and did just that while filling her in on the across-the-street neighbors. Annie settled back on the couch and found a comfortable spot. Closing her eyes, she acknowledged that she might have missed many Wednesday night services because of fatigue and choice, but for the first time in years, she actually acknowledged that Wednesday night services even existed.

A life outside of work and family existed.

One she suddenly realized she missed.

* * * * *

"She sure can sleep." Joe sat in the rocking chair by his dad's kitchen door and rocked back and forth. He told himself that the movement was what kept him awake. But he knew the truth. The woman sleeping on his dad's couch had his attention and then some.

He was amazed and conflicted by his feelings. He could sit here and watch her all evening.

"You should head home," Max said, interrupting Joe's thoughts. "Willa's here. She brought the medicine, and she'll take care of me. I'm fine. You, on the other hand, look like you're half-dead."

Half-dead didn't begin to describe the way Joe felt. His eyes felt dry, his head ached dully, and every once in a while he zoned out completely. He'd done it during church tonight. He'd been sitting straight up, he knew that. His eyes had been open, he knew that. His Bible lay open to Romans, he knew that. What he hadn't realized was when class ended. Instead, while the people around him gathered their belongings, corralled kids, and said their good-byes, he'd just sat there, unmoving, until Frank, also looking fatigued, said, "Time to head home, boy."

If Joe didn't do something, he'd go from half-dead to sound asleep now, at his father's house. He cleared his throat and said, "Every single person asked about you."

What he didn't tell his father, because he didn't need any more razzing, was how many people asked him about Annie and why he hadn't brought her to church.

"And I was mentioned in the prayer," Max said.

"Two of them," Aunt Margaret called from the kitchen.

"I only heard one," Joe muttered.

"You were sleeping during the second one." Willa entered the room, water glass in hand. She handed it off to Max and gazed down at Annie before sweeping up Max's dirty dishes. "Not quite as soundly as my daughter, though."

"The neighbors across the street came home," Max said. "She thought it was you and went all quiet. Then she promptly fell asleep while I was talking—right in the middle of a sentence. I wasn't even preaching."

"No one would fall asleep during one of your sermons." Margaret came into the room and shook her head as if appalled by the thought. "They wouldn't dare."

"Should we just cover her up, leave her here?" Joe asked.

"No, we definitely can't leave her here," Willa said. "She's never liked surprises, and although Max is winning her over, she's still not completely convinced that he isn't the boogeyman. I'll wake her up, and we'll head over to Margaret's."

"Oh, we chatted tonight," Max said. "I've won her over."

"I can carry her to Margaret's," Joe offered.

Both his father and Willa looked at him as if he'd spouted two heads.

"You awake enough?" his father asked.

"She wouldn't like that a bit," Willa said. "Not that I don't appreciate the offer." She sat on the edge of the couch and gently pushed

Annie's bangs away from her forehead. Then Willa gave a little chuckle and pulled the kitten from the crook of Annie's elbow. "I'm glad this little fellow didn't get squished."

"Make sure she changes her clothes before she crawls into bed," Max said, nodding at Annie. "Kittens that young have no control."

Willa only tsked.

Annie mumbled something, and Joe wished he could hear her words.

"I know, baby," Willa said. "And I'm sorry to wake you, but we need to head home."

Annie sat up. Her hair was back to the mussed stage that Joe was starting to think was his favorite look. This time, when she spoke, Joe could hear her words.

To his surprise, he didn't like them one bit.

"Home, Mom? Really? Can we go home?"

Chapter Thirteen

....

There was a time, Joe thought wryly, when he could do what he wanted, when he wanted, and how he wanted—unless someone needed his veterinary services.

Somehow, he'd lost that carefree existence.

And this morning, when his eyes opened at five, he knew exactly who to blame: a golden-haired woman who'd landed—uninvited— in the middle of his life and now occupied almost all of his thoughts.

If he could get her out of his mind, he could go back to sleep and wake up at a decent hour, like seven.

Instead, he put on shorts and a T-shirt, let Jacko out into the backyard after making sure he had plenty of food and water, and headed toward 138th Street and a private drive called Mr. Goodcents Subs and Pastas.

What he really wanted to do was go to his dad's and wait until Annie showed up.

That, of course, made no sense.

Only a few souls were out at this ridiculous hour on a Thursday morning. Before becoming a vet, Joe had never been particularly fond of the early morning sun, but he'd learned long ago that being a vet wasn't a nine-to-five job, and that sometimes, if he wanted to work out, he needed to be there at five thirty when the facility opened.

Right now he had two goals: work up a sweat and work out his feelings for Annie Jamison. Last night, when she'd mumbled her happiness about *going home*, he'd felt something he'd not felt for a long time.

Fear.

Parking was plentiful at this early hour. The front desk attendant was on the phone, so Joe didn't have to answer questions or make small talk. He signed in and headed for the locker room to stow his belongings and then went into the weight room.

Fifteen leg presses and fifteen lying leg curls later, every bone in his body was awake and complaining and his mind really wasn't on the fifteen seated cable rows he was about to do.

So, Annie wanted to go home. Well, he couldn't blame her. Her adventures here in Bonner Springs couldn't count as fun. Plus, judging by the one-sided phone calls he'd been privy to, Annie was failing miserably at the task assigned to her: to bring her mother home. Willa would be here quite a bit longer, maybe weeks, and she was quite happy fussing over Max.

It almost made Joe believe in love at first sight.

Almost.

Time spent on the flat bench press convinced him that thinking about love at first sight and working out both caused pain.

He decided to stop thinking about Annie.

Instead, he'd think about all the things he had to do. First, how to keep his practice going. This meant he needed to find a personable receptionist who wasn't always thinking about greener pastures.

Then, too, he wasn't the only veterinarian in town—plus he was the new kid on the block. Sometimes he had hours in his schedule without business, hours that worried him.

Unfortunately, thinking about work only proved that work was about the only thing he'd been thinking about for the last two years. He needed a life. He needed to date now and then and have fun. And, sad to say, his social life was a small congregation with only two or three single women, all of whom he'd known forever and who felt more like sisters than potential dates. Joe looked around the gym. It was pretty empty, but even if it were full, he doubted he'd see even one woman who appealed to him like Annie did.

She'd appealed to him ever since he found her on the side of the road.

Joe chuckled. In some ways, Annie was like Jacko. He'd rescued her, loaded her into his truck, brought her into town, and now he wanted to keep her.

His final routine involved dumbbells. Quite honestly, he knew who the biggest dumbbell of all was. Joe Kelly, for wasting time at the Y when he could be with Annie.

He checked his watch. If he showered now, he could make it to his dad's in time for breakfast. Everyone would be there, including Margaret, who now thought that Max's house was a bit more, make that *a lot more*, interesting than television.

Joe had to agree. There'd not been a dull moment since Annie arrived, and she'd only been here four days.

That's all.

Unbelievable.

He wasn't exactly sure what Annie's morning plans were. He

assumed she'd eat with her mom, his aunt, and his father. But then, so far, her mornings had been anything but typical. Just like his. Dutifully, he wiped the seat of the machine he'd just vacated and headed for the shower. He didn't want to waste another moment at the gym.

He could pretend showing up at his dad's was the act of a dutiful son, but chances were he wouldn't fool anybody. Anyone seeing Joe turning into his father's driveway and hopping out of the truck would notice that he was hurrying toward something. They'd know it wasn't his dad.

It was a woman.

The wrong woman. One who wore fancy sandals and didn't like things to be dirty. One who obviously had been raised with lots of money and had never owned a pet.

She was everything he wasn't.

And she was exactly what he wanted.

And, honestly, it scared Joe to death.

* * * * *

"We were expecting you," Dad said.

Kansas sunlight spilled through the white and yellow kitchen curtains. Joe blinked, unsure whether his dad looked so happy because Willa was cooking breakfast or because Joe showed up.

Of course, his dad still might be on painkillers.

"Orange juice or milk?" Willa asked.

"Joe's a milk drinker," Margaret answered, as she handed Willa a glass.

"Where's Jacko?" His dad almost stood but, a short grimace later, changed his mind. He looked much better than he had yesterday.

Joe took his regular seat and tried to act nonchalant. No way was he asking where Annie was. "He's roaming the back acre of the clinic."

His dad raised an eyebrow. "You never leave him behind, except for church."

"I'll go get him in a little while."

Dad wasn't finished with the interrogation. "I figured you'd sleep until noon."

"No, I've got the whole morning booked with patients." Joe checked his cell phone to see what time it was. "In an hour, I'll be with my first appointment of the day, a potbellied pig. Luckily, it's pretty routine. I'll be trimming his hooves."

"I've heard potbellied pigs make good pets." Willa put a plate of pancakes in front of his father. "Like a cat or dog."

"Except most cats and dogs don't get up to two hundred pounds."

"One of my clients has a Saint Bernard," Annie said, coming into the room. She was pocketing her cell phone and looking quite pleased with herself. She continued, "Clementine weighs almost two hundred pounds."

Aunt Margaret promptly started singing. By the time she got to the third "Oh my darlin'," Joe's dad hushed her. Margaret, thanks to a slight hearing problem, never quite realized just how loud she really was.

"That's the exception, not the rule," Joe pointed out, purposely ignoring his aunt.

"Just sayin'," Annie said breezily and headed over to the stove. She picked up the bowl containing the pancake batter and checked its consistency before adding some water and stirring.

Joe's mouth watered. Yes, he was hungry, but it wasn't food that had him on the edge of his chair.

Annie poured some batter on the grill and picked up the spatula.

"You're on vacation." Her mother took the spatula from her and pointed toward the chair next to Joe's dad. "And don't think I haven't seen that folder of work in your bedroom as well as the jewelry supplies. Did you know that forty percent of all women feel guilty when they take time off work? Stop feeling guilty. Rachel's doing just fine. You need to have some fun."

"I'm not on vacation," Annie said. "And I'm not here to have fun. I'm here to help you."

"I don't need help. Now that you know I'm safe," Willa admonished, finishing the batch of pancakes Annie had started and putting them on a plate for Joe, "you can have fun. I insist."

"Now that I know you're safe," Annie said, "I'm going home."

The kitchen grew quiet. Even Margaret, who'd ignored Joe's dad, stopping singing and stood perfectly still as if movement would unleash some emotion she wasn't willing to deal with.

"When?" Willa asked, after a moment of silence stretched on way too long.

"I've got a flight out Sunday afternoon."

"Only three more days? I wish you'd stay another week," Willa urged gently, "like you originally planned."

"I agree," Margaret said. "You just got here. We've enjoyed having you. You leave now, you're like one of the wildflowers that sneak into my garden. You grow, amaze everyone with your beauty, and then you're gone before anyone can fully appreciate you."

"I think that's the nicest thing anyone's ever said to me."

Annie poured herself a glass of milk and sat down. "I'm already a nervous wreck, thinking about Cathy handling the Fountain Hills show alone."

"Cathy will be fine," Willa said. "She's a natural at selling jewelry. Go ahead, stay a little longer."

"I am staying a little longer. I really should leave today, but I want to finish looking for the coins." Yes, that was the reason she'd chosen a Sunday over a Friday departure. It had to be. "I need to get back to work on Monday. Rachel needs me."

"It would do Rachel good," Willa said, "to run the business by herself for a while. She'll never know what she's capable of if you don't give her a chance."

"I really hope you're right, Mom."

"So, you're leaving Sunday?" Joe asked. It wasn't the news he'd hoped for. Things would be too quiet in Bonner Springs, too quiet at his dad's house.

Lonely.

"My flight leaves at three," Annie said. "That gives me plenty of time to help Mom find the coins."

"There's no hurry to find the coins," Joe's dad said.

"None at all," Willa agreed, "and I don't need any help, but feel free to look. If you find them, you can have my share of the reward."

His dad didn't look convinced. "You don't need to be crawling in my cabinets and getting all dusty. Why don't you just consider your time here a vacation and have some fun? I'm sure Joe wouldn't mind showing you around."

"I can do that," Joe offered. After all, three more days might convince him she didn't belong in Bonner Springs, wasn't someone he needed to rescue and then keep. "Jacko and I know all the nooks and crannies that make Bonner Springs special."

"Where is Jacko?" Annie asked. "He's usually with you."

"Back at the clinic. I left him there when I went to work out this morning."

"Long time since you've hit the gym," his dad remarked. "You've mentioned starting up again, but you really haven't gone since—"

"I go now and then," Joe interrupted, "when I have time."

"You go," Margaret said, "when you have something in your head that you need to work out."

There were times, Joe thought, when he questioned his decision to settle back in Bonner Springs where everyone knew exactly what he was thinking and doing, sometimes before he did. Luckily, Annie didn't seem to care one way or the other if Joe regularly worked out or not.

"Seems weird to see you without Jacko," she remarked.

"Where's Boots?" Joe asked.

"In the living room on the couch. I've wrapped him in a towel. He's safe and comfortable."

Margaret shook her head, a Cheshire smile on her face, and asked, "How are you going to make yourself leave him behind when you go back to Tucson?"

"Okay," Annie acknowledged. "You were right. I'm not leaving him, I'm keeping him." Then, giving her mother a searching look, she continued, "Mom can bring him home when she's finished here. He'll be older and able to go longer without food. Besides, it's just a short plane ride." She switched her attention to Joe. "I want to leave him here for now, while he's such a tiny baby, just in case he needs you."

"Maybe you should stay," Joe suggested. "He needs more care than I can give."

But Annie was shaking her head, looking both guilty and sad. "It's hard to miss work."

"Work shouldn't be your whole life," Willa muttered, loud enough for Annie to hear but soft enough for Annie to ignore.

"We're a new business," Annie said, reaching down and playing with a bracelet on her wrist.

Joe suddenly realized this was what she did when she felt nervous, and he wondered why talking about OhSoClean would make her feel that way.

"Every start-up company demands dedication," Annie continued. "And really, I have to get back to it. I'm missing the bazaar in Fountain Hills this weekend. Cathy's doing it for me, but she doesn't know the different types of gems. And if someone were to try on a ring or something, and then just walk off without paying, she might not even notice. Me, I'd chase 'em down."

Willa looked like she had more to say but chose not to.

"I'll take good care of Boots," Joe promised.

Anything to put the sparkle back in her eyes. Anything to return her to that pleased-with-herself bounce from earlier this morning.

* * * * *

In a way, Joe Kelly made Annie long for something she didn't have, like free time and pets. When she was young, she'd always been busy with school, church, and friends. Since she'd hit her midtwenties, she'd been busy with work.

She'd never had a pet.

Being too busy came with a high price tag, one that Annie hadn't even been aware she'd been paying.

Maybe that's why when Annie booked the flight, she'd planned a departure date for tomorrow evening, but when the computer popped up to the reservation page, for no reason other than pure desire, she'd chosen a Sunday afternoon departure date.

She was tired of being too busy.

"I've never owned a cat." For some reason, Annie felt almost apologetic. "But I've always wanted one."

Her mother put pancakes in front of Joe and explained. "My late husband didn't like cats."

Annie nodded. "Dad was allergic to animals."

"All animals?" Max asked.

Annie thought for a moment. "I never thought to ask that, but for sure dogs and cats. I'm not even sure he'd have been open to the idea of fish."

"Bill wasn't allergic to animals," her mom said softly. "He just didn't like them around. He wasn't fond of dog or cat fur, said it got on clothes and into food. Plus, when we went to friends' homes and they had pets, he complained about the smell."

"I didn't know that." But in truth, Annie wasn't as surprised as she should have been. Her dad expected a clean house, demanded it sometimes.

"I want to take you to my museum," Max said. "But I need to get my car back first, and, hopefully, all the tools Willa left like crumbs on the side of the road. Willa's got some stuff in the backseat, too, that we need to fetch home."

"I was planning to do that today, Dad. My last appointment is at two."

Max shook his head. "It's too much for one man. I'll hire—"

Joe interrupted. "It shouldn't be too hard. Annie, if you want, you can come with me. You can see the land that belonged to Dad's family. You were so impressed with Blue Sunflower Farm, you might find what's left of my great-great-grandparents' place interesting."

"I'd like that."

"It was smaller than the Whittakers' place, more a gentleman's farm. They only lived on it a year. Then they packed up and moved into town."

"Why?"

"My great-grandpa was a preacher. The farm was supposed to pay the bills, because preaching certainly wasn't," Max answered. "However, he spent so much time in town, taking care of his flock, that his wife wound up doing the farming. Not only was she not very good at it, but they lost money."

"She didn't like the farm, said it was too hard," Margaret added.

"I'm not sure I could be a farmer's wife," Annie said, getting up to pour herself a fresh cup of coffee. "From what I've seen and read, it's hard work around the clock, not an eight-to-five job."

"Just as much today as yesterday," Max agreed.

"Got that right," Joe said. "I've heard stories about my great-grandfather from the time I was little. Dad not being a farmer, well, it's a generational thing. Most of the Bonner Springs congregation think that having members of the Kelly family as preachers for more than a hundred years counts for something."

"I'm the first Kelly," Max said, "to actually make a living on a preacher's salary and not have to do a side job."

"It helped that he inherited this house, paid for," Margaret said. "Plus, Elizabeth wasn't one who needed things. She didn't care much for the newest car or the newest technology. She was mostly happy just taking care of Max and Joey and her animals."

"Joey?" Annie almost spit out her coffee.

Joe frowned at Margaret, but she just grinned in return.

"I'd make a good preacher's wife," Annie's mom said.

For the second time in a single morning, the kitchen went silent.

Chapter Fourteen

....

When Annie finally tore her eyes away from Joe, who was carefully watching his father, she noticed Margaret—an unmoving, unsmiling Margaret. Neither her mother nor Max noticed. They were too busy gazing at each other, looking happy.

Margaret's reaction didn't quite make sense. No way should Annie's mother's words have been a surprise. Not if they weren't a surprise to Annie, who'd arrived on the scene a mere four days ago.

And they certainly shouldn't cause anguish.

Yet, here stood Margaret, who, from almost the moment Annie arrived in Bonner Springs, had been a cheerleader, welcoming both Jamisons into her home, filling them in on the Kelly history, sometimes tagging along on Max and Mom's outings—when her favorite show wasn't on the television—and keeping the path well trod between the two houses.

Joe, for his part, had stopped eating. His expression wasn't as easy to gauge as Margaret's. It was more guarded.

Annie stood, silently gathered her dishes, and took them over to the sink. Margaret turned and leaned against the countertop, gazing out the window. Annie could see Margaret's house, with its simple white clapboard and amazing yard. Annie didn't know anyone who gardened, but just a few days with Margaret and she could already tell the Mexican hats from the bluebells. And Margaret had already started her vegetable garden with tomatoes, peppers, and beans.

It was pretty much what Annie pictured for herself in a few years, only she pictured hers in Tucson red brick and some adobe. The yard would be desert-scape instead of lush green grass and flowers. If Annie were lucky, she'd have an orange tree as well as cacti. Maybe, just maybe, she would learn to garden when she needed to take a break from making jewelry and running a business.

Margaret finally turned from gazing out the window and spoke to Annie's mom. "Technically, Max is no longer a preacher. He retired. You wouldn't be a preacher's wife."

Max took his eyes off Annie's mom and looked at his sister, as if just noticing she was there. His words were strong—not exactly reassuring—but more purposeful, as if he'd suddenly regained something he'd lost.

"Once a preacher, always a preacher," he said. "I may not stand behind the pulpit, but there's not one ministry I'm not involved in. In some ways, I have more time now to spread the gospel."

"I was just kid—" Annie's mother began.

Margaret held up her hand. "No, please," she said. "Really, this is great news. I'm happy for you. It just took me by surprise. That's all."

Unfortunately, while her words said "happy," her eyes glistened with tears.

"There is no news and no need to be happy," Annie's mom continued. Max might have completely missed the expression on his sister's face, but Annie could tell that Willa was starting to notice. "It was just some friendly jesting."

"I'm not jesting," Max said solemnly. "And I'm very happy. Happier than I've been in years."

Margaret nodded. Her lips shaped into a half smile that Annie recognized, a smile Annie used often enough herself. It was an I-can-live-through-this kind of smile.

Max was reaching for her mother's hand.

Margaret turned to the sink, her back to her brother, and started doing dishes.

Joe stood, walked over to the sink, and gave Margaret his empty plate. She took it without looking at him. He stood so close to Annie she could feel the heat of his skin, feel the hard muscles in his arms.

From where she stood, Annie couldn't tell whether his smile matched his aunt's or was more contemplative. Then he was at the back door and heading outside with a simple "Bye, everyone." The screen door almost closed behind him when he turned to add, "Annie, I'll pick you up sometime after two."

Then he managed a quick getaway.

Once the door swung shut behind him, Annie hoped she could do the same—a quick getaway. She needed to think, needed to have something constructive to do with her hands.

"I'm not quite done searching the kitchen, but I'll leave it for now until you guys are through in here." Annie wasn't sure if they even heard her. She cleared her throat and asked, "Mom, what rooms have you searched?"

Her mother didn't even pause. "The basement, attic, living room, and Max's study. You and I went through the porch the other day."

Which left the bathroom, Max's bedroom, and Joe's bedroom. "I'm going to take apart the bathroom," Annie said.

That got their attention. Max looked faintly alarmed. Margaret even stopped washing the glass she'd been working on for five minutes.

"She's not being literal," her mother assured them.

"Of course not," Annie said brightly as she backed out of the kitchen. "And whatever I take apart, I can put back together. Sort of. Probably."

"It's a good choice," her mom said. "You'll have plenty of time to finish searching and putting everything back into place before you need to get ready to go help Joe with Max's car."

At the door, Annie took one more look at the scene before her. Unfortunately, that moment of hesitation took away any chance of getting away quick and easy. Margaret swirled her washcloth inside a glass. Her head was slightly bowed, the half smile still in place.

A clandestine tear dropped into the dishwater.

It was too much for Annie to deal with right now. Something about Margaret gripped Annie's heart like a vise. The vise had nothing to do with her mother and Max and everything to do with the pain, mixed with longing, she'd seen in Margaret's eyes.

It was a look Annie had seen many times, looking back at her from a mirror.

Turning, she headed for the stairs and up to the main bathroom. It was a simple room, really, with a combination bath/shower, a sink with a cabinet underneath, an oval-shaped toilet, and a hamper. An ugly brown carpet failed to brighten the room.

Annie sat on the toilet lid and frowned at the carpet. She didn't feel like crying, not a bit. Really, she was happy for her mother. Max seemed like a wonderful man. Her only fear was of change. Things were changing way too quickly, and the fact that the changes were for the good didn't make acknowledging and accepting them any easier.

Change was an interesting thing. After all, if she found the coins, things would change again. After all these years, would people care that Kyle Hicks didn't take them? At the most, the coins would either be money in the bank or a family heirloom restored.

Annie doubted if Max cared about the money or if Joe needed an heirloom.

Okay, maybe Joe might care, a little. Annie still wasn't sure why the loss of the coins ended a friendship, especially since Kyle's part in the theft was never proven. It didn't make sense.

Lots of things didn't make sense, like Annie's feelings for Joe. The man was a mystery. He had a way with animals and, yes, a way with women. Annie was most impressed with his heavy-lidded expression, those dark brown eyes that seemed to ask questions she didn't know the answers to. They hinted at suggestions Annie wasn't ready for.

Might never be ready for.

Speaking of change, it was best for Annie to focus on the here and now. The future she most wanted was one without surprises, not one in Bonner Springs. She was building two successful businesses from scratch, not starting over, and time was a taskmaster she shouldn't ignore. She had her plane ticket purchased. Yes, that was what she needed to focus on.

Rachel was ecstatic—a two-man office was so much better than one. She wanted Annie home now, today, in the office in a matter of hours.

Beth, of course, wanted Mom on that plane, too. No way was

Annie going to tell Beth that Mom's adventure might—would probably—turn into the happily-ever-after kind. Not with Beth's engagement on the rocks.

Cathy's only complaint was that she couldn't leave her studies long enough to hop a plane and visit Bonner Springs and meet Max. For some reason, Cathy thought it important to meet Joe, too. Annie thought Cathy just might get along with Joe. She didn't gravitate toward peace and quiet like Annie did. She would think getting lost in a cornfield—and spending the night sleeping in a car—great fun. Cathy always managed to look beautiful and would continue to look beautiful even with pet hair on her clothes.

Annie wasn't sure she wanted Cathy to meet Joe, yet. For the first time, Annie really didn't want the little sister who was everybody's favorite to be everybody's favorite.

Not when it came to Joe.

* * * * *

Joe looked at the woman sitting next to him. Well, not exactly next to him. Jacko was in between. It was almost three in the afternoon, and he'd picked her up just ten minutes ago. So far, the only conversation, somewhat stilted, had centered on the weather. Maybe Annie was just as leery about bringing up their parents as he was. In an effort to keep communication open, he said, "So, you didn't find anything in Dad's bathroom?"

"Your father stockpiles Irish Spring soap. He has enough to last fifty years."

"I knew that."

"The carpet was ruined, though. I tried so hard to be careful when I pulled it up."

"That carpet's been there since I was a child. It's older than me," Joe said. "I wouldn't worry."

"Mom went to the store and bought a cute blue oval rug. It's down and she's already talking about going out with your dad and picking new tile and then buying a new shower curtain and some towels."

Joe would let Annie redo his attic bathroom anytime she pleased. Unfortunately, he doubted they made cute blue oval rugs that small. As for new tiles, he doubted he'd need more than four. His bathroom was definitely a one-man unit.

"Your dad's been on the phone and Internet all day, looking to replace his cell phone. Seems his contract was up, so he can get an upgrade if he wants it."

"It took him a year to figure that phone out," Joe protested.

"Tomorrow I'm doing your bedroom," Annie continued. "Saturday, I'm hoping Mom and I can do your dad's bedroom. After that, I think we're done."

Something about picturing her in his bedroom, going through his childhood belongings, was discomforting. "You're not going to find anything in there. I lived in that room off and on for eight years after the coins went missing. If they were in my bedroom, I'd have found them."

"You'd be surprised at where things turn up."

"Like in cornfields," he teased.

"You're never going to let me live that down, are you?" Annie reached down to stroke the top of Jacko's head.

"Never."

Kansas, for some reason, was behaving. There was only a hint of a chill in the breezy May air. Annie wasn't quite dressed for exploring an old, falling-down farm, but she was dressed perfectly for appealing to a young, red-blooded male. Her white dress was long, with a brown belt emphasizing her waist. Not made for climbing trees but definitely made for being chased. Tennis shoes had replaced the sandals she'd worn the last time they'd been there.

Her hair was loose, just long enough to tuck behind her ears if she wanted, and because it was blowing in the breeze, she wanted.

A red sweater was carefully packed in a bag she'd brought along.

They left the Bonner Springs city limits.

Every once in a while, he pointed something out, like who lived on a certain farm and how he knew them. She now knew which cornfield his high school class liked to party in after football games. She knew the corner where he'd had his first car wreck. She even knew the name of his first date, at the tender age of sixteen, and the restaurant where he'd taken her.

Annie stretched before putting her hand on Jacko's head. The dog nudged his nose into the palm of her hand, encouraging some serious petting. Annie obliged, even taking the time to stroke the dog's ears.

Annie's hands were small, delicate, her nails painted a pale pink. She was more compact than the women he'd dated. In vet school, his female classmates were usually big girls with boisterous laughs who had little use for the latest hairstyles or much jewelry. Of course, they were busy getting a hands-on education with cats that swatted at dangly earrings and horses that nibbled on hair.

Annie was small and girly, yet he saw in her what he liked best about those women he'd been close to in college. She was willing to get her hands dirty, willing to do what must be done, and quite good at it.

When they passed some cone-like white structures, she sat up. "I don't remember these from last night."

"You couldn't see them in the dark. This is an old ammunition plant. It's huge. It would take a whole day just to explore. It closed down when I was little."

He watched her as she stared out the window. She was counting the white structures, her mouth silently saying the numbers. He was fascinated by watching her lips move, but he had to keep his eyes on the road.

"There's more than a hundred," he said. "Every once in a while the paper reminds us that this place is not really closed, it's just on standby."

They passed an orange billboard that advertised the plant. From their spot on the road, four water towers and a few bunkers were visible.

When they left the ammunition plant behind, Joe said, "I was so glad when we finally found our parents last night because in the back of my mind, I was thinking I wouldn't like to explore this at night."

"I'm glad you mentioned our parents," she said, too casually. "I couldn't read your expression this morning after my mom said she'd make a great preacher's wife."

He'd wondered when she'd bring it up. Of course, in some ways, she already had. Her mother was buying bathroom rugs, talking new tile, and such. Her mother wouldn't make a good preacher's wife; she'd make a good wife. And if Joe thought about it long enough, he knew his father had been lonely.

He knew one of the reasons his father had stopped preaching was because he thought a preacher's wife as important as a preacher. Joe's mom had always been right by Dad's side, helping organize potlucks and baby showers, teaching Bible classes and going along when a woman's presence was necessary.

Without a helpmate, his dad felt hindered, and he'd wanted more for the congregation.

"I always told Dad he should get remarried, even encouraged it," Joe admitted. "I wasn't exactly prepared for him to meet someone from out of town and fall in love in a matter of days, but it is what it is and I'm okay with it."

Annie opened her mouth to say something, but Joe cut her off. "And your mother is quite nice."

"She's more than nice," Annie said, somewhat defensively. "He's lucky she'll have him."

Joe only nodded.

This morning, when the kitchen had gone so quiet after Willa's announcement, Joe had looked at his father and witnessed something in his eyes that had been missing for four years: fulfillment.

And, selfishly, even while Joe somewhat rejoiced for his father, he couldn't help but think that having Willa for a stepmother meant having Annie around, too.

Annie was getting used to dog hair.

Joe was getting used to Annie.

Chapter Fifteen

....

"'Ask and it will be given to you; seek and you will find; knock and the door will be opened to you.'"

"What?" Annie and Joe had been riding in companionable ease since Joe admitted he'd wanted his father to remarry and was okay with it.

Okay with Mom.

"It's Matthew 7:7. I was thinking about my dad. When Mom passed away, it made him an eligible bachelor. There may not be many single women my age at the church, but there are plenty of single women his age."

"So, you're saying he dated a lot?" Annie asked.

"He didn't date at all," Joe replied, "until now. And I'm wondering if he ever prayed about it."

"Prayed about what, dating?"

"Well, yes, finding the right woman."

"I'll bet that not in a million years did he think the answer to his prayers would be an armchair detective from Tucson, Arizona."

Joe chuckled and stopped the truck. "You're right about that. Especially one who leaves his tools in a pile by the side of the road." Hopping out, he quickly gathered a stack of tools—one Annie hadn't even noticed—and tossed them in the back.

"Just think of all the fun they'll have," Annie said when he got back behind the wheel, "and all the stories they'll get to tell about the way they met."

As they pulled off the rural route and onto an almost obscure drive leading to something she couldn't see, Annie tried to stop evaluating herself and whether or not she was okay with Max and all the fun he'd be having with her mom.

It was easier said than done.

So, Joe had *told* his dad to get remarried, even encouraged it. Why hadn't she expressed the same sentiment to her mother? Why hadn't her sisters? Granted, Joe's mom had been gone longer than Annie's dad, but still, Mom had been a widow over a year now, and she was fairly young, only in her early fifties.

Had her mom been petitioning God about being lonely?

This was not something she wanted to share with Joe as he parked the car on packed grass in front of a broken-down farm.

"My dad always called this the Chicken Farm."

"Why? Did his family mostly raise chickens?"

"No, they had a little bit of everything. It was called the Chicken Farm because Great-Great-Grandma would sell fresh eggs and fryer chickens to the members of the church."

Annie immediately thought back to the Whittakers and the way their cows stood at the fence and how much she'd liked their chicken condo. What remained of the Kelly Farm, the Chicken Farm, however, looked nothing like the Norman Rockwellish Blue Sunflower Farm or any of the farms they'd passed while driving down the country roads. No, what Annie was looking at looked more like a Tim Burton creation with peeling gray-weathered wood and a collapsed roof.

Jacko barked once as Joe parked the truck. The dog clearly liked visiting the old Kelly place and wanted out. Annie opened the door, braced herself as Jacko scampered over her, and watched as he raced toward the farmhouse, around the corner, and out of sight.

"He's thinking about rabbits," Joe said.

"I hope he doesn't catch one."

"He hasn't yet, although one time I had to chase him for over two miles before getting him to turn back." Joe came around the truck, and before she knew it, he was holding out a hand to help her down. She couldn't remember the last guy who'd been so gallant. "That's why I put the bandanna around his neck—so I can see him while I chase him."

She stood by the door of his truck and studied the farmhouse, trying to picture it as a home with a wife, a husband, and a few kids running through its door. What remained of the house was too broken for Annie to fix, even in her imagination.

"Why haven't you sold this place? I mean, you have to pay taxes on it."

"Sense of family, sense of commitment, I don't know. Mom talked about living here. She even drew her dream house. I have the drawing somewhere in my stuff. Just think of the animals we'd have kept. Dad neither felt the urge nor felt we had the money."

"You should turn this into your vet practice," Annie said. "I mean, you're only in the office two days a week and it's really small. If you moved out here, wouldn't it be easier to build exactly what you want?"

"I like the way you dream, but dreams don't solve the reality of student loans. A vet practice is a huge investment. I'm just now building my clientele. I haven't been around long enough for anyone to feel the type of loyalty necessary to drive all this way. Plus, in order to live and work out here, I'd have to tear the farmhouse down and start from scratch."

He was right. Not only was the wood gray-weathered, it was also rotted. The glass was gone from the windows, and even though there weren't that many, not only had the weather been allowed inside but also animals.

The landscape, however, promised more. Grass swayed in the wind. In the distance, wispy cirrus clouds streaked across the sky until they seemed to dip and touch the land.

"Imagine," Joe said. "No electricity, no running water, no phone service, no public transportation. No wonder my ancestors moved to town. Every time my mom brought up moving out here, Dad told her stories to discourage her. He'd talk about the hardships. He'd talk about having to scrub drainpipes with lye and about cows getting into buttonweed and dying."

"It would be fairly easy to get electricity here now. The lines run down the road already. I can't imagine your mom letting the stories discourage her."

"They didn't, not really. She knew Dad wanted to stay in town, and she knew he needed to be near the church." Joe's hands were in his jeans pockets, but his look—which hadn't left her face even once during this conversation—was intense. Annie felt the touch of his expression and it made her shiver.

"Wives tend to give up a lot for their husbands," she said softly.

Joe nodded.

The porch looked ready to collapse, and Joe shook his head when she started to head for it. "Let's try the back."

The back of the house was worse than the front. Whereas the front looked like someone had, at one time, wanted it to be presentable, the back looked like no one had paid any attention to it, ever. The porch was just flat, rotted wood. There were no eaves, no arches, nothing to distract from just a straight up-and-down look.

"They were sensible," Joe explained. "When they built this, it was more important to care for the animals, the family, and the necessities."

Stepping on the porch, Annie peered in through the gaping hole where a door once hung. The room she stared at had to have been the kitchen. Nothing was left except dirt on the floor, the dim smell of animals, and a few holes in the ceiling. Turning, she looked out at the plains. The wind was rippling anything willing to bend. It did the same to her hair. She brushed it out of her eyes and tried to figure out where the barn might have been. Finally, she saw a spot of land where the grass wasn't nearly as tall and where a patch of barren dirt remained. "Is that where the barn was?"

Joe stopped peering in the kitchen and turned to survey the land with her. "My dad has always thought so. It's almost completely gone back to nature. Don't sell yourself short. For not growing up in the country, you have good instincts—both with the land and its creatures."

Joe stood so close that Annie almost stepped away. Not because of any other reason than she felt herself losing her breath, thinking about touching him, and wondering why…why this man affected her so.

Maybe it was because she was out of her comfort zone, away from her sisters, her work, and because the person she was supposed to be helping—her mother—didn't need help at all.

Jacko barked, and Joe whistled. The dog burst from the grass, jumping in exuberance, and raced to Joe as if to say *Yes, I'm still alive, but I'm busy just now* before turning to go back to whatever he'd been doing.

Annie stepped down from the porch and started following the sound of Jacko's barking. The distant sun began its descent. She liked it here, liked exploring, and liked the ideas that were starting to form in her mind.

Joe followed, every once in a while reaching out to steady her or guide her away from what he must consider dangerous territory. Annie thought about laughing at him for being overprotective, but she rather liked it.

Chapter Sixteen
....

Joe meant to take care of his dad's car first and then explore. That was the practical, sensible thing to do. That way, if darkness came more quickly than expected, they could hop in his truck and head for home.

Once Annie had stepped toward the old farm, like a moth to a flame, he'd left behind the practical common sense that had always been a part of his life and become helpless to do anything but follow and answer her questions, tell her about the past, and try to understand just why he enjoyed being with her so much. Maybe it was because she didn't know all his stories. Everything he shared with her was new. She asked questions no one else did; she paid more attention than he was used to.

She didn't remind him of the females he knew in Bonner Springs, the ones he'd hung around with all his life, the ones who knew all his stories and didn't act like they were special.

Like he was special.

She paused before the sea of blowing grass that Jacko had disappeared into and went down to her knees, reaching for something he couldn't see. After a moment, she came back with a bright yellow wildflower. It looked the same as the hundreds that were positioned across the grass.

"I love this color. I need to do something with earrings and this shade."

He nodded because he didn't know what else to do. It was a wildflower, nothing more. He didn't see what she did.

"The garden was here," she continued. "It's close enough to the house that your great-grandmother could get to it easily, but far enough away that the kids had a backyard to play in and that what they used for fertilizer wouldn't waft into the house."

Joe doubted she could tell where a garden had grown more than a hundred years ago. He also wondered if she knew that the fertilizer from his ancestors' day was manure. More likely she was imagining where she'd put a garden and why.

"Do you garden?" he asked. This wasn't a pastime he imagined her having.

"No, but your aunt Margaret's sure proud of her flowers and garden and has told me some things. I think I'd like to garden. Something about all the neat rows really appeals to me. I love tomatoes."

"My aunt loves tomatoes, too, and grows way too many. She starts giving them to my dad in June. Soon she's giving them to everyone she knows and even people she doesn't know, complete strangers she meets on the streets. When she wrote to me in college, she spent more time telling me about her garden, especially the tomatoes, than she told me about what was happening at home."

"You know much about gardens?" Annie asked.

Suddenly Joe wished he did, wished he'd listened closer to Margaret and all her talk. "I know about pulling weeds," he finally offered.

Actually, he never wanted to pull weeds again, but for Annie maybe he'd make an exception. "You've gotten to hear about my family," he said. "Now, tell me about yours."

She sat, cross-legged, smiling in the last of the sunshine and pulling a few sunflowers into her lap. Her bracelets clinked against each other, adding a purely feminine melody to the sound of the Kansas wind.

"I've met Dad's parents," she said. "I've had dinner with them, five whole times. They weren't the touchy-feely kind. I got the idea they had a hard life. Dad didn't share many stories except for hating to ride in the backseat when they took trips. That's a funny thing to remember, don't you think?"

"As an only child, I can tell you that always sitting alone in the backseat is incredibly boring. I, at least, had video games. I doubt your dad had anything."

"He said he used to sing in the car, but his mother made him stop. Whenever we went to church, he'd turn to whatever page the song leader requested, but then he'd just stand there. He wouldn't sing a word."

"You like to sing?"

"Mom and Cathy are the singers. Mom often leads singing for the ladies' class at church." Annie smiled, and suddenly Joe realized that she missed her sisters, even though she spoke to them on the phone every day. "Cathy sings karaoke. She won a prize once for singing 'You're So Vain' by Carly Simon. I like to sing, but my voice isn't anything to get excited about. On my mom's side, Grandpa leads singing at the church. He's good."

"That's one thing I don't do," Joe admitted. "Lead singing. My voice scares people. The few times I have, Agnes Miller sings louder than I do so there's some hope the congregation will stay on key."

Annie laughed. "My grandpa, Mom's dad, would love you. His job took him a lot of places, even Japan sometimes, for years at a time. Grandma always went with him. They flitted in and out of our lives. But they sent cards and pictures and brought back great presents. They sent me a rock tumbler when I was just eight. I think that's how I got involved in making jewelry."

"No cousins?" Joe asked.

"None I'd recognize if I passed them on the street. You?"

"No cousins. You know my aunt Margaret. She never married. Grandpa had one sister. I know she married, but they moved to Texas, and I never heard about any kids."

"I think my favorite thing in life is my sisters. I talk or text with them every day."

"You solve their problems," Joe pointed out, "or at least try to."

As if to prove his point, her cell phone went off. She took it out of her pocket, glanced at it, and then said, "It's Beth."

"I'm going to find Jacko. Then we probably need to head to my dad's car before it gets dark."

She nodded and pushed a button before putting the phone to her ear. As he took off through the grass following the sound of Jacko's happy barking, he heard Annie order, "Stop crying and tell me what happened."

He paused and shot her a questioning look, but she waved him away. Clearly, she didn't need him.

* * * * *

Beth was not the sister who cried. Annie didn't cry much either. Cathy was the one who cried at Hallmark commercials. She did enough crying for all of them.

Not today. Today Beth was making up for lost time. Through the phone, Annie could hear the sobs and imagine the endless stream of tears that didn't allow for conversation. What words Beth did attempt were so broken, they couldn't be understood.

Annie didn't need the words. Beth had already told her that Charles had asked for breathing room. In the world of dating, when a guy asks for breathing room, it really means *I-don't-want-to-breathe-in-the-same-room-with-you*, not right now and possibly not ever.

While Beth cried, Annie stood and watched Joe walking through the tall grass. The fading sun shimmered on his dark hair. He stopped and Annie had to strain to see why. She hadn't realized there was a creek. Even as she watched, Jacko bounded out of the water, shaking his fur and apparently giving Joe a bit of a shower.

Joe didn't seem to mind. He ran at the dog and Jacko backed up, then ran forward, initiating a game of cat and mouse that seemed well orchestrated. In a full-out run, Joe took off after Jacko, and the sound of Jacko's barks were the stuff of laughter and joy. After a minute, Jacko let Joe catch him, and boy and dog—er, man and dog—slowed down to a companionable walk.

Until Jacko took off after what appeared to be a rabbit.

No wonder Joe took Jacko everywhere. They were a team.

She hoped there would be time to come here again. She wanted to join in the game. And she wanted to know what kind of tree Joe was heading for. It was huge and black and unlike any tree she'd seen in Tucson.

Finally Beth calmed down enough to say, "He. Asked. For. His. Ring. Back."

"Did you give it to him?"

"No, it was a gift." Ever the lawyer, she added, "I can prove the three criteria that make it a gift. He bought it for me, he gave it to me, I accepted it. I'm not giving it back. I'm flushing it down the toilet."

"Don't do that." Annie was well aware that the ring cost more than her car, make that her last two cars put together.

Beth's silence meant she hadn't really decided what to do.

"So, what happened?" Annie asked. "Why did he call the wedding off?"

"I don't know what happened. He called me on the phone. He said he'd been thinking and that he wasn't happy. Apparently, he hasn't been happy for a while and just now decided to clue me in. He thinks it's me."

"Thinks it's you? He had no definite reason?"

"The only thing he was willing to say is that I tend to talk too much when we're out with people he wants to impress. He says I draw the conversation to what I'm interested in, whether I agree with popular opinion or not, and that I forget that somewhere down the line he wants to go into politics and that I should be agreeing more with the people I'm talking to and sharing more positive things about him."

"There are no positive things about him," Annie said.

"Yes, there are!" Beth protested.

"Okay, okay." Annie backed down. In a month, Beth would be more likely to agree that there was nothing good about Charles

Simon Reinfeld. Right now, she was still reeling, still thinking she had imagined his phone call.

"Why don't you take a few days off and come down here? You need to meet Max." No way was Annie going to say how nice he was and that now it looked like Mom would most likely be sporting a wedding ring sooner than Beth.

"I can't. I'm working on a big case. Plus, tonight I'm meeting with the criminal justice teacher. Hopefully, I'll find out something from him that will convince Mom to come home once and for all since nothing you're doing seems to be working." Beth had stopped crying, although an occasional sniff punctuated her words.

"Everything is fine here. Mom is fine. Quit worrying about her. Cancel the meeting with the criminal justice teacher."

"I can't. I'm worrying about everything, including you."

"I'll be home on Sunday night. Grab Cathy. It's time to find out how school's really going, and let's have a sisters' night out."

"That might be good," Beth agreed. "I'll call you after I have coffee with the professor."

"I can't believe you're still going to meet him tonight."

"Believe it. It's better than staying home and having a pity party."

Annie almost felt sorry for the professor. Beth would be in a mood. "I'm sure the professor will tell you that Mom's an adult and we don't need to worry."

"I'm sure the professor will tell me as little as possible," Beth grumped. "Schools and privacy laws leave very little room for conversation."

Annie ended the conversation as Joe walked up, Jacko by his side.

"You ready?" he asked.

"I am, but if there's time, I want to come back. There's so much left to explore. You didn't tell me there was a creek, and I want to see the big tree that you were standing next to, and I want to see—"

"You're talking about the black walnut tree." He glanced at his watch. "I wish we did have time. You'd like the wild raspberries and gooseberries that grow here, but right now we need to head to Dad's car before it gets dark."

In daylight, exactly what happened and what could have happened were even more pronounced. Max's car was several yards off the road. The ditch he'd almost crossed was about five feet wide. The front wheels had almost made the leap. They were resting against the mud and dirt of the berm, with the front bumper on the edge.

"This is not going to be fun," Joe muttered.

Annie had no clue where he'd begin.

"Traction is going to be a joke" was Joe's first assessment. Nevertheless, he positioned his truck so the rear was toward Max's car. "At least I don't need to worry about being in the way of other cars. No traffic out here."

"No one to stop and offer help," Annie said glumly.

The look Joe shot her implied she wasn't helping, either.

Joe waved Annie out of the truck. She found an old tree stump to sit on. Unfortunately, he didn't let her sit for long.

Next thing Annie knew she was back in his truck, in the driver's seat, and Joe was in his dad's car to make sure it was in neutral. Jacko ran back and forth between Max's car and Joe's truck, unable to decide where he belonged.

"We need a tow truck," Annie advised, loud enough so Joe could hear. "A real one."

After a moment, he yelled, "Move forward until you don't feel any more slack."

"I won't recognize when I don't have slack. I've never helped tow anyone before." She pressed the gas pedal, and his truck moved forward, its wheels spinning. She watched as the Cadillac tilted a bit, not enough to be called a lurch. To Annie's thinking, lurching would be good, because then the car would be heading her way. Instead, the car slid down, and it looked like the front bumper separated from the body.

"Back up," Joe yelled. "Turn the other way. Try to move forward gradually."

She felt the wheels spinning again. Jacko started barking. Over in his dad's car, Joe was saying something and she doubted he really wanted her to know what it was. Still, when things quieted down, she asked, "What next?"

He jumped from the car, looked at the front bumper, shook his head, and walked back toward her and said what she already knew. "We're calling a tow truck." He flipped out his cell phone and punched a few numbers, and after a moment, one was on its way.

"Can we go back to the creek while we wait?"

"If we have time, but first we need to unhook the tow strap and move my truck out of the way. Plus, I need to get Dad's and Willa's belongings out of his car."

It took only a moment for Joe to unhitch the tow strap. After he'd put everything back where it belonged in the truck's toolbox, Annie followed him to Max's car. It took a while longer to clean out the backseat. There were two bags with purchases her mom had made. Joe handed them down.

Annie opened the bags and gasped. "Paint supplies."

"Your mother paints."

"She used to, before she married my father and we all came along."

"Why'd she quit?"

"I just told you. She married my father and we all came along. She no longer had any time."

"Then she didn't want to paint or she would have made time."

"Spoken like a true male," Annie said. "You have no idea what it's like to work and raise a family and try to find time for something you love, like painting or making jewelry."

"Sure I do." Joe put one hand on each side of the door frame and started to lower himself out. "My mom managed to do it and take care of animals. I watched her, and Dad and I helped."

Annie reached up to steady him. She half-believed him, that in his mother's situation, both Joe and his dad helped. Her mother didn't have that luxury. Annie's father wasn't the kind who would have encouraged a hobby like painting, no matter how good at it Mom was.

That's when the car shifted. The bumper separated from the car and the car nosed its way down in one abrupt motion.

Annie scrambled backward but not fast enough. The door caught her on the chin. She'd barely registered pain when something heavy knocked her down. The next thing she knew, Joe's dark brown eyes were a mere inch away from hers and her chin didn't hurt at all.

"Are you all right?" he asked.

Luckily, she was. She'd already been moving out of the way

when the door hit her chin, and it more or less helped her along without really hurting her. "I will be when you get off me."

"Oh, right." He eased up and rolled to the side before jumping up and offering a hand to her.

"We've managed to make things worse, huh?" she asked.

Joe looked at his dad's car and then back at her, still just inches away. The fingers that had clasped hers to help her up were still tightly gripping her hand. They were rough and warm and strong.

Annie wasn't sure she ever wanted to let go.

Moments went by, but time didn't seem willing to allow for words. His fingers had just gone to her chin, to gently touch the area where she'd been bruised, when a horn sounded.

The tow truck had arrived.

Joe tugged her toward the side of the ditch and helped her up. She didn't need his help. She had a scratched chin, not a broken ankle.

A man was climbing down from the tow truck, a vehicle unlike any tow truck Annie had ever seen. It was huge, with a winch-like thing taking up most of the space in the rear. The operator's red shirt matched the lettering on the side of his vehicle: KC Towing. He reached in the front seat and drew out a clipboard. When he turned around so they could see him, Joe stopped.

"What is it?" Annie whispered.

"It's not what is it, it's who is it?" Joe replied.

That's when the man came close enough for Annie to read the name stenciled on his shirt.

Kyle Hicks was home and did not look happy to see them.

Chapter Seventeen

....

"When did you get back?" Joe asked.

The expression on his face, the way he stood so nonchalantly, and the matter-of-fact tone of his voice all seemed to imply that it was just another day, just two men who happened to be acquaintances suddenly meeting up with each other after a few years.

But Annie knew better. This had been Joe's best friend until their senior year. Their shared memories were a foundation that should not have been made of sand. It should have stood the test of time when the rains came, the streams rose, and the winds blew. It made no sense that it fell with a great crash. Not over something like coins gone missing and misplaced accusations. No, there was something else. Something Joe either didn't know or wasn't telling her.

It appeared that Kyle had no intention of answering Joe's question, of acting like anything besides a tow truck driver.

Annie stepped forward, one hand held out, and Kyle somewhat reluctantly shook it. "I'm Annie Jamison. Joe's told me so much about you, about your friendship. I'm glad I've gotten to meet you."

He looked a lot older than Joe, rougher around the edges. His skin, like Joe's, was tan from long hours spent outside. His hair, light brown and thin, was mostly under a baseball cap that read CHIEFS and was a lot longer than Joe's. His handshake was as firm as Joe's, his skin as calloused.

Kyle looked from Annie to Joe, his expression dour, his lips turned down in a frown. "I'm still the subject of most conversations, huh?" he asked.

"My mom is an armchair detective," Annie explained. "She's here to find the coins." As an afterthought, she added, "Among other things."

That pronouncement at least wiped some of the attitude off Kyle's face. He looked at Joe. "She kidding?"

"No, my dad actually hired her mom. He was thinking about moving and wanted to make one last effort."

"Well, good luck with that," Kyle said to Annie, heading back to his truck. "Quite a few people think I took them. You probably need to be detecting me."

"Nah," said Annie. "That would be a waste of time. Joe said you didn't take them. We think they're somewhere in the house."

Kyle shook his head and said to Joe, "You still live with your dad?"

"No, I have my own veterinarian practice and live in the apartment upstairs."

"Where?"

It took Annie a moment to realize Kyle wasn't just making small talk. He was filling in a form with pertinent information. In quick succession, Joe provided not only his phone number but also his insurance card, followed by a signature that he was good for paying whatever insurance didn't and that if something went wrong during the retrieval, he wouldn't hold the company responsible.

Once the paperwork was finished, Kyle headed toward Max's

car. Jacko looked up at Joe and Annie inquisitively and then followed Kyle as if to say *Someone needs to make sure this guy doesn't steal the car.*

"Did your old man start drinking and driving?" Kyle asked when he got close enough for a good look.

"No, apparently a cow and her calf were in the road and he really went out of his way to avoid hitting them." Joe made his way toward Kyle. Annie leaned against his truck and waited. In the silence of the Kansas outdoors, she could hear every word they said.

"Dad broke his ankle when he fell getting out of the vehicle."

"Lucky that's all he broke." Kyle did a quick assessment before saying, "You realize this is probably totaled."

"Just the bumper," Joe said.

Kyle disappeared under the car and after a moment reappeared and stood, brushing off his pants. "Your dad was making some good time. The way the car shot across the ditch, hit the other side, and then crumbled, I'm thinking the crossmember is bent, which means he's going to lose his axle. Insurance companies usually total before taking a chance that there'll be a domino effect of costly repairs."

Joe looked accusingly at the car, as if it were somehow to blame for all the bad luck his dad had suffered. Then he returned to his original question. "When did you get back?"

"I moved to Kansas City just over two months ago. I've been working the tow truck three weeks. It's a job."

"Did you recognize this address when they gave you the call?" Joe asked.

"Yes, but since I operate the boom truck, I've been called to this area twice already for the offroad retrievals. I didn't realize it would be you."

"Would you have taken the call if you'd known?"

"I'm not sure," Kyle admitted. "But I've not been with the company long enough to pick and choose my assignments. I figured I'd run into you sooner or later, I was just hoping the later would take a bit longer."

"I was at your parents' house last Sunday night helping birth a bull calf. They didn't mention that you'd returned to Kansas."

"They don't know."

"Kyle!" Joe's exclamation was so loud, so sharp, that Jacko barked and ran over to him.

"I don't want to get their hopes up until I'm sure I'm going to stay. If they know I'm in Kansas City, they'll start talking taking over the farm. I'm not ready for that." Kyle headed for his tow truck and leaned inside, doing something with a calculator and writing down things on his clipboard. It only took him a minute before he returned to where Joe waited. "This isn't going to be cheap. You know that?"

"I know it," Joe agreed. "If it's going to be totaled, maybe I should just hook up a chain and pull it out."

"Not with your truck. You'll wind up with two damaged vehicles."

It took almost an hour for Kyle to situate the winch securely and lift the Cadillac from the ditch. Once the car was on solid ground, Kyle handed Joe some paperwork to sign and said, "Do you want me to take it to Ed's?"

"If you take it to Ed's," Joe said, "then the fact that you've returned won't be a secret any longer."

"You're the customer. You make the call."

Joe didn't hesitate. "What's the best auto repair place in Kansas City?"

Relief washed over Kyle's features. Unfortunately, the men moved back toward the truck just then, and Annie could no longer hear what they said. She saw Kyle's lips moving and Joe nodding. Then, Joe put his hand on Kyle's shoulder and said something. After a moment, it looked like the two men were praying. Annie almost lost her breath at the sight of them, one so lost and the other so solid.

Could they be praying?

Annie thought back to her last attempt at prayer. All she could come up with were the words *help* and *please*. No doubt, if the two old friends were praying, those words would be used.

They shook hands and Kyle headed to his truck, hoisted himself into the driver's seat, and, with a quick wave, started the engine and drove off.

Joe watched with Jacko at his feet. Neither moved until the tow truck disappeared from sight, and then slowly Joe walked over to where Annie still waited.

"You want to know what I just realized?" he said.

"What?"

"All the players are back."

She raised an eyebrow. "What players?"

"Aunt Margaret's back, Missy's back, and Kyle's back. From that night when the coins went missing. Everyone who left has come home."

"Margaret left after that? You didn't tell me." Annie felt indignant, like a key piece of information had been kept hidden.

But Joe wasn't listening. He was staring at the empty dirt road. All that remained of the tow truck was a billowing swirl of dust heading away from them.

"Now, if we can just keep everyone home."

The look he sent Annie made her want to be part of the everyone. Forever.

* * * * *

The drive back to Bonner Springs went by quickly. Annie tried to talk about Kyle, even asked if they'd prayed together, but Joe didn't seem inclined to share. The only comment he would make was, "I can't believe he hasn't let his parents know where he is."

So they drove mostly in silence until they reached the city limits. Joe offered to feed her, but it was dark and they were both tired. "I'll just make a peanut butter and jelly sandwich," she said. "Your aunt makes the best jelly."

"She does," Joe agreed. "She's a master at anything to do with growing things."

"You said she went off to teach…"

"In Nebraska, teaching horticulture at the university. She was what they call a visiting professor. She doesn't have a master's, just a two-year degree. But they needed someone who knows tomatoes, and that would definitely be my aunt. She's had a hundred or more articles published in garden magazines. She's spoken at more conferences and club meetings than I can count. People drive here from all over the United States just to get advice from her."

People often asked Annie for advice about cleaning. For the first time she wondered just how passionate she was about her cleaning business. Was she passionate enough to write articles or lecture? For so long, being the one who kept things neat defined her. But was she passionate enough to want to clean, or run a cleaning business, for the rest of her life?

Annie shifted in the seat. Here in Kansas, sitting next to a handsome veterinarian, it was so easy to think that life could be entwined with faith, hope, and love. Oh yeah, her time with Max was having an influence. But Bonner Springs wasn't her home. It wasn't where her job was and it wasn't close to her sisters.

So why, then, was she so content?

* * * * *

"You could have called," Margaret said, opening her front door and stepping out on the porch. Her house was silent, the usual noise from the television absent. "I was starting to think we'd need to send a posse out looking for you two like we did for your parents."

"We wound up needing the tow truck." Joe didn't mention who the tow truck driver was.

"I could have told you that," Margaret grumped.

Joe had made it to the porch by that time. When he reached down to rumple his aunt's hair, Annie was again struck by how tall he was. While Margaret shared a lot of Joe's and Max's features, she wasn't nearly as tall. She shook him off but smiled while she did it. "I need to go tell Willa you're back. She was starting to worry."

"And if she wasn't worried," Joe said, "Aunt Margaret would convince her she needed to be."

"Every family has a worrier," Annie said. "In my family, it's Beth."

"I thought you'd said it was you." Joe sat on the cement steps leading down from Margaret's porch. Jacko circled three times and settled down next to him.

"No, you said it yourself. I'm the one who fixes things. I don't have time to worry. I'm too busy." As if to prove her words, the music from her cell phone sounded. She checked her caller ID, saw it was Beth, and said, "I need to take this."

Something flickered in his eyes that vaguely resembled disappointment.

"Her fiancé called off the wedding," Annie explained. "She's hurting and needs me."

He nodded and left her on Margaret's porch. As he walked away, Jacko trotted dutifully next to him, looking back at Annie as if to say, *Are you crazy? Why are you letting us leave? We don't want to leave.*

She opened her mouth, wanting to ignore the phone in her hand and tell him to come back.

But they'd been together almost six hours.

She wanted six more hours.

Her phone stopped singing. Annie glanced at it, thinking that she needed to let Beth wait until morning. Beth was a big girl. She started to stand, intending to run after Joe. She could come up with something to say, some unimportant comment, something to keep him there for a while longer. Unfortunately, at that moment, Margaret opened the door and said, "Boots is in your mother's room. They're both almost asleep. She says she's glad you're home."

Home.

There was that word again.

Home.

Where was home? She was beginning to think it wasn't Casa Grande, where she lived with her best friend and work was her life. Was it Tucson? Nobody was there. Not her mother, not her sisters.

Never before had Annie felt so alone.

There was a Scripture that her mother used to quote to the girls when they were younger. Now Annie wondered if Mom had been reassuring herself or trying to teach them.

"Many are the plans in a man's heart, but it is the LORD's purpose that prevails."

As she'd done a mere thirty minutes ago, she watched a vehicle, Joe's vehicle, disappear from sight, and suddenly, for the first time, that Scripture made perfect sense. Leaving Annie to wonder at all the decisions in life, the twists and turns, that had brought her here to Bonner Springs, Kansas.

* * * * *

Her phone rang again. Without thinking, she hit the ANSWER button.

Before she could even say hello, Beth started in. "Mom's going to be fine."

"I've been telling you that."

"Yes, but the professor of her criminal justice class seems to think the same thing."

"So you believe him and not me?"

"I believed you, but I was starting to think you were being swayed by the preacher's son."

"Huh?"

"Oh, come on. Even Cathy has figured out that this Joe character is popping into our conversations a bit more than necessary. And our proof? Why are you flying home Sunday afternoon instead of tonight? You're the one who's so concerned about the Fountain Hills craft show and how Cathy will do by herself selling your jewelry."

"Cathy's not concerned."

"You're right. Cathy thinks the world is perfect. I'm worried."

Exactly what Annie didn't want. Beth deciding to worry about Annie as well as Mom. Time to change the subject.

"Has Charles called?"

Sometimes silence was the only answer necessary. After a moment, Beth said, "I've had my cell phone on the whole evening. I've checked it a hundred times. Mom's teacher even asked me if I needed to be somewhere else."

"You didn't flush his ring, did you?"

"No. If we make up, I'll need it."

Need, not want? How interesting.

"I'll be home Sunday night," Annie said. "I already have my plane ticket."

"Changing the subject to my love life isn't enough to convince me that nothing is going on between you and this Joe character."

"Joe is just a nice guy who happened to have some free time and is showing me around Bonner Springs and Sunflower a bit. There's nothing else going on."

Margaret snorted.

Before Annie could turn around, the porch door creaked shut. Margaret was back in her living room. Soon the television blared so loud, even Beth remarked, "Where are you? A restaurant or something?"

"No, I'm at Margaret's."

"What time is it there?"

"It's a little after nine."

"It's not quite that late here. I just left Mom's teacher. He had a class to teach, but we'll probably get together again. He thinks it's amazing what his students are doing, but there's a catch. He doesn't think they'll be doing it for much longer."

"Why?"

"Wendy apparently has dropped out of the class because of illness."

No surprise that. "What about the guy, the one doing the computer?"

"I get the idea this professor isn't worried about him, per se, but I've asked a couple of the other students in the class. They all know what's going on and think Computer Boy has flaked out. Apparently, he got a job doing something with web pages and no longer has time for anything else."

"Does that mean he's no longer helping with the Armchair Detectives?"

"Not sure. I'll call Alice later tonight when she gets out of class. She, by the way, will probably soon cease to be an armchair detective."

"Why?"

"She's been offered a job as a tour guide for some company that does Arizona day trips."

Annie almost laughed. Her mother had gone three states away, chasing a dream of doing something interesting, and instead, because of a whim that four people actually brought to brief fruition, she'd found something that was beginning to look a lot like love.

Maybe she wasn't the only one.

Chapter Eighteen
....

Mornings had always been Annie's favorite time of day. Growing up, she'd gotten out of bed—usually about five—before the rest of her family and had done what she needed to do without anyone offering suggestions or getting in the way. She'd liked the solitude and the feeling that she'd set the mood for the day.

Since arriving in Bonner Springs, she couldn't seem to control anyone's mood, and mornings weren't so calm.

First, Margaret's morning shows began at five. Annie's favorite time of day, at least back in Casa Grande. Here in Bonner Springs, getting up at five was a given, thanks to a house that fairly reverberated from the television's noise. Annie's next choice—at least if she wanted a little solitude and quiet—was getting up at four. No way. Especially since Bonner Springs was the land of late nights and no sleep

Second, mornings meant phone calls. And lately, all the phone calls had to do with problems Annie needed to solve and was too far away to do much about. Very frustrating.

Third, if she kept eating breakfast at Max's house, she was going to be ten pounds heavier when she returned to Casa Grande. It was enough to make a girl think about jogging. Instead, after eating another wonderful breakfast prepared by her mother, Annie put

Boots's box on the kitchen counter, helped herself to a third cup of coffee, and made her way up the stairs to Joe's bedroom.

Max and Mom busied themselves downstairs getting ready to head to Kansas City so Max could talk to the auto repair place himself. Since Max didn't have a car, this meant borrowing his sister's.

"Can't believe Joe sent it so far away. What was he thinking?" was Max's only comment as Mom helped him out the door. He smiled the whole time, clearly glad to be getting out of the house, and not as perturbed as he pretended to be.

Mom merely shook her head and said, "Annie, do you really need so much coffee this early?"

"Yes, I really do," Annie said without turning around. She might as well have not answered. Her mom had already helped Max down the stairs and onto the front walk. Annie was left in Max's eerily quiet house.

"I'll probably need a fourth cup," she told herself as she turned on the radio in Joe's room and started stripping down the bed. She tossed the bedding in the hallway, propped the mattress up against a wall, and felt all along the seams. While the mattress was off, she ran her fingers over every nook and corner of the frame. Then she went through the jumble of items under his bed. She found his senior math book, some class notes—complete with messy handwriting—still inside, a pair of blue and white tennis shoes, curved with use, and a couple of magazines dealing with trucks. She sat on the floor and kneaded the homemade quilt, just in case the coins had gotten lost in an errant tear.

Her cell phone warbled. She checked the text message and replied "yes" to Joe's invitation to meet for lunch. Eleven was early, but she knew he needed to plan his day around appointments.

She pulled the drawers out of his dresser and noted only two contained the remnants of his childhood clothing—namely, T-shirts. Every drawer was emptied and every piece of clothing gone through. It didn't take long. Obviously, either Joe or his father had a hard time throwing away Kansas City Chiefs T-shirts. Although Annie hadn't noticed Joe wearing the sports logo since she'd been there.

No, right now he seemed to prefer dark blue T-shirts that stretched across his torso and showed the muscles that came with his trade.

Her cell phone rang, snapping her out of her daydream before she could start thinking about any more parts of Joe worth contemplating.

"I passed today's quiz!" Cathy announced after Annie managed a brief hello. "If I can get at least a C on the final test, my daily average will be enough to pass the class."

"*Muy bueno*," Annie said.

"Words good, accent bad," Cathy responded. They spent the next twenty minutes discussing Beth. Finally, Annie said, "I need to go pretty soon. I'm tearing apart Joe's childhood bedroom. So far I know he has bigger feet than I thought, did poorly in math, and has kept every Kansas City Chiefs shirt he's ever owned, starting from birth."

Cathy chuckled, then asked, "Why are you searching without Mom?"

"She's busy taking care of Max. I don't leave until Sunday, and if I find the coins, Mom said I could have her share of the reward. It seems like OhSoClean is falling apart while I'm gone, so having earned something while I'm here is a good idea."

"What's happening with OhSoClean? I thought you had more business than you could handle."

"We're doing fine, sort of. But in the week I've been gone, girls are calling in sick and we've got some unhappy customers. I'll be doing catch-up when I return and we'll definitely lose some money."

"I don't think I'd ever want to run my own business," Cathy said. "I like it when someone else has to deal with all the headaches of customer service."

Annie bit her tongue and didn't tell Cathy that being a teacher meant being on the front lines and dealing with parents and government both. Cathy would learn soon enough, and she'd do fine.

At twenty-two, it was all right if your biggest concern in life was passing a Spanish class.

At twenty-seven, the biggest concerns needed to be paying bills and keeping the peace. "These things happen," Annie said. "If I find the coins, I can leave here knowing the job got done. There are no loose ends."

"You don't consider Mom a loose end?" Cathy asked.

"No, Mom's fine. Chances are, next time I visit Bonner Springs, you'll be with me, and we'll be attending Mom's wedding. Don't tell Beth."

Cathy didn't even gasp. Just said, "I'll start shopping for a new dress."

After ending the call, Annie decided to check in with Rachel. She tried both the work number and Rachel's cell but only got voice mail.

Not good.

Wishing she could be in two places at once, she finished going through the corners of the drawers and even turned them upside down to look at the bottoms. Nothing. She took everything off the shelves and ran a broom along the back edges. Dust trickled down.

Sitting on his bed, she started going through the mementos

from the shelves. Not that she thought she'd find the coins; maybe she thought she would find out more about the man. Joe had left trophies behind and lots of pictures, too. She'd noticed them the first time she'd passed by his room the day she arrived, her clothes covered in dog hair, irritated at him, and wanting to wash up.

She had dog hair on her pants right now, and she'd not even seen Jacko this morning.

It didn't bother her at all.

The photos that were framed were all professional. She saw Joe, maybe ten years old, in the bottom left-hand corner of one picture. He held a baseball bat and stared straight at the camera with a huge goofy smile on his face. At the top of the picture was the whole team. There were probably five pictures of the same ilk, only Joe and his team got older and sometimes the sport was football. His smile changed from goofy, to serious, to cocky.

Annie liked them all.

Joe also had lots of loose snapshots. There were pictures of two little boys making snowmen with a big brown dog in the background. The boys were so bundled up Annie had to really study the photos before figuring out Joe was the one rolling the snowman body. Then there were two boys, not so little, skateboarding and definitely not bundled up. Both teenagers wore low-slung jeans and black T-shirts. There were family photos, too. Joe's mother was almost always in the center, a gentle hand on both her husband and Joe. In one of the last ones, Annie recognized Kyle Hicks. He was older now and leaner, but the shape of his face was the same, as were his eyes. She went back to the earlier photos and confirmed what she already knew. Kyle was the snowman builder and one of the skateboarders.

"They were friends from the time they were born, just two months apart." Margaret stood in the doorway.

Annie almost dropped the pictures. She'd been so engrossed in studying Joe's history, she'd not heard the front door open, footfalls on the stairs, or anything.

"Joe's the older, but Kyle had a brother and so figured things out first. He dragged Joe along. It was good for Joe. I don't think he ever felt like an only child."

"Must have really hurt Joe when Kyle left."

"Yes," Margaret acknowledged, coming into the room and sitting down next to Annie on the bed. She gave her the box with the kitten in it so Annie could take over the feeding. As they switched, Boots meowed as if afraid he'd never eat again. "I came to see what you had planned for lunch. I could make us some sandwiches."

"I'm meeting Joe. Want to come with me?"

The invitation was automatic, but Annie almost immediately wanted the words back. She was leaving in two days. She wanted to be alone with Joe, with no one else vying for his attention.

"No, you two go on. I don't mind eating alone." Margaret took one of the photos from the pile and studied it. "This was their senior trip. They went to Worlds of Fun in Kansas City. Both Max and Elizabeth went along as chaperones. I think this was one of the last times Joe and Kyle had a good time without accusations and suspicion interfering. It was just a few weeks later the coins went missing."

"I work with my best friend. We were afraid it might hurt our friendship, but it hasn't. We have different strengths and weaknesses."

"I got the idea your partner wasn't doing her share?" Margaret queried.

"No, it's that she's not good at doing my share, too. Plus, Rachel's not one who likes to tell people what to do, and when you're in charge, you pretty much have to. Together, we're a good team; apart, we somewhat flounder."

Margaret laughed. "I guess we all need someone like that in our lives." She sobered. "If we're lucky."

Annie thought about yesterday morning. She opened her mouth to ask if Margaret wanted to talk, but Margaret was looking at yet another picture: one of Joe and Kyle, wearing football jerseys, their arms around each other's shoulders. "Luckily," Margaret said, "Joe went off to college a few months later."

"You know everyone in town, everyone who was at the party that night. What do you think happened to the coins?"

"I wish I knew what to think. I always sort of liked Max's theory that someone off the street saw we were having a party. The door was wide open—not that Max ever turned anyone away—and they came in, saw an opportunity, and took it. Er, took the coins, that is."

"Why would they take only three when there were nine altogether?"

"Three were out of the display mat. Maybe they didn't see the others."

"Who first accused Kyle?"

Margaret didn't hesitate. "Me. It seemed so obvious, and the kid acted guilty. Of course, when Elizabeth got back, she thought the same thing."

"What did Kyle say?"

"That he didn't take them. That he felt bad he'd taken them out of the mat and that he felt he should pay for them. He offered to pay twenty-five dollars a month until he got a full-time job."

"Max didn't take him up on his offer?"

"Max said if Kyle didn't take them then it wasn't Kyle's problem. Then, the kids graduated, and I left for Nebraska and my teaching job. When I came back a few years later, the whole thing had died down, except the friendship never recovered. For the most part, Kyle left Bonner Springs and never looked back."

Annie knew that wasn't quite true. He'd looked back two months ago.

Taking another photo from the pile, Annie showed it to Margaret. "So no one really considered Missy, Marlee, or Billy to be the thief? Or even Cliff?"

"No. Anyone who's met Billy and Cliff know they'd return a penny if they found it on the ground. Marlee was engaged, and her boyfriend's family owns the restaurant in town. They're not hurting for money. Missy, now, that girl couldn't hold on to a dollar if it were glued to her hand."

"Why didn't anyone suspect her?"

"Her family gave her all the money she ever asked for. That was high school. She was a princess. It wasn't until after high school that suddenly nothing went right in her life."

"Like?"

"Never going to college, one job after another, things like that. She's back now and seems to be trying to make good. For a while I hoped she'd get with Joe. But now I can see she wasn't meant for him."

"Who is she meant for?"

"I don't know. Maybe if Kyle Hicks hadn't left town... But Joe needs someone like you. Someone not afraid to put him in his place. Someone strong."

Strong? Annie had never thought of herself as strong. Beth was strong. Cathy, for all her quirks and struggles, always came out on top. That was strong.

Annie just accepted things, moved forward, did the best she could.

Margaret set down the picture of Joe and his high school friends and picked up one of the family shots. Joe must have been five or six. He was wearing a Spider-Man costume and showing his fake muscles. Her face softened.

Annie finished feeding the kitten and put it on the bed. It curled up—more like collapsed—against her leg. Reaching over, she put her hand on Margaret's. "Why were you so sad yesterday? Are you upset that my mom and your brother really like each other and might actually consider marriage? I realize it's happening fast. Joe and I—"

"I wasn't upset."

"No, you were sad. I could see that."

"How old are you?" Margaret asked abruptly, suddenly withdrawing her hand.

"Twenty-seven."

"You don't have a boyfriend?"

"No. I've dated a couple of guys, but no one I could imagine being with twenty-four/seven. I'm not in a hurry."

Margaret nodded. "That was my problem, too. I wasn't in a hurry. I dated some young men, especially when I attended the Christian college over in York, Nebraska. One of them even let me know he wanted to propose."

"But he didn't."

"I didn't give him the chance." Margaret clasped her hands together in her lap, her expression woebegone. "The minute I realized how serious he was and how serious I wasn't, I stopped hanging around with him. I would cross the street, hide in bathrooms, and even stay in my dorm room to avoid him."

"You shouldn't marry if you're not sure," Annie said. Lord knows she'd said that often enough to Beth. Beth, however, was sure. At least she'd been sure until yesterday.

"Yes, but I spent my youth—high school, college, and beyond—thinking that I would meet the perfect man for me. I didn't want to be single. I wanted a husband, a family. But every guy I dated had some flaw I couldn't seem to overlook."

Annie wasn't sure what to say.

Margaret shook her head. "Max met Elizabeth in elementary school. I think from that first meeting they knew, the whole town knew, they'd get married. Sometimes I think the whole town knew I wouldn't."

"Oh, I don't think so."

"Elizabeth's been gone four years now. The casserole brigade started just a few months after her passing, and Max, at first, didn't seem to notice. Then, when he did, I think it scared him."

"Casserole brigade?"

"Single women over sixty who see an unattached male and try to get to him through his stomach."

"Oh."

"Then your mom swoops in, and in a matter of days, he's not only in love, but so is she."

Annie nodded.

"Why couldn't it happen to me?" Margaret said. "Why couldn't the armchair detective have been a guy? A widower who took one look at me and said, 'There she is, someone who likes watching the news and football. Someone who thinks staying home to eat soup and sandwiches, not casseroles, is greater fun than going out to eat. Someone to take long drives with.'

"Oh, Margaret. I'm sorry. I had no idea that's what was bothering you."

"No one does, and I shouldn't have told you. I don't mind eating alone, but I just didn't realize that I'd be eating alone forever."

"Come to lunch with us." This time Annie meant it.

Margaret hesitated. "What time are you going?"

"Eleven."

"That's right when one of my shows is on. Plus, I have a few other things I need to do."

"Like?"

"Like take care of your cat."

"Boots can come with us."

"No, really, you kids go on by yourselves. And please don't share what I told you with anyone. I'm almost sixty, set in my ways. I don't know why it hit me so hard yesterday. I guess it just reminded me of what I missed out on." She pushed herself off the bed and seemed to try to shake the melancholy mood. "I shouldn't have burdened you with this. You're too young to understand."

"Not true. My oldest sister has been engaged to the same guy for years. She met him on her first day of law school, and they've been together since. Even when he goes out of town, he calls her on the phone." Annie decided not to mention that when he called, he had a list of things for Beth to do. Nor did she mention that every day had ended yesterday. "Then, my little sister, Cathy, she's a magnet. She walks into a room and the guys flock to her. She always knows what to say. Me? I'm quiet. Most guys want a little more excitement."

Margaret shook her head. "That's not it. You just demand a little more than the first guy you see or every guy you see. Maybe I was a little like that, but I thought there'd be some Harrison Ford–type guy just around the corner."

"I'm more a Matt Damon kind of girl," said Annie.

Margaret nodded. "I want to say that's sensible, but I'm not sure. I do know if I'd have been sensible I'd have stayed with the guy from York College. By the time I figured out he was a catch, he'd gotten away."

"I'm sorry."

"Me, too. He married one of my friends. They have three children, nine grandchildren, and are about to become great-grandparents."

"You keep in touch with them?"

"Oh yes, somewhat. They send me a Christmas card every year. She used to thank me for breaking up with Robert."

"So, what was it you didn't like about him?" Annie really wanted to know. Maybe he was short or had yellow teeth. Maybe he had dandruff or smelled funny.

Margaret looked at one of the professional photos lying on the bed of Joe and his parents. "I can tell you what I thought it was. He wanted to be a preacher and I didn't want to be a preacher's wife."

Before Annie could comment, Margaret continued, "Now that I'm older and wiser, I can tell you how foolish I was."

"Okay, tell me."

"I didn't realize I could plant a garden anywhere and it would grow."

Chapter Nineteen

....

Margaret decided to help. She picked up the bedding from the hall-way and headed downstairs to the laundry room. "I'll search around there a bit, even though I know you've already done it."

"Actually, we've not been down there yet."

After Margaret walked away, Annie got started putting things back where they belong, dusting and feeling along crevices the whole time. She'd just about finished when the doorbell rang.

She listened for Margaret's footfalls on the stairs but didn't hear them, so she headed down to the front door.

Kyle Hicks waited.

"Oh, hi," he said uncomfortably. "I was hoping to talk to the minister, to Mr. Kelly."

"He and my mother are heading for Kansas City to the place you took his car. They'll be back in a few hours."

"I tried his cell," Kyle said.

"It fell out of his pocket the day of the accident and landed in the water. He's got a new phone, but I don't know the number. You had his old one?"

"I've always had his number."

"Joe's in town. He's at work. You should go by there," Annie suggested. "He'd love to talk to you, and he could tell you the new number."

"Kyle Hicks, is that you?" Margaret said the obvious as she emerged from the basement stairs.

"Hello, Miss Kelly. I was hoping to talk to your brother."

"I'll let him know."

Kyle took a step back, surveyed the house, and said, "Everything looks the same."

"Everything is the same," Margaret responded. "Including your welcome here. Would you like some tea or a glass of water?"

Kyle gave a half smile. "No, I think I'll go bother Joe. We have some things to catch up on."

The look he shot Annie told her she'd be near the top of his list of topics.

* * * * *

"About time you got a serious girlfriend."

"Used to be, people carting cats and dogs were the only ones walking through that door," Joe quipped, too surprised to do anything else. "Although, just twenty-four hours ago, a potbellied pig opened it with his snout. Today, it's you."

Yesterday all Joe felt at seeing Kyle was a longing for the old days. Today, what he felt was anger, irrational and unwanted. And, it was twofold. First, a true friend doesn't just walk away when something goes wrong. He stays and fights.

But Kyle had walked away, not even trying to fight, and disappearing for years, leaving Joe—who had been raised believing reconciliation was not a choice but a way of life—feeling frustrated.

Second, there was Annie, whom Joe was meeting in a mere ten minutes. Funny, he'd wanted to have a serious talk with Kyle for years, and at this moment, all he could do was joke about a ridiculous pig and think about what was more important.

Annie was leaving the day after tomorrow.

Joe looked at the clock again. Almost eleven. He had clients coming in at ten after twelve. They were using their lunch hour to take care of their pets. If Joe wanted to enjoy a nice lunch, think forty-five minutes, with Annie, he pretty much needed to leave now.

He didn't move.

"Yeah," Kyle agreed. "I'm here. Seeing you yesterday made me realize it was just a matter of time. I needed to make it to my parents' place before they found out from somebody else that I'm back."

"I won't tell them. Annie wouldn't, either."

"That's beside the point." Kyle came the rest of the way into the room and sat on one of the many chairs in the waiting area, not too close to Joe but not the one farthest away, either. Joe figured Kyle was unsure of his welcome.

Joe was feeling a bit unsure himself.

Kyle's eyes settled on Jacko. "Where's Pepper?"

"He lived to be seventeen. I put him down a few years after you left. He was in pain. This is Jacko."

At the mention of his name, Jacko got up off the floor and went over to sniff Kyle.

"Pepper had a good long life." Kyle scratched Jacko behind the ears and looked around the room. "You've changed it up since the other vet. I don't remember his name. We never used him much."

"He didn't do large animals, so he wouldn't be your family's first choice."

"You do large animals," Kyle said matter-of-factly. "That's why you were out at my parents' house. You didn't tell me that they've been selling stock off and even some of the land."

"Not an easy thing to work into a conversation with someone you haven't seen in a decade and someone who wasn't exactly thrilled at the encounter. Plus, I'm not sure your parents would have appreciated me sharing that information."

"I went out there this morning, right at breakfast time. I figured if I put it off, I might never go. They look older."

"Don't we all."

Kyle certainly had aged. There were black circles under his eyes, and he'd lost enough weight so that his cheeks were sharp. He'd always been sturdy, husky, and muscular from working the farm. Now he was lean and his body seemed full of nervous energy.

"Mom opened the door. I didn't even get to say a word. She just started crying. My dad came running into the kitchen and started yelling. He thought I'd said something to her. When he realized she was crying because I'd come home, he started crying, too."

"Wow" was all Joe could think of to say. It was hard to imagine Kyle's father crying. He was a silent rock of a man who rarely showed emotion, at least that Joe had seen.

"Yeah, wow."

After that, Joe didn't know what to say and moments stretched to minutes. Joe knew that if he didn't say something, anything, Kyle would simply get up and walk away.

Again.

Grasping at the first idea that came to mind, he said, "I've always kinda wished the Bible would have shown the reaction the prodigal's mother had. I mean, if the father was happy enough to throw a feast, what did the mother do?"

Kyle laughed wryly. "She cried, cooked the feast, and then cried some more. Dad had to physically help Mom step back so I could get in the house. I'm thinking if we added the prodigal mom, no doubt the parable would have doubled in size and that chapter would be longer."

"So, are you back? Or just stopping through?"

"I'm back. I haven't been happy anywhere else. I should have come home a long time ago, but once I left, it just seemed easier to stay gone."

"Easier for who?"

"You sound like your dad."

Unbidden came a Bible verse that Dad had quoted over and over from the book of Proverbs: "A man's wisdom gives him patience; it is to his glory to overlook an offense." For the first time, Joe got it. The irrational, unwanted anger he'd felt started to ebb, replaced by relief. His dad was right. The Bible did provide answers if one took the time to listen. Joe wondered what the Good Book would say about his feelings for Annie.

"Well," Joe said, "I probably sound like my dad because I listened to him counsel people for years. I'd be surprised if I didn't sound a bit like him."

Kyle leaned back in the hard plastic chair. This once, Joe was grateful he didn't have a room full of owners and pets. Ignoring the clock and the ever-moving minute hand that robbed him of time with Annie, Joe asked, "Are you ready to talk?"

Kyle started to say "About wh—" but stopped short. Even he knew denying they had anything to talk about was ludicrous.

"I stopped by your house," Kyle admitted, "thinking I'd talk to your dad. But your girlfriend answered the door."

Joe didn't correct him.

"So, I came over here. I guess I need to talk. I haven't told my parents everything yet, and maybe I won't, ever. But I gotta get this off my chest. You're a preacher's kid, so does that mean you're bound by the same restraints as your dad?"

"Meaning?"

"If someone confides in you, you keep it secret."

"I can't believe you'd even ask me that. It makes no difference that I'm a preacher's kid. I'm your best friend. If you told me you'd stolen the coins and there was no chance you could return them or the money they got you, I'd keep it a secret—even from my dad— if you asked."

"You still consider me your best friend, huh?"

"I never stopped."

Looking first at the floor, then at the ceiling, and then back at the floor again before finally meeting Joe's eyes, Kyle said, "I got her pregnant."

Not what Joe was expecting.

"Who?"

"Missy. She told me that night, at your party, right after I was in your dad's office looking at the coins."

"Oh wow" was all Joe could say.

"Oh wow is right," Kyle said. "You were following me around, try-ing to find a moment alone with me to see if you could ask her out.

I was going to tell you to go for it. I was wanting to ask Marlee out because she'd broken up with Dwayne, even though I and everybody else knew it was only temporary. And here comes Missy, pulling me into the bathroom, all weepy-eyed, telling me she was pregnant."

"I didn't even know your relationship had gone that far," Joe admitted.

"Once. It just took once. All I could think about was having to tell my parents. They were still reeling from my brother. Oh, the grandbaby was helping to patch things up, on both sides, but just the thought of sitting down across from my dad and telling him that it looked like son number two wouldn't be going to college, either— man, I didn't have the courage. Missy's parents, they would have freaked, too."

"I think I understand."

"So," Kyle continued, "I'm feeling all numb, and then your dad comes and asks me about the coins. Did I take them? I hadn't. But I probably looked guilty."

"So what did you do after graduation? Why aren't you and Missy together? What about the baby?" Joe had a dozen more questions, but those seemed the most important.

"Missy and I decided not to tell anyone, not until we figured out what we were going to do. We headed to Denver. We talked about getting married, having the baby, and then with the baby, coming home and breaking the news to our parents. It would be easier, a done deal, not so much heartbreak, and hopefully they'd see we were doing what was right."

It made sense now, both Kyle and Missy disappearing at the same time.

"Missy always looks sad," Joe said.

"Huh?"

"I'm just saying, Missy always looks sad."

"I guess that's true," Kyle admitted. "She has a lot to regret. So do I."

"Okay," Joe urged, "you went to Denver, got married, had the baby…"

"We went to Denver. I think in the back of my mind, I thought she'd taken the coins. But she hadn't. We had no money. I'd never realized what it felt like to be poor. I got a job as a busboy in a restaurant. She got a job at a grocery store clerking." Kyle looked up. "We didn't love each other. We were young and stupid. We didn't get married. She wouldn't let me touch her. We were roommates, nothing else. I've never been so unhappy in my life. And, Missy, she cried every day. She missed her family, her sister."

"Did Marlee know?"

"Yes, but she'd been sworn to secrecy. And so did your dad. I called him. I had to talk to someone."

Joe let out a breath. All this time, his dad had known the truth about Kyle and the coins. No wonder he always simply said, "Kyle didn't take the coins."

"Go on," Joe urged.

"We were at the doctor's office one day. It was time to get the second or third sonogram. I don't remember which. I tried so hard to be excited. This one would tell whether I had a son or a daughter. I prayed so hard. I was hoping that the minute the doctor told me, I'd feel that push—you know, the 'I'm gonna be a daddy' moment."

"And?"

"They said, 'It's a girl.' I smiled, I waited, and nothing happened. I just felt like I was going to throw up."

Joe didn't know what to say. Kyle was the youngest in his family, so except for a few cousins, he hadn't been around little ones. Yes, his brother had a son, two now, plus a daughter, but when Kyle left, little Brandon wasn't even a year old.

"And Missy?"

"She felt the same way. It was probably the only thing holding us together, the way we were feeling."

"I had no idea. I would have stood by you, helped even." Joe checked the clock on the wall. "Look, I need to make a phone call. Annie expected me to meet her for lunch." He took his cell phone from his pocket and punched Annie's number. He'd waited too long, he knew it. He so wanted to see her, but Kyle was emptying words he'd kept bottled up for years. It didn't take a preacher's son to see the kind of hurt that came from the soul.

Annie answered on the second ring.

"I'm not going to be able to make it." Joe looked at Kyle. His friend looked ready to bolt.

"I already figured. I take it Kyle found you."

"Yes."

"Well, I'm already sitting at a table, waiting to order. Your aunt's with me. We're solving all the world's problems."

"Then this works out just fine. Margaret's great company. Kyle has already been to his parents' house. We're talking—"

"—for the the first time in years. I understand. Go for it. I guess this means it's no secret he's in town."

"Exactly. Go ahead and tell Margaret. You want to get together tonight?"

"Margaret already knows. She was helping me look for the coins when Kyle knocked on the door. And your dad called just a minute ago. He's making plans, something about dinner."

"For you or both of us?"

"I'm pretty sure all of us."

Across the room, Kyle waved his hand to get Joe's attention. When Joe finally looked, Kyle said, "Go ahead and meet her for lunch. I've got some things to do."

"I gotta go," Joe told Annie, ending the call and redirecting his attention to Kyle. "Not a chance. If anything, I'll take you to lunch."

"I won't be hungry until next week," Kyle said. "Mom was flustered. She insisted on feeding me and then she made food like she used to when she had a full house. Poor Dad, I think he ate breakfast for a second time just to keep her from crying again."

"It lets you know how loved you are."

"There you go, sounding like your dad again. Maybe you should have been a preacher."

Joe had heard that suggestion a thousand times. He'd considered it, but he'd not been too keen on the idea of being at everyone's beck and call during difficult times. His dad dealt with life *and death*. Life, Joe could do. He didn't mind serving on the table, helping with the buildings and ground, or pitching in to help someone move.

It was death he was uncomfortable with. He'd gone with his dad to a few hospital visits. Watching someone during their last days on earth made Joe feel helpless, and he didn't like that feeling.

And when his mom died, he'd known administering to the

dying wasn't his gift. He couldn't talk, couldn't think, couldn't reach out to the others when pain and sorrow went that deep.

So, he served four-legged friends instead of two-legged ones. And he did get the calls that interrupted meals and he did have to put some animals out of pain. But he could talk, think, and try to soothe their owners.

After a moment, Joe said, "It wasn't my calling."

"And being a father at eighteen wasn't mine," Kyle admitted.

"So, what did you do?"

"We were lucky. One of the girls Missy worked with recommended a great obstetrician, a member of the church. He introduced us to his minister." Kyle chuckled. "We actually started out meeting him for marriage counseling. We were still thinking we'd get married. But eventually, the sessions turned to deeper issues. After one session, Missy and I stayed up all night talking. We knew there were couples out there who desperately wanted children. We decided to give the baby up for adoption."

"That was the bravest thing you could have done," Joe said.

"It didn't feel like it at the time."

"Why didn't you come home afterward?"

"I guess I didn't want to have to face the truth. I was okay with giving the baby away. Well, not okay. How can you ever be okay with giving away something so tiny, so special? But I was at peace with the decision."

"That doesn't explain why you didn't come home."

"If I were at home, the fact that I had a secret would be the elephant in the room, any room. There would be no place I could go where I'd be able to escape the memory of what I'd done and hadn't done."

Joe nodded. It made sense.

"It gets worse," Kyle said.

Joe couldn't imagine how.

"After all was said and done, we signed the papers and stayed together for the next few months, just existing. Finally, the baby was born. I saw her just once as they wheeled her out of Missy's room. There were a few more papers. Then, when Missy and I parted ways, you know what I realized?"

Joe was almost afraid to ask. "What?"

"That somewhere along the way, during that whole mess, I fell in love with her."

Chapter Twenty

. . . .

Annie's cell phone rang at almost three. She was once again standing in the middle of a bedroom with a mattress leaning against a dresser and going through the bedding looking for tears. Pulling the phone from her pocket, she hit the TALK button. She thought for sure it would be her mother, but it wasn't. Instead Rachel's usual matter-of-fact voice said, "We've had another catastrophe."

"What? And did you say *had*?"

"Yes, I said had. I took care of it. It was the Shermans."

Annie closed her eyes. The Shermans had been the house that took them from a struggling paycheck-to-paycheck ragtag group of three women with Rachel in the office and Annie plus one other woman cleaning the homes, to Rachel and Annie in the office, Annie cleaning houses part-time, and five employees cleaning houses full-time.

"Suzette was cleaning their chandelier."

"That's a monster job. I've done it a few times." What Annie remembered most was how many crystals there were and how each one required, per Mrs. Sherman's orders, individual attention. "So what happened?"

"Suzette had laid out the tarp and was on the ladder spraying the entire fixture with cleaner. She's not crazy about heights, you know."

"I know."

"The son came home. One of the dogs came running in, skidded, and got tangled in the tarp."

"Not good. They have German shepherds."

"No, not good. The tarp somehow got tangled in the dog's feet and when he took off, the tarp came with him and the ladder didn't have a chance."

"Poor Suzette. Is she all right?"

"Broken wrist."

"And the Shermans want us to pay for the chandelier," Annie finished. That was it. The end of their business. Yes, they had insurance, but if they used it, their rates went up. The Schonbek chandelier was a twenty-thousand-plus piece, and was one of Mrs. Sherman's favorite possessions. She'd tell her friends and they'd all find a new cleaning service. Soon, there'd not be enough money to pay the monthly insurance.

"Mr. Sherman had me on the phone while I was at the emergency room with Suzette."

"That's rude."

"I think so, too. I hung up on him. I don't have to listen to someone yell at me about something I had no control over."

"What did you do?"

"I called your sister."

"Beth helped you out."

"She didn't just help me out. She drove here from Phoenix, went to the Shermans' house, spoke to his staff and kids—they all saw the accident—and called him on the phone to talk about workman's comp."

"So, he's not asking for restitution?"

"Not anymore, and he's going to pay Suzette's hospital bills as well as her wages while she's recovering. Plus, for now at least, we're still their cleaning service."

"Good job."

"I also went through the applications we had on file again, and I sent out e-mails to ten women. Three have already gotten back to me and two of them sound like potential employees. I'll need to replace Suzette, at least for a month or two. Plus, three people stopped by today and asked for rates."

"Everything else okay?" Annie noticed that Rachel said "I'll need to replace Suzette" instead of "we'll need to replace Suzette..."

"No, nothing else. It was a good day except for Suzette's accident. No one called in sick and I caught up on all the work I was behind on."

"Because you're doing my job as well as yours."

"Because I'm learning to do your job as well as mine. This was a good experience for me. I should have been taking on more of a hands-on role long ago. I didn't realize how many issues you dealt with day to day."

Annie had no more than hung up from talking with Rachel than the phone sounded again. This time it was Beth.

"Thanks for helping," Annie answered the phone, skipping the usual hello.

"It's the first time I've seen your office. It's not what I pictured. Better. You've got quite a little business going. I'm impressed."

"We've doubled our clientele in just two years. If this keeps up, I won't be cleaning houses part-time at all. I'll work in the office with Rachel and—"

"And then you can devote more time to your jewelry."

"Yes," Annie agreed. "So why aren't you at work today? I thought Fridays were your busy days."

"Every day is my busy day. I had some things to do, very mental health, so I cleared my desk as best I could yesterday."

Beth never took days off. "What did you do?"

"First I had breakfast with Dan."

"Dan?"

Beth sighed, clearly exasperated that Annie didn't know everything. "Dan O'Leery. He's Mom's criminal justice professor. I told you all about him already."

"I don't think I've ever heard his name. Did you find out anything new?"

"No, but I'm going rock climbing with him weekend after this."

Annie sat down, cross-legged, amidst the sheets and pillows and old shoes that made up the mess in the middle of Max's bedroom. He'd not had an old math book under his bed, but he had enough black shoes to keep Tommy Lee Jones and Will Smith outfitted for a decade. Some of them even had old socks, black also, tucked inside. "You're bouncing back quite nicely."

This time, Beth's silence wasn't long lasting. "I went out for lunch, too."

"With Dan?"

"No, with Charles."

If Annie hadn't already been sitting, she'd have fallen down. "Did he want to make up?"

"Yes, he did."

"And what did you do?"

"I gave him back his ring."

"Ohhh," Annie said, suppressing the urge to shout with joy. "I wish I could have been there."

"Stop. I still love Charles, just not enough to marry him. I even thanked him for breaking up with me. I mean, do you know the kind of life I would have had with him?"

Annie nodded, glad that Beth couldn't see her. She knew exactly the kind of life. Beth would have had expensive chandeliers and a staff and a husband more concerned with keeping up appearances than keeping promises.

"Anyway, I just wanted to check base, tell you that the Shermans have no intention of taking any further action. Plus, I'm going to work with Cathy this weekend at the Fountain Hills Bazaar."

"You're kidding." Beth had never expressed an interest in Annie's business.

"She needs help in Spanish. Now that I'm not at Charles's beck and call, I have some downtime. I'm tired of having to pencil my sisters in between commitments. I figured I could do flashcards or something with her when the booth isn't busy."

When Annie finally ended the call, she stood and started putting Max's bed to rights. A funny feeling accompanied her. It wasn't until she finished going through every single drawer that she realized what it was: a vague sense of discomfort.

She didn't feel needed.

It was a strange and oddly exhilarating feeling.

* * * * *

"I can't believe you sent my car so far away. What were you thinking?"

Friday nights at the Bonner Springs Café were hustling. Joe didn't answer as he followed his dad through the crowded restaurant and made sure he didn't bump into anything with his crutch as he shook hands with or greeted practically everyone in the room. Even little Katie, who'd been sitting at a booth coloring, stopped working on her princess picture and stood up to give his dad a hug. Behind them, both Willa and Annie were talking to Marlee, probably exchanging stories about *the girls*.

When the ladies finally joined them, Joe slid into the bench next to Annie while his father settled in next to her mother.

"Now's probably a good time to tell you," Joe said. "Kyle's back. He was the tow truck driver."

His father's mouth opened and closed. He bowed his head for a moment, and Joe knew he was talking to God. When he looked up, Joe continued, "He hadn't let his parents know he was back yet. He was trying to get up the courage. I didn't want to interfere, so I had him tow it to Kansas City instead of here."

"I understand. I'd have done the same thing."

"He went to see his parents this morning," Joe continued. "He's moving back. He came by my practice. We had a long talk."

"He came by the house, too," Annie said. "He'd tried your cell phone and had been unable to reach you."

Joe's dad nodded. "They gave me an upgrade, and I've still got to learn how to use it."

"He told me everything," Joe said.

His dad nodded again and quickly looked around the restaurant. "Missy working tonight?"

"I don't know."

His dad leaned forward, concern etched across his features. "Does Kyle know she's back in town?"

Joe suddenly got it. "I didn't tell him, not directly. I told him she always looks sad. Surely he knows—"

His dad stopped nodding and shook his head.

"Oh man."

"Are you gentlemen going to fill us in on the other half of the story we're hearing?" Willa asked.

Joe's dad put his hand on Willa's. "Sorry, I can't believe I'm talking shop." He looked at Annie and changed the subject. "I'm glad you're willing to eat here twice in one day. Their Friday night fish fry is the best in town."

"The only one in town," Joe added.

"I'm definitely going to miss this place," Annie said. "But Casa Grande has some decent restaurants, especially Mexican. You'll have to come visit. You can meet my friend Rachel, and we'll show you around."

"I'll do that," Joe said.

In some ways, he found it hard to believe she'd be leaving day after tomorrow. Aunt Margaret had said it best, although Joe couldn't exactly remember the words. Something along the lines of Annie being like a wildflower, blooming in strange soil but only for a short while.

Someone else's words echoed in Joe's thoughts. Kyle's. "Somewhere along the way, during that whole mess, I fell in love with her."

Missy came to the table then. Joe resisted the urge to stand up and hug her. His dad wasn't so restrained. "How's my girl?"

LOVE FINDS YOU IN SUNFLOWER, KANSAS

"I'm doing okay. It's busy tonight."

Missy wasn't one for small talk, hadn't been in years, and now Joe knew why.

She took their orders and headed toward another table. Joe met his father's gaze. They shared a look. Lately, all the Scriptures that Dad had quoted through the years were coming in handy. All Joe could think of at the moment was Galatians 6:2: "Carry each other's burdens, and in this way you will fulfill the law of Christ."

"So." Joe's dad turned his attention to Annie. "I see I have the cleanest bedroom in three states. You found a pair of shoes I'd forgotten I owned. Where were they?"

"Way under the bed."

"But no coins were under there."

"I've looked through all the rooms Mom said she'd not gotten to, although I need to spend a bit more time in the basement. Margaret searched down there today. If the coins are in your house, they're not in a place I—we—can find."

"That's okay. I've got another twenty years to look for them."

"Decided not to move, Dad?"

His father looked straight at Willa when he answered. "Exactly."

Missy came with their salads and drinks. Joe wished he'd seated himself so he could see the door, but his dad appeared to be keeping a constant vigil. Still, Joe turned in his seat often enough that Annie must have noticed.

"Are you expecting someone else?"

"I hope not."

"Kyle?" she guessed.

"I really hope not."

Missy returned again to fill their iced teas, and Joe's dad changed the subject. "What did you think about the old homestead over in Sunflower, Annie?"

"I thought it was great. I could just picture what it must have looked like in its prime."

"Think you could live there, in the middle of nowhere?"

"I think it would inspire me to make a completely new line of jewelry. I've always been a garnet, peridot, turquoise kind of girl, but yesterday got me thinking about all I could do with pressed flowers. My fingers are itching to go home and experiment."

"I could live out there," Joe said. "Last night I sat down and really looked at my practice and future. My small animal clientele are mostly people from church or friends. I'm competing with two other vets. My large animal clientele is just about everyone in a forty-mile radius, friends and strangers. And it's growing because I'm not competing with anyone. Last night, I started surfing the 'net and looking at clinics that focus just on farm animals."

"No more dogs, cats, or squirrels?" his dad asked.

"Oh, I'd still do them, just not on scheduled days. I think what I want is a fully equipped mobile veterinary unit. Right now, that would cost more than I could afford."

"I doubt pet people would drive all the way out to Sunflower just to have their cats spayed." Willa finished her salad. She started gathering everyone's plates so Missy could remove them easily.

"No, but people who own cows and horses also own cats and dogs. They wouldn't need to come to town or even come to me. I'd already be on their property and prepared."

"I like the way you're thinking," his dad said.

The moment their meal arrived, his father's cell phone rang. Checking the number, he said, "I have to take this." He carefully stood, positioned his crutch, and slowly headed toward the back of the restaurant where it was a little less noisy.

"This always happens at mealtime," Joe warned Willa.

She looked him squarely in the eye, not hesitating. "I've already figured that out. It doesn't bother me a bit."

He noticed she wasn't eating but was waiting for his dad to return. "I guess that means you're staying?"

Willa looked at the back of the restaurant. Joe followed her gaze and saw that his dad was sitting on a stool by an old pay phone. He was talking and nodding and then talking some more.

"I shouldn't say anything until Max is here," Willa said.

"Oh, go ahead," Joe encouraged. "I think Annie and I know what you're going to tell us."

Willa looked back at his dad again. He smiled and waved.

"Mom," Annie said. "I think it's great and so do Beth and Cathy."

"Beth thinks it's great?" Willa sounded doubtful.

"Charles broke up with her."

"Yes, I know, but I don't think Charles breaking up with her would suddenly cause her to tell me it's all right if I marry again."

"You're right. I think it was having breakfast with Dan O'Leery this morning."

"She had breakfast with Professor O'Leery? Now this I didn't know."

"She's going rock climbing with him next weekend."

"I guess," Willa said, "this means she won't be flushing Charles's ring down the toilet."

"She's already given it back."

"You're kidding," Joe said. "That happened fast. She was going to flush the engagement ring?"

"He deserved it," Annie and Willa said together.

Joe held up his hands. "Okay, okay. Boy, you Jamison women stick together. I'd better warn my dad."

"Pshaw, you don't need to warn him. He already knows and appreciates it. I told him I wouldn't marry him until all my girls gave their blessing." Willa looked down at her left hand. "The best thing about love at fifty is you're mature enough to appreciate it."

Joe noted the ring. He also heard the gasp Annie gave. Surely she wasn't surprised.

"Apparently, he went to Annie's website and ordered it. He had it shipped first class, and it just arrived this morning." Willa held out her hand so Joe could see. "White fossilized coral has always been my favorite of all the rings Annie designs."

"Okay," Annie said. "You can keep him."

"I'm glad to hear you say that. Because we went to the county clerk and got the marriage license today. Come Monday, we'll have fulfilled the three-day waiting period. The only thing I was worried about was you girls." She looked at Joe. "And you. Are you okay with this?"

Joe nodded, amazed by how okay he was.

"That's one of your designs?" Joe looked at Annie. "You make wedding rings?"

"Well, what Mom's wearing is not exactly a wedding ring, but yes, I design rings."

Joe looked at the back of the restaurant. His dad relaxed against the wall, nodding at something the person on the other end of the phone was saying, and looking more content than Joe had seen him in years. Then Joe's dad stood up, his expression worried. His crutch fell to the ground. The crash Joe heard, however, was not from his father's direction. It was from near the entrance of the restaurant. Joe turned and saw Kyle standing in the doorway.

Missy was frozen in place, a tray with four teas and a salad balanced just over her shoulder—her pale face looking lost and guilty at the same time.

Marlee, however, wasn't frozen in place. She was bent over, hands reaching to pick up shards of broken plates while she said, "Katie, don't move. Stay there."

Katie didn't listen. In a heartbeat, the third-grader was next to her mother saying, "I can help."

Joe took one more look at both Missy and Marlee's faces and did the math. In that moment, he figured out something he doubted even Kyle knew.

Joe knew who was raising Kyle and Missy's little girl.

Chapter Twenty-One

. . . .

Joe was out of his seat and to the front of the restaurant in record time. "Kyle, good to see you. Come on outside. Let's talk."

Eager didn't begin to describe how quickly Kyle moved. "Mom said Missy worked here. I thought I'd drop in, say hi, all very low-key. What just happened in there? Why did Marlee freak out?"

"How long has it been since you've seen Marlee?" Joe asked when they made it to his truck. Jacko, elated at the presence of his owner and an extra person who might pay attention to him, jumped at the window and barked. Joe made a motion, and Jacko sat on his haunches, silent and waiting.

"Not since I left here. When did she dye her hair black?"

"About five years ago." Joe had to remind himself that Kyle had no clue what chaos he'd just caused. For a moment, Joe allowed himself to think that maybe he was wrong. Maybe Katie wasn't Missy and Kyle's daughter.

"I guess she wanted to look more like her mom," Kyle mused.

More like she wanted to look like Katie because Katie had black hair, just like Kyle.

His dad would know, right? Joe had been gone around the time Katie was born, and being in vet school—for a boy who'd always had a hard time cracking the books—was time consuming.

And Joe couldn't recall Marlee looking pregnant.

"Look," Joe said. "Tonight's probably not the perfect time for you to be talking to Missy. It's a busy Friday and she's working. How about I talk to her and try to set something up?"

"I have no intention of bothering her. I just want to find out how she's doing. I had no idea her sister would freak out. Missy looks great. Is she married or something?"

This was Joe's dad territory, not Joe's. Joe didn't have a clue if what he was doing was helping or hurting matters. He glanced at the restaurant entrance. Through the window he could see Missy still waiting on tables. Joe couldn't see Marlee, but that didn't mean anything. She could be in the kitchen or simply beyond Joe's view.

"She's not married, and she's only been back a couple of years."

Before Joe could say anything else, his dad came out the door and went to Kyle, giving him a quick hug. "Good to see you. Joe said you two had run into each other."

"I'm glad we did, or I might not have gotten up the courage to come to town."

Dad nodded. "Lots of things to get straightened out, that's for sure. You have plans tomorrow morning?"

"Just helping around the farm."

"Think you can stop by the church around nine?"

"Why?"

"Missy's working the lunch shift, but she wants to talk to you, so I suggested an early morning meeting."

Kyle nodded. "I'll be there."

Both Joe and his dad watched as Kyle headed for his truck, jumped in, and drove down West Kump Avenue. They watched as his vehicle slowed at the bar on the corner. Its parking lot was as filled as the café's. The biggest difference was the lack of children exiting cars and being caught up in parents' arms, the absence of whole families coming together.

"No answers there," Joe's dad said softly.

"He knows that." Still, Joe was relieved when Kyle sped up and turned at the intersection. Both men stood for a while.

"I don't envy you," Joe finally said. "Tomorrow's meeting is not going to be fun."

"No, it's not, but life isn't always fun. It's ups and downs and everything in between. Still, now that Kyle's back in town, maybe some healing can take place and some fears can be alleviated."

"Like Marlee's?"

"That I don't know." Dad leaned against the car, resting his crutch against the door handle and looking up to where the stars were already starting to show their faces in the darkening sky. "But I can tell you one thing. I'll be praying about it, and God's timing is spot-on."

"Willa told us you're getting married."

Dad laughed. "I knew when I left her alone with the two of you, she'd tell. What do you think?"

"I think it's great. I think God's timing is spot-on." Joe swallowed. He meant the words. He really meant them.

"I haven't felt this good since…" The words tapered off.

"I know, Dad."

His father nodded. "I was married to your mother for thirty-five years. I loved her. I've been asking God could there be someone else. I, personally, didn't think so until Willa arrived. I knew the minute

I saw her at the baggage claim there was something special about her. On the drive home from the airport, I was thinking that this was a woman I'd never be bored with. By the time I pulled into the driveway, I knew I wanted to be pulling into the driveway with her the next twenty years if she'd let me."

"Love at first sight," Joe agreed.

His dad picked up his crutch and positioned it under his arm before heading toward the café. He chuckled. "Hard to believe, isn't it?"

Joe held open the door and followed him to the table where Willa and Annie waited.

"Not at all."

* * * * *

Saturday, Annie woke up way too early and headed for Max's house, more specifically, his basement. What she really wanted to do was work on the last of her bracelets, but her time in Bonner Springs was running out. Four hours later, she finished.

She hadn't found the coins.

She had, however, found a calendar from 1952 as well as some rusty old toys that probably had been Max's at one time.

She knew better than to call her sisters. With the time difference, she'd be calling them during the rushed prep time. Fountain Hills was one of the busier shows—and she had to trust them to handle it for her.

With time on her hands—she knew they wouldn't be eating at Max's this morning as he had an early morning appointment and

Margaret's idea of breakfast was a Pop-Tart—she headed back to Margaret's and settled in her room to work on her jewelry. When she finished with that, she began to pack. From his box on the dresser, Boots made a few mewling sounds and then fell asleep.

How could the kitten be so content when in a little over twenty-four hours, Annie would be on her way home?

She should feel a whole lot more excited.

"Honey?" Annie's mother poked her head in the door, taking in the neatly stacked jewelry supplies and half-packed clothes. "Oh, good, you're awake. Feel like coming with Margaret and me into town to do a little shopping?"

Two hours later, her mother had picked out her wedding dress—a sensible blue, not-quite-to-the-calves-length creation. Annie dutifully sent photos from her cell phone to her sisters' cell phones. Everyone approved, and Cathy immediately called to say that she'd seen a purse in the booth right next to theirs that would be a perfect match.

Her mother nodded. "That can be my something new to go with my something blue."

"How's everything?" Annie asked Cathy as she carried the phone to a bench located outside the changing room and sat down.

Beth took over the conversation. "I didn't realize how much fun this is. Cathy's a natural. Half the time, I think people are buying the jewelry because they think it's a bidding war. She puts it on, looks admiringly at it, says how great it looks, and then talks as if she's going to buy it. Pretty soon, they're practically pulling it off her finger or wrist."

"But she doesn't know the name of the gems, where they're mined, or their history."

"No one's complained."

"Sales are good?"

"We've taken in over six hundred so far."

Annie checked her watch. It was just past noon. Cathy and Beth had only been doing business for three hours. Unheard of.

"What did you sell?"

"Two bracelets and some rings."

After ending the call, Annie did a little dance and then went to find her mother and Margaret, who were more than ready for lunch. Apparently Max had called and was already at a fast food restaurant near his museum.

"About time," he said.

It took all afternoon to go through the Wyandotte County History Museum, as Max was not only slow moving—thanks to the crutch—but also a wealth of knowledge. By the time they left, Annie could have passed a test on the Shawnee, Delaware, and Wyandotte Indians, felt like she knew the Founding Fathers, and had a sudden urge to buy a quilt after looking at all the ones on display.

"We'll do the National Agricultural Center and Hall of Fame next time you come," Max said. Turning to Annie's mother, he asked, "When are we getting married?"

He'd asked this question at least a dozen times already.

"Exactly one week." She leaned over and kissed his cheek. "Cathy takes her final at ten thirty. She and Beth have two o'clock flights. They'll arrive at four."

Mom reached over and took Annie's hand. "Are you sure you need to go back to Arizona, just to turn around and come back here?"

"I need to get home, see how work's going and some other stuff. Plus, I have a show the weekend you're getting married. I've either got to find someone to work it or cancel." Annie hadn't agreed to fly out with Beth and Cathy next week, so she'd not purchased another plane ticket. If all went well finding a replacement for her next weekend bazaar and with OhSoClean, she was hoping she could get back to Bonner Springs a bit earlier, like Wednesday.

"I could sure use your help getting Max's backyard ready for the wedding," her mother continued.

"I can't believe you're not getting married in the church," Margaret grumped.

They'd had this conversation already also. Max and Elizabeth had been married in the Bonner Springs church. Mom didn't want to get married in the same place. She wanted a new beginning for both of them. Plus, they wanted a small wedding. Max's backyard limited the number of people who could attend. They'd have a reception that night at the church. Everyone would be invited.

"You going out with Joe tonight?" her mother finally asked.

Annie had checked her phone a dozen times. For a cell phone that usually spewed out a hundred calls a day, her BlackBerry was uncharacteristically quiet.

"He hasn't called."

"Saturdays are busy," Max said. "Lots of people wait until the weekend to bring their pets in."

"Did you know that twenty percent of people prefer their pets' company to their spouses'?" her mom asked.

"You didn't learn that in your criminal justice class, did you?" Annie asked.

"Ah, no," Mom admitted. "I read it in one of the vet magazines at Max's house."

Max leaned over and kissed her. "You don't have to worry about that, honey. I'll always prefer your company."

"You don't have a pet," Margaret said.

"I take care of animals for Joe all the time. That counts," Max reasoned.

For once, one of her mother's statistics gave Annie pause. Wherever Joe was right now, Jacko was certainly with him. And Annie hoped they were both with Kyle. That was why she didn't call him.

It wasn't until the evening meal—chicken prepared by Annie's mom—that Joe finally showed up. He looked tired and somewhat subdued. Margaret immediately stood up, made him a plate, and put it in the microwave.

Joe sat down next to Annie. Jacko licked her hand and curled up at her feet. He looked exhausted, too.

"We spent all day at Blue Sunflower Farm," Joe explained. "I think he herded children all day."

"That'll do it," Margaret said.

"Everything all right?" Max asked.

"Two gilts gave birth. Each had ten piglets. Each wound up with five dead. Cliff and I spent all afternoon trying to figure out why."

"Did the gilts fight each other or something?"

"No, Dad, that's the first thing we looked for, no sign of that. Neither mama was overweight. I didn't see any moldy feed, not that it's the season or that Cliff would let that happen."

Annie's first thought was to say, "This might not be dinner table conversation," but stopped. Those words were what her father would be saying. Joe was a vet. He was talking about his day just the way she and her sisters talked about their days. She reached down and gave Jacko's head a caress. Something else her father wouldn't allow: a dog at the table.

"I'm sorry," Annie said.

Joe looked at her and smiled. Suddenly, Annie thought she could listen to pig stories—both happy and sad—all evening.

"They asked about you," Joe said. "Cliff was surprised you weren't with me. I'm going back out there tomorrow after church. Want to come with me and see the piglets? We're invited for lunch. You can leave from there to the airport."

"I'd love to see Blue Sunflower Farm one more time," Annie said, "That's a good idea."

The microwave dinged. Joe stood, got his plate, and then sat down before asking Annie, "So, what did you do all day?"

"We went shopping for a wedding dress."

Joe raised an eyebrow. "This soon?"

Everyone nodded.

"The wedding's next Saturday," Max said. "I know it's fast, but why wait when it's what we both want?"

"I'm pretty sure I'm free. I'll check my calendar when I get out to the truck."

"Good. You're the best man whether you're free or not."

"Sometimes it has to be pleasure before business," Annie said. "I'm still trying to figure out what to do. I have a show next weekend. My sisters can't work it, they'll be here."

Everyone looked at her.

"Honey, we can wait a week or two. It's not—"

"Are you kidding?" Annie shook her head. "I'd a million times rather be at your wedding than sitting in a booth by myself selling jewelry."

"So you're going to cancel?" Joe asked.

"You won't be able to get your money back?" Mom said gently. She'd worked alongside Annie a few times, especially early on.

"I'm not worried about the money. Life happens." Annie smiled a wry smile. "The problem is that the people who put on these shows have long memories, and next year either I won't have a spot or I'll have a spot next to the booth selling onion-scented candles."

Mom started to say, "Honey, really, we—"

Annie held up a hand. No way was work more important than her mom's wedding. "No, I'm sitting here thinking. I'll find someone to work it. Maybe Rachel. She's come along once or twice. She's not comfortable in a crowd, but she needs the money and I'll offer to pay her a percentage, just like I do when she handles the website. At least she knows what each gem is."

"Go call her," her mother urged.

As if cued, Annie's phone sounded. Picking it up off the table and checking caller ID, she said, "It's Cathy."

* * * * *

Annie took her phone and headed out to the living room. Jacko didn't even give Joe a *Do-I-have-permission* look, he simply followed Annie.

Joe understood completely. He'd follow Annie just about anywhere, too.

Instead, since the call might be private, he kept eating.

"What!" Something had Annie excited. So excited that her voice rose and everyone in the kitchen heard her words.

"You're kidding! Janice from the *Jack and Janice Morning Show*?"

"She's about to get married, too," Willa said.

Margaret set down her fork. "Who?"

"It's a show back home. The *Jack and Janice Morning Show*. They've been in the area for years. I've met Janice a time or two. She's friends with one of the ladies from church. I doubt she'd remember me, though." From the living room came, "My flight gets in at six. Yes, tell her I'll meet her. Yes, thanks, bye."

Joe kept eating.

Annie came flying into the room. "Janice from the *Jack and Janice Morning Show* was at the Fountain Hills craft show. She stopped by my booth and looked at the jewelry."

"That's great," Willa said. "What else?"

"She wants to order some special items to use as gifts for people in her wedding, and she wants me to be on her show sometime this week. I'm supposed to meet with her tomorrow evening to discuss the details. She's leaving on an eight o'clock plane to research some honeymoon locales. I'm arriving at six. We'll meet right in the terminal at seven. Oh man, I wish I could update my website right this minute."

"This could be your big break," Willa said.

"My fingers are itching," Annie gushed. "I wish I had more of my stuff here. I could work all night putting things together. I can hardly wait to get home."

What Joe heard, though, was Annie really saying she couldn't wait to leave.

Chapter Twenty-Two
....

Sunday morning the ladies didn't head over to Max's house for breakfast. Instead, they vied for bathroom privileges and checked out what each other was wearing. Annie had never seen her mother so content.

In the week Annie had been Margaret's guest, she'd gotten to know the older woman and realized that for Margaret, having a full house was equivalent to a blooming garden. Nothing made her happier.

She was already planning how to make room for Beth and Cathy, even though Max had plenty of room.

Annie hadn't brought any church clothes so she was wearing her best pair of jeans and one of her mother's shirts.

Why had she really stopped going to church? How had prayer stopped being a natural part of every day? Annie knew part of the answer. Time management or, rather, time mismanagement. OhSoClean took up forty to sixty hours a week, especially when they first started. Then, when the jewelry business took off, Annie poured all her spare moments into designing jewelry.

In Annie's world, she pushed God aside one step at a time. Then she'd pretended she hadn't noticed His apparent absence.

"I'm sorry, God," Annie whispered. At least that was better than a constant drone of *please* and *help*. It felt better, too. "I'm sorry, God. I didn't even realize how empty my life had gotten without You in it. I thank You for bringing me to this place. For introducing my mother to Max."

Annie gulped. When her mom married Max, Annie would, in essence, become somewhat of a preacher's daughter.

If someone had mentioned this last week, Annie would have shrugged it off. Beth would have laughed. Maybe she'd still laugh. Her emotions were raw, thanks to Charles. Only Cathy would smile and say, "Awesome."

The sister who always seemed happy, always seemed to glow, was the one who knew the Lord intimately. Cathy prayed a lot.

Today, thinking about going to church, and praying, and the changes that were about to happen in her life, Annie felt both awe and fear.

Awe that the Lord had blessed her so much; fear that somehow she wasn't worthy.

Heading out of the guest room, she cornered Margaret by the front door and said, "I need a Scripture about prayer."

"You're going to need to narrow that down a bit. The Bible spends a good deal of time on prayer."

"I want one," Annie confessed, "dealing with someone who didn't pray enough but changes."

"I'll tell you my favorite, then. It's in Second Chronicles, the seventh chapter. It says, 'If my people, who are called by my name, will humble themselves and pray and seek my face and turn from their wicked ways, then will I hear from heaven and will forgive their sin and will heal their land.'"

Annie repeated it to herself and then smiled. "It's about change and how change is good."

"Exactly," Margaret agreed. Putting her arm around Annie's shoulders, she whispered, "And you better change your shoes, because we need to leave for church."

Annie looked down. Instead of tennis shoes, she wore bedroom slippers.

"Not that God cares, mind you," Margaret said. "But I doubt if my nephew plans on giving you much time to change your shoes. He's going to want all your time, since you're flying out today."

Annie knew that, and after just six days she had only one thing to say about Joe Kelly and his wanting to spend time with her.

"Thank You, God."

* * * * *

The church was about the same size as the one Annie had attended in Tucson, only here in Bonner Springs it was surrounded by lush green grass instead of rock.

Annie followed her mother, Margaret, and Max through the entrance and into the foyer. People of all sizes, shapes, and ages gathered, all talking excitedly and seemingly glad to be at church.

Annie shared that feeling.

Max immediately started an awkward move-the-crutch, shake-a-hand, move-the-crutch-again path through his throng of friends, who treated Willa like they'd known her all her life.

It wasn't hard to feel accepted. The minute Max and Mom finished their greetings, people turned to Annie. For the next five minutes, she heard how nice she looked, how lucky she was to have a momma like Willa, and the question, "Where's Joe?"

"Thank you. Yes, I do look like Mom. I'm not sure where Joe is. I'm sure he'll be here."

All she knew was that he'd been more than tired last night and left right after eating. Annie spent her time on the laptop googling the *Jack and Janice Morning Show*. There were all kinds of photos of Janice, some professional and some candid. Annie had zoomed in, studied the jewelry Janice wore, and made notes. By the time she finished, Annie figured out that Janice loved the color red. This meant Annie would be looking at spiny oyster, possibly some rhodochrosite, or maybe even red jasper. Janice was also more into display than subtlety, so Annie needed to go big.

After three hours, she had an idea about what Janice really wanted and what she could create to show her. She'd draw on the plane, sketches that would turn into Janice's dream jewelry.

Annie had spent most of the night tossing and turning, thinking about the sketches. That explained why she was so tired at church.

The last person to shake her hand with his calloused work-roughened one was Cliff Whittaker. "Did Joe tell you about the pigs?"

"He did."

"Sure was a shame to lose half. But the ones alive are prime. I hear you're leaving today. I told Joe to bring you by first. Mona's already planning on you staying for lunch."

"He mentioned that. I'm not sure we came up with any definite plans."

"You ever see a baby pig?"

"I've been to the state fair a time or two."

"In Arizona, right?"

"Of course."

Cliff pshawed. "Them pigs are runts."

Annie laughed. "I believe you."

"I'll remind Joe," Cliff said as he walked off.

The adult Bible school class was in the main auditorium. Just as the lesson began, Joe slipped in and sat beside Annie.

"You were almost late," Annie whispered.

"I had things to do," he whispered back. "And I'm never late for church unless it's an emergency."

For the next forty-five minutes, the Sunday school teacher spoke about "Why Come to Services?" Then there was a ten-minute break for people to go gather kids from Sunday school and also for those who didn't come to Sunday school to arrive and find a place to sit.

Annie took the opportunity to run to the restroom. There were five women already there. They each agreed that she looked like her mother, was lucky to have Willa as a mother, and wanted to know what she thought of Joe.

They didn't really give her time to say what she thought. Instead they told her what they thought. It all boiled down to whoever finally caught him—and many had tried—would be a very lucky gal.

Annie went back to her seat feeling somewhat torn. If this were Arizona and Joe was a Casa Grande or Tucson veterinarian, she'd feel very lucky.

Her mother leaned over. "We're invited to the Whittakers' for lunch, too. I can hardly wait to see their place. Max has told me all about it. And Mona Whittaker is a painter. You didn't tell me."

"She paints sunflowers. You saw the blue ones I brought home."

"But you didn't tell me who made them."

A low murmur went through the auditorium. Annie's eyes followed the wave. In the back of the church, Kyle followed his parents to a pew.

Joe leaned over and whispered to his dad, "You see Missy or Marlee?"

"Missy's in the back. I didn't see Marlee."

"If Missy's here, then we have some hope that everything will work out. Right, Dad?"

"I'm praying for it."

The main sermon was from Matthew 13: the sower. Just down from Annie, Max turned the pages of a well-worn Bible. Occasionally he wrote something down in a blue spiral notebook. Next to him, Mom had her Bible. It was newer, and Annie remembered Cathy urging them just three Christmases ago to chip in for it. Cathy realized before her sisters that the term "large print" meant something to their mother.

Annie might have chipped in for the Bible, but today was the first time she'd really looked at it.

She hadn't even packed her own.

Twenty minutes later, Annie knew that when it came to church, she had become the one who'd fallen on thorny ground. She also knew when it came to love, she was the one without roots.

And at the moment, all she could think about was Margaret's Scripture, about how to change. Unfortunately, there just wasn't time to dwell on what could be.

After the last "amen" and as the auditorium emptied, Annie found herself drawn once again to two words that tumbled through her mind when she attempted to pray: *please* and *help*.

* * * * *

Joe parked his truck in front of Cliff's house. Annie was behind him in her rental. His dad and Willa were behind her. They were already running late, thanks to every single member of the church wanting to talk to his dad and the Jamison ladies. Add to that Annie's need to stop by Margaret's and gather her belongings, and Joe doubted that he'd have a moment alone with her.

He should have offered to take her to the airport. He could drive her rental. But then, how would he get back? It made no sense to ask his father to come fetch him. Although Dad would have volunteered eagerly.

Annie stopped her vehicle and stepped out. Immediately, three of Cliff's grandchildren surrounded her. As Joe moved to join her, Jacko at his heels, he heard the youngest one ask, "Where's your kitten?"

"Right now Boots is with Miss Margaret. She's going to watch him until I can take him home."

"Where's home?"

"Arizona."

"Where's that?"

Joe left her to fend for herself—Jacko, the traitor, stayed with her—and went looking for Cliff. He found him in the barn, looking at his gilts. He pointed to one old girl. "She's due anytime. I worried about her the whole time I was at church, prayed really. God hears prayers about pigs. I wonder if yesterday was a fluke or if I'll lose more."

"I don't know," Joe said honestly. "I thought about it all night, and the only suggestion I have is they need to be restricted."

"Easier said than done," Cliff responded. "These mobile pork chops are masters of escape."

"Well, I think probably your gilts got into something they shouldn't have."

"Then why didn't all the piglets die?"

"I'm thinking the weak ones died and the strong ones lived."

"I guess I'll get me some of these hog panels I've been reading about. They're expensive, but losing ten piglets is expensive, too." Cliff looked sheepish. "Plus, the grandchildren cried. Can't have that."

Annie came into the pen, stepping carefully even though she had long ago exchanged the sandals she arrived in for tennis shoes.

"Can I touch one?"

"Yes, but just for a moment. They get cold away from their mamas. Let me fetch one," Cliff offered gallantly, beating Joe.

Joe checked out the remaining gilts, all the while keeping an eye on Annie. He could hear her talking to Cliff, commenting on the fact the piglets' eyes were open, remarking how round their stomachs were.

After a moment, Annie was ready to return the piglet to its mama, and they all headed for the house. Inside, Willa and his dad were looking at photograph albums.

"You're in quite a few of them," Willa said to Joe.

"Preachers' kids do a lot of visiting."

"Oh," said Cliff, "and it couldn't possibly be that you were over here every weekend wanting to ride the horses."

Cliff turned to Annie. "He started helping my boys after school. They hated grooming the horses and giving them indoor showers. Not Joe. He liked everything."

"Especially my cooking," Mona hollered from the kitchen.

Joe wound up in the same spot, Annie next to him, but the best news was that the extra chairs Mona had put around the table meant close quarters. Having Annie so close was bliss and torture. She would be gone in just an hour.

Love at first sight wasn't working out as well for Joe as it had for his father.

"So," Cliff said. "Kyle Hicks is back in town. Think he'll stay?"

"I hope so," Joe's father replied.

"I take it you two ladies didn't find the coins."

"No," Willa said. "We've searched the house top to bottom."

Joe's father beamed. "It's cleaner than it's ever been."

"You giving up?" Mona asked. She was sitting next to Willa.

"No," he answered, "just no longer in a hurry."

"Seems odd that you never found them," Cliff said.

"I always said someone from off the streets came in and took them."

"That makes no sense. If someone came off the streets, you'd have fed them and converted them," Cliff pointed out.

"If only it were that easy."

"Did you put the rest of the Stellas in a safety deposit box like I suggested?"

"I did. But I took them out yesterday."

Joe looked from his dad to Cliff. They'd had this conversation a dozen times, minus the clean house portion. The Stellas had caused so many problems. At least most people blamed the Stellas, that is. Joe now knew the bigger picture.

Max continued, "I took them out because of something Joe said at dinner Friday night. He was talking about my great-grandfather's land, how it might be to live out there and start a large animal operation, complete with a mobile unit."

"That would be great," Cliff said, and his two sons nodded.

"Dad, it was just talk, for the future."

"This is your future. I'm giving you the Stellas. I suggest you sell them. Start your dream. I lived mine. I wouldn't change even one thing, especially the last few weeks with Willa and Annie here. Friday night was the first time you forgot about the past, what you owe, and what's in your way, and really told me your dream. You've worked hard. Make it come true."

"Dad, use the money and take Willa on an extreme honeymoon or something."

"Been there, done that," Willa said. "I have all the T-shirts I need. Besides, I have to help take care of Annie's kitten. Having a vet in the family is more important than a honeymoon."

"Honeymoon?" Cliff said.

"Honeymoon!" the rest of the Whittakers echoed.

"We haven't even talked about a honeymoon." Joe's father suddenly looked willing to investigate the possibility.

"Our honeymoon will be in Arizona when we go retrieve my belongings."

For a moment the conversation changed to the upcoming wedding. Then Mona, the voice of reason, asked, "How many Stellas you got?"

"Enough to start Joe's dream, whether it be a stationary or mobile clinic," Max said. "If Joe wants something bad enough, he knows how to go get it."

Annie smiled. "I can hardly wait to see this all happen. It gives me reason to come back often."

Joe didn't want that. He didn't want her to come back often. He wanted her to stay.

* * * * *

It felt like leaving the Waltons, only with no John Boy. Even as they were getting into Max's car to head back to Bonner Springs, Annie's mother and Max gave Annie a bunch of last-minute directions. "Tell Cathy she can live in the house rent-free for the summer if she doesn't go to summer school. Tell her to find a job. I don't want to put the house on the market while Tucson is in such a real estate slump."

Max added his few. "Pack up and send the rest of your mom's paint supplies if you can't bring them on the plane next week. She's excited to start. Oh, and send a few of her completed paintings. I'll hang them in the living room."

Joe merely smiled and gave her a hug.

It didn't really feel like a hug. It felt like so much more. Annie allowed herself to get lost in it for just a moment, but she had a plane to catch and couldn't let the touch of this man distract her.

He's just a guy I met on vacation, she told herself. Only she hadn't been on vacation, and now—thanks to Mom and Max getting married—he'd be something more.

He sure felt like something more.

And then she thought she heard a whisper: "Don't go."

But she wasn't sure, and she pushed her way out of his arms before he could say it again, say it louder, and maybe change her mind.

She didn't want to go.

She had to.

Janice and her very publicized wedding could be her big break.

She headed for her car, keeping her gaze on the driver's side door, the steering wheel, and her luggage in the back. The tears pooling in her eyes were just happiness for her mother. Yes, that was it. Annie knew exactly where her jewelry was packed. She needed to concentrate on that. If all went well, between the online store and what she'd made here in Bonner Springs, she could convince Janice that Jamison Jewelry was the right choice for wedding party gifts.

Getting a spot as part of their morning show would be more exposure than Annie had dreamed of.

It was all she had worked toward for the last four years.

She hadn't dreamed of nor worked toward a boyfriend or marriage or kids.

Of course, she hadn't known Joe existed.

Which is why she needed to drive away fast.

It took an hour to get to the airport, check in her luggage, turn over the keys, and finish the paperwork on the rental. With a mere twenty minutes until her flight was called, Annie settled down in an uncomfortable black chair and took out her laptop. Maybe she could google and find a few testimonies about her jewelry and use them as a selling point. Maybe she could figure out which ones to pitch to Janice and why.

Her cell sounded just as she was starting to shut everything down.

"Honey," her mother said, "is there any chance that Jacko got in the back of your rental car?"

"No. He'd not only have crawled up to sit with me, but I'm sure he'd have been barking to get back to Joe. Why?"

"When Joe went to leave the Whittakers' place, he couldn't find

Jacko. They've searched everywhere on the farm. Right now, Joe, Cliff, and both of Cliff's sons are out driving around looking. Max and I are headed out there, too. I'm just trying to think of someplace, anyplace, that Jacko could have gotten off to."

"Oh, wow. Joe loves that dog."

"Yes, and he's worried that Jacko might have fallen in a hole or that a coyote or something got a hold of him."

"I didn't even know that coyotes live in Kansas."

"They do."

Annie closed her eyes, picturing Jacko and Joe. He'd be frantic. "Oh, Mom. I hope everything turns out all right. Keep me posted."

Just as Annie turned off her cell, the overhead speaker announced her flight. Quickly, she put her laptop away and grabbed her carry-on.

A line formed and Annie headed for its end. As people gathered behind her—jostling, talking, or just leaning against loved ones—she stepped to the side and let them pass.

What was she doing?

"You getting on?" It was a scraggly-haired boy in loose jeans and a T-shirt, carrying a skateboard.

When she didn't answer, he said, "Are you all right?"

Her feet were glued to the floor. She wanted to move, wanted to get on the plane. She had plans, things to do, important things to do.

The skateboarder waited. Annie looked at his shirt. It had Jesus on a skateboard, doing some kind of jump. The words underneath proclaimed, "Through Him I can do all things."

"I'm fine now. Thank you. I've decided not…" Her voice faltered. "I've decided not to leave."

She had something important to do.

She turned, laptop and carry-on belongings bumping against her side, as she hurried back to the car rental kiosk.

* * * * *

Joe had been everywhere. He'd been over almost every acreage of Blue Sunflower Farm. When finally convinced that the Whittakers could handle that part of the search, he headed for his great-great-grandfather's place. That was within the distance Jacko would travel. Now he was driving aimlessly, stopping every once in a while to get out and shout Jacko's name.

Where to go? Where to go?

Surely he wouldn't lose his dog on the same day he'd lost Annie.

He slowed the vehicle as a weathered orange and yellow sign came into view. The Sunflower Ordnance Plant. As a kid, he and Kyle had found a hole in the fence and explored the place. They'd barely scratched the surface it was so huge, but what they did see was run-down and fascinating, full of history and full of debris.

Joe drove down one of the dirt roads, parked his car by an old white sign stating Speed Limit 35, and exited.

"Jacko! Where are you, boy? Jacko!"

Only the wind gave any kind of answer. If Joe had been worried about Jacko falling down a hole or something, then the Sunflower Ordnance offered a wealth of opportunity.

It wasn't hard to get in. Joe merely climbed over a rickety fence and looked around. The trees were full of leaves. The fence went on for miles. There were water towers, four of them, and an old stone cottage to explore. Once Joe turned from the cottage, he headed toward what looked like bunkers. The way they were built made it look like their roofs were made of grass.

His cell phone rang. It was Dad checking to see if he had located Jacko. Joe quickly filled him in on where he was and where he had been. Another call interrupted. It was Cliff, checking to see if Joe had found Jacko. When the third call came in, Joe simply let it go to voice mail and then listened to the message just long enough to determine that Frank Miller had joined the search.

Joe felt a little like the shepherd who'd gone in search of one sheep. He used to wonder how one sheep could be so important. But over the years, as he fought to save a solitary, crippled bird, a wounded, homeless dog, or a suffering horse, Joe had learned why the shepherd left the flock to go after one.

If Jacko wandered away from a crowd, Joe would be searching, desperately searching. Each and every one of God's beings was special in its own way.

He started walking between beamed structures that looked like giant upside-down hives. He'd made it to the last one when in the distance he heard the sound of a vehicle. Whoever it was, they'd completely bypassed the dirt road and the rickety fence. They must have found a way in that he hadn't. He wished they'd hurry up and park so he could listen for Jacko.

Joe didn't recognize the car. It was silver and four-door. The driver took a moment, then finally stepped out.

Annie!

She spotted him almost immediately. Cupping her hands around her mouth, she shouted, "Did you find him yet?"

"No," he hollered back.

She stood perfectly still and so did Joe.

He took a step toward her, but she held up her hand and cocked her head. Did she hear something? After a moment, she came toward him. "I don't hear anything but the wind."

"Me, either."

"Where have you already looked?"

Quickly, Joe filled her in.

"Every time I'm with one of you Kelly men," she joked, "you have me searching for lost things."

He recognized her words as a feeble attempt to lighten the mood and appreciated it.

"Which way have you already gone? I'll head the other."

Joe shook his head. It was starting to get cold and the sun was fading fast. It was too dark and too dangerous to let her search on her own. Besides, she had those silly sandals on again, and a jacket that wasn't nearly warm enough. And this place was huge, deserted, and he wanted her beside him: safe.

"Just come with me." He moved toward the end of a driveway, and she followed. From where they stood, nothing was on the horizon. The place was deserted, empty, void.

"We'll find Jacko." She glanced around, taking in the area. Joe didn't miss the look of helplessness on her face. This wasn't a house she could tear apart, wash, and then put back together. "Okay. Where do you want to start now that I'm with you?"

"I've already started," Joe said. "The real question is, where do we go next? I won't lie. I'm getting worried."

She reached out a hand. Her fingers gently entwined with his.

She hesitated, looking down at her feet and then at the vast area they needed to explore.

"I feel… I don't know which way to go." Her voice caught, and he loved her for it.

"Me, either."

"I hate this," she admitted. "This isn't a situation that has a rule book. I hate not knowing what to do." She turned to face him. Taking a deep breath, she suggested, "Let's pray?"

"I've been praying from the moment I realized he was gone."

"I've not said a prayer. How about you say one with me?"

She was not a woman who prayed. She'd admitted as much to him. Yet, here she was asking.

He clasped her hand close to his side. The evening sky seemed to grow darker even as he bowed his head. "Father, we thank You for how You watch over Your flock. Tonight we're searching for Jacko, just a little dog. But he's not little to our hearts and he's a big part of our lives. Please help us find him. Guide our steps. Thank You for bringing Annie to my side to help. Amen."

"Please and help," Annie murmured.

"What?"

"Lately, every time I've prayed, those two words have taken the lion's share of my prayers."

"They're powerful words," Joe agreed. He started walking again, her hand still tucked against his side.

She didn't say anything, just walked with him, pausing every time he did, listening to the silence. His phone rang and he shut it off. If they were going to find Jacko, they needed silence.

In the distance the lonely sound of a train echoed. There were birds, black shadows against a gloomy sky. This was a desolate place, forgotten by man and time.

Joe came to a complete halt. He couldn't walk one more step. The night's fingers chilled his skin, finding their way under his coat and causing a shiver to go up his spine.

"I—"

"Shhh," Annie whispered.

That's when he heard it. A bark.

He looked at Annie, waiting to see what she did, waiting for another bark so he'd know which direction to go.

It took only a moment, but the bark came again. Joe still couldn't decipher the direction, but Annie didn't seem to have any trouble. She took off running. Joe followed.

She was faster, but Joe had to take a breath every now and then because he soon figured out that every time he called Jacko's name, the dog barked in answer and helped draw them to his location.

They arrived at the end of a driveway. An uneven pile of dirt was at one end. Overgrown grass and a few tumbleweeds were at the other. Next to the pile of dirt was the hole Jacko had fallen into, a hole so deep that while they could hear his echoing bark, they couldn't see him.

"I'd suggest we call 911, but last time I did that, you laughed at me."

"Nine-one-one doesn't exist here." Joe got down on his hands and knees, peering into the hole. "I can't tell if he's hurt or not."

"We could call the sheriff," Annie suggested.

"What's he going to do? Get down on his hands and knees and peer into the hole?"

"Right. So what's your idea? Does it involve your truck, me behind the wheel, and a tow chain?"

Joe thought for a moment. "That's not a bad idea. Personally, I like any idea that involves you. Good thing you showed up. I need someone who knows how to spin wheels."

Annie looked around. "You might want to spin your wheels a little faster. It's starting to get dark."

Joe got busy searching through the back of his truck while Annie made a few phone calls to let people know Jacko had been found. Finally, when it seemed they had run out of ideas, he came to Annie with a pet carrier. "Your tow chain idea might work. I can lower this into the hole and if he gets into it, I can hoist him out."

"Not a bad idea." The carrier Joe held was sturdy black canvas and had a zip top. "You think the top could hinder him from getting in?"

"I'm not sure."

"We don't want that. If he gets in, he has to be able to get in all the way or at least as much as possible and be as balanced as possible."

A moment later, Joe had cut off the zipped top.

"You think he'll know to get in?"

Joe shook his head. "He's smart, but right now he's scared."

"How did he get out here?" Annie asked.

"My guess is he chased a rabbit, but we'll probably never know." He looked at her. "How did you get out here?"

"Mom called me to see if there was any chance Jacko had hidden in the back of my rental car."

"He was with me when you took off. No chance of that," Joe said.

"I know how much he means to you," Annie said softly. "I

wanted to help. I was heading to Blue Sunflower Farm to help look and happened to see your truck."

The wind blew stronger and Joe took the step he'd meant to take earlier. He cupped Annie's cheeks and pulled her to him.

* * * * *

Please. Help. Thank You.

The kiss was nothing like the hug. It didn't make her feel lost. It made her feel alive.

His lips were demanding and so was the rest of him. He enveloped her in a tight hug until she wasn't sure where he ended and she started. Then, when her knees had almost given out, she said, albeit mutedly, "If you keep kissing me, I won't have the strength to help you save Jacko."

"Consider that kiss a preview." Joe slowly stepped away, letting go of her piece by piece—lips first, body next, hands last—grinning like he'd just won something. His eyes were on her as he started attaching the pet carrier to the tow strap.

Annie went to her car, pulled out a paper bag, and brought it over. "I stopped at McDonalds, but nothing tasted right. I just wanted to find you."

The hamburger went into the carrier. Joe hunkered down next to the hole to try to manage the carrier so it stayed upright and the hamburger didn't fall out.

It was slow work. Soon Cliff and his sons joined them, shouting words of encouragement and helping to balance the tow chain. Then Max and Annie's mother showed up, not a bit surprised to see Annie.

Even the sheriff showed up, joking about trespassing and toxins, and bringing with him a high-beam flashlight so that Joe could finally see and encourage Jacko. After a few trial-and-error runs where Joe thought Jacko was in the bag and probably even Jacko thought he was in the bag, the carrier crested the top and Jacko burst from the hole. He flew right by Joe and went straight for Annie.

"I know how you feel," Joe said.

"Then let her know," Max encouraged.

"I already did, but I'll do it again."

The second kiss was better than the first. It even came with applause.

Chapter Twenty-Three

....

"I can't believe you're getting married," Cathy said. "This is so much fun!"

Beth added, "Me, either. And in Kansas. And you barely know the man."

"I thought we'd been all through this," their mother said. "We all agreed that love at first sight is possible."

Annie looked at her mother's reflection in the full-length mirror in Margaret's bedroom. She looked gorgeous. Her dress was cobalt satin with silver accents, a shell neck, and crystal-embellished shoulders that included a draped overlay. The purse Cathy brought from the craft bazaar was indeed a perfect match, right down to the silver fastener. White shoes finished the outfit. She'd worn it for her wedding and now she wore it for Annie's.

"I'm glad the purse came in more colors than blue," Cathy said.

Holding the white purse Cathy had given her, Annie nudged in next to her mother. Unlike her mother, Annie wore a full-length A-line wedding gown with a sweetheart neckline, chapel train, and bolero. It had come with pearls, beads, sequins, and rosettes, but Annie and her sisters made short work of eliminating the accessories that it came with and replacing them with Annie's handmade pieces.

Janice from the *Jack and Janice Morning Show* had arranged for the transformation from retail to one-of-a-kind to be filmed. Since the show had aired, Annie's website had doubled its business.

Janice, it turned out, was a dog lover. She understood perfectly the reason that Annie had canceled their Sunday evening rendezvous. She had been willing to reschedule the meeting. When they'd finally met, they'd instantly clicked. Outside, right now, were Janice and a cameraman, who was filming a portion of Annie's wedding, to be featured on a future "How We Met" episode.

The camera had Mom all nervous.

"Did you know," she told Annie and her sisters, "that the average wedding costs twenty-five thousand dollars and only allows for a hundred and forty-six guests?"

"Where did you hear that?" Cathy asked.

Beth just rolled her eyes.

"That's a down payment on Joe's mobile lab," Annie said.

"Hurry up, ladies." Margaret hustled in, her cheeks red, her eyes glittering. "We need to get downstairs. I saw the groomsmen come out of Max's back door. They're already on the back porch." Margaret had taken on the role of wedding planner when she'd realized Annie wanted an outdoor wedding. It was convenient since, one, Annie had been living with Margaret for the last month, and two, the wedding would take place right next door.

"You're busy," she'd told Annie. "Working as Joe's receptionist is time consuming, and you need to keep up with your jewelry."

Margaret especially was in charge of flowers.

"I believe in love at first sight." Cathy sighed.

Their mother kissed each of them and went outside. In a moment, she'd be walking Annie down the aisle and giving her away. Max couldn't do it, as he was performing the service. There was still time. Mom could stay with her daughters, offering advice, adjusting straps, and helping with makeup, but she couldn't stand still. She wanted to greet people, gush about her daughters, and enjoy every moment.

She was still very much a honeymooner herself and couldn't seem to contain her excitement.

Annie stood behind her sisters and peered through Margaret's basement window at Max's backyard. She was careful to stay out of sight as she noted the people gathering.

Friends she'd made in the last month living in Bonner Springs, Kansas.

Every chair was taken. Missy was sitting on one side of her grandmother. Marlee, with her husband and daughter, were on the other. The Whittakers were all there. They'd brought what looked like a hundred wooden blue sunflowers. Margaret and a few others had spread them throughout the backyard.

Not what Annie or Margaret had had in mind, but they matched the bridesmaids' dresses and, even more important, they were given in love.

The Hickses had adopted Rachel, who had flown in late last night. Annie was still negotiating the signing over of her portion of OhSoClean to Rachel, with Beth acting as legal counsel. Little by little, Annie was planting her garden here in Kansas.

Rachel had brought along her father, who was acting as an usher. During rehearsal this morning, he'd talked about some of

Rachel and Annie's escapades when they were young. He'd had the bridal party in stitches, and a few times, Annie's mother had frowned. "I didn't know that."

A few stories included Annie's father—stories that made Annie ache for her dad on this special day.

Rachel's dad, surprisingly, knew a lot about flowers and had spent the day helping Margaret. He'd been the one to stand on the ladder and hang flowers on Max's back porch. Max was too busy, and Margaret disliked any ladder that went higher than three steps.

Annie scanned the audience and found Dan O'Leery sitting in the third row. The criminal justice teacher, in a way, was responsible for all this.

He was responsible for something else: Beth's good mood.

Nevertheless, the only Jamison girl who didn't believe in love at first sight had to ask yet again, "Are you sure you know what you're doing?"

"I've never been so sure in my life," Annie answered.

The music started, and everyone settled down.

"Can you see?" Cathy whispered.

"Yes."

As if orchestrated, the sun slid from behind a cloud. A faint breeze made the flowers seem to nod. Down the aisle came Annie's grandparents, Grandma's arm entwined with Frank Miller's while Grandpa walked behind. Frank and the sheriff were also acting as ushers. Mostly they'd fetched more chairs as the small wedding turned into a fairly big wedding. Annie resisted the urge to count. Most anyone who knew Max assumed they were invited even if they'd not received an invitation.

At the same time, Joe stepped to the gazebo to stand by his father.

He didn't look nervous at all. At his feet was Jacko, wearing a bow tie. If anyone happened to look at the upstairs bedroom window, they'd see Boots resting on the sill, enjoying the wedding. Okay, enjoying the sunshine.

By Joe's side was Kyle, all smiles, and looking less antsy than he had two months ago.

As far as Annie knew, he'd been friendly with Missy these last two months but nothing more. Annie shook her head. Prayers were a wonderful thing. She'd said many over Kyle and Missy. When it came to Marlee, Dwayne, and Katie, though, she wasn't sure exactly what to pray.

Joe said Katie was Kyle and Missy's biological daughter.

But Joe wasn't sure if Kyle knew.

Max was counseling all involved.

Also by Joe's side was Billy Whittaker, looking uncomfortable in his suit, but smiling nonetheless.

Margaret beckoned. "It's time."

Cathy went out first. Her dress was a royal blue that shimmered as she made it to the back of the gathering and started up the aisle. It had kerchief sleeves, hugged Cathy's torso and waist, but then had just enough flare at the bottom to let her silver shoes peek out. The dress not only matched many of the flowers, but it complemented the stones in Annie's gown. Cathy looked like a princess as she made her way to stand at the bottom of Max's back porch steps.

Beth followed, always regal, head held high, looking more like a queen.

Annie closed her eyes and whispered, "Dad, I'm sorry you couldn't be here to give me away. But, oh, Dad, I'm so happy."

The wedding march began. Annie put one foot before the other and stepped out onto the grass, and the music changed. She had wanted nontraditional and upbeat. She walked across the grass, escorted by her mother, to the Dixie Cups singing "Going to the Chapel." When she made it to the front and Max asked, "Who gives the bride away?" her mother and sisters all said, "I do," before her mother sat down on the front row.

Joe waited at the top of his back porch. It had been painted and now was a riot of flowers, thanks to Margaret and Rachel's dad.

She'd only known him but two months, yet she'd been waiting for him forever.

She climbed up the three steps and stood next to him, her back to the audience. Max started the ceremony. "Dearly Beloved..."

Oh, how true the words were. Annie looked across at Joe, at his dark eyes that were saying what he couldn't—since he wouldn't interrupt his dad: *I love you.*

Annie smiled and giggled. This was her wedding. She needed to savor it.

I love you, too.

Finally, they exchanged rings.

That's when Jacko suddenly decided to interfere. He'd been sitting patiently, close to Kyle. The first sign of trouble was a low rumble in the retriever's throat. Then his nose went to the wooden flooring and he started moving.

There were a few snickers from the audience. Billy tried to gently nudge Jacko back to his previous position.

Joe snapped his fingers. Jacko looked up, acknowledged Joe with a *But I'm busy* look, and then followed his nose to the back corner of the porch and barked.

A barking dog during a wedding is not peaceful. The first few barks ended the actual "You may kiss the bride" kiss, but not the taste or lingering sensation on Annie's lips.

I'm Mrs. Kelly, she thought. *Annie Kelly.*

Then Jacko went ballistic, digging at something. Billy had followed Jacko and now was on his hands and knees. "I'll calm him down," he promised. "Something's got him all worked up."

"Jacko," Joe scolded under his breath.

Annie only laughed and pulled Joe closer to steal another kiss while the audience wasn't looking.

"Hey!" said Billy as a blue sunflower tumbled down, pretty much on his head.

The audience stood, not looking at Annie and Joe but back at Billy, who pulled up a loose floorboard and then reached his hand into the opening. "There's something down here."

"Maybe this is not the time," Max suggested. The audience heard him and nodded.

But Billy wasn't listening. The look on his face said he felt exactly like Jacko and wouldn't be happy until he had whatever he was going for.

"Maybe it will be of more interest after the newly married couple walks down the aisle," Max said.

Billy pulled a tangle of leaves and dirt and other things from the flooring. "It's a packrat nest!" He sorted through it, froze, and then stood. "Go ahead," Billy suggested, "announce them as Mr. and Mrs. Joe Kelly and then come here. I've got a surprise." He returned to his place by Joe's side, grinning the whole time.

"You know this is on film," Joe said. "For eternity, you'll be known as the groomsman who ditched part of his good friend's wedding to look for hidden treasure."

"There are worse things," Billy returned.

"I present to you Mr. and Mrs. Joe Kelly." Max wasn't done. Before anyone could move, and it looked like plenty wanted to, he added, "Please pray with me." Every time he said the word "help" or "please," Annie felt the pressure of Joe's hands squeezing hers. They were one…, Annie thought.

When he said amen, the audience applauded. Annie tucked her hand under Joe's arm, but instead of walking down the porch steps, both she and Joe held up just-a-minute pointer fingers at their audience—an audience that was crowding forward—and followed Billy to the corner of the porch. Kyle and Annie's sisters were right behind.

Billy went down to his knees and started showing off his finds. Annie had to laugh when she saw the treasures—the treasures he'd interrupted her wedding for. He held up some yellow plastic trash bag ties, a tiny piece of a tire, and a bunch of soda lids, the old-fashioned kind from the glass bottles, among other things.

"Dad, did you know you had a packrat?" Joe asked his father as Annie's mother and Margaret came closer to see what was going on.

"No, I'd have chased him out."

"I think he's long gone, but he left a few things behind." Billy's eyes were wide as he opened his right hand.

Three gold coins.

"I don't believe it," Margaret murmured loud enough for everyone to hear.

"Wow, oh wow," Kyle said. He turned, pushed through the

crowd on the porch, and scanned the audience until he found his parents. "Mom, Mom. They found the coins." Max didn't hesitate, merely shouted, "Rejoice, for what was lost is found."

Joe looked deep into Annie's eyes. His eyes weren't on the coins, and his body language said that he didn't even notice they were in the middle of a crowd. He leaned close, so close she could feel the heat of his body, and said, "I've already found what I've been looking for."

"Me, too," she whispered in his ear and instigated a third helping of the "you may kiss the bride" portion of the wedding.

About the Author

....

 Pamela Tracy is an award-winning author who lives with her husband (who claims to be the inspiration for most of her heroes) and son (who claims to be the interference for most of her writing time). She was raised in Omaha, Nebraska, and started writing at a very young age. While earning a BA in journalism at Texas Tech University in Lubbock, Texas, she picked up the pen again—only this time, it was an electric typewriter—with which she wrote a very bad science fiction novel. Pamela has written contemporary, historical, and suspenseful fiction, all in the romance genre. In 2009, she won the ACFW Book of the Year award for short romantic suspense. She has also been a Holt Medallion winner and a RITA Finalist.

POST CARD
CARTE POSTALE
Love Finds You

Want a peek into local American life—past and present?
The *Love Finds You*™ series published by Summerside Press
features real towns and combines travel, romance,
and faith in one irresistible package!

The novels in the series—uniquely titled after American towns with romantic or intriguing names—inspire romance and fun. Each fictional story draws on the compelling history or the unique character of a real place. Stories center on romances kindled in small towns, old loves lost and found again on the high plains, and new loves discovered at exciting vacation getaways. Summerside Press plans to publish at least one novel set in each of the fifty states. Be sure to catch them all!

Now Available

Love Finds You in Miracle, Kentucky
by Andrea Boeshaar
ISBN: 978-1-934770-37-5

*Love Finds You in
Snowball, Arkansas*
by Sandra D. Bricker
ISBN: 978-1-934770-45-0

Love Finds You in Romeo, Colorado
by Gwen Ford Faulkenberry
ISBN: 978-1-934770-46-7

*Love Finds You in
Valentine, Nebraska*
by Irene Brand
ISBN: 978-1-934770-38-2

Love Finds You in Humble, Texas
by Anita Higman
ISBN: 978-1-934770-61-0

*Love Finds You in
Last Chance, California*
by Miralee Ferrell
ISBN: 978-1-934770-39-9

*Love Finds You in
Maiden, North Carolina*
by Tamela Hancock Murray
ISBN: 978-1-934770-65-8

*Love Finds You in
Paradise, Pennsylvania*
by Loree Lough
ISBN: 978-1-934770-66-5

*Love Finds You in
Treasure Island, Florida*
by Debby Mayne
ISBN: 978-1-934770-80-1

Love Finds You in Liberty, Indiana
by Melanie Dobson
ISBN: 978-1-934770-74-0

Love Finds You in Revenge, Ohio
by Lisa Harris
ISBN: 978-1-934770-81-8

Love Finds You in Poetry, Texas
by Janice Hanna
ISBN: 978-1-935416-16-6

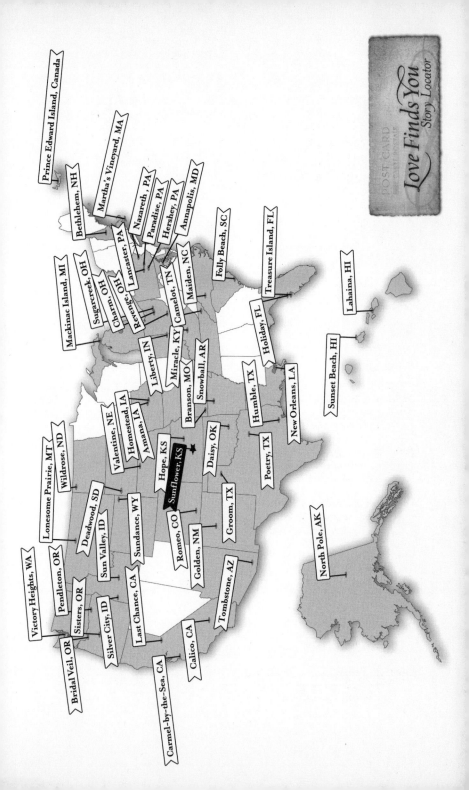